4.

LOOKING
F·O·R
JAKE

ALSO BY CHINA MIÉVILLE

King Rat
Perdido Street Station
The Scar
Iron Council

MACMILLAN

LOOKING FOR JAKE

A·N·D
OTHER
STORIES

CHINA MIÉVILLE

First published 2005 by Del Rey Books
an imprint of The Random House Publishing Group, New York

This edition published 2005 by Macmillan
an imprint of Pan Macmillan Ltd
Pan Macmillan, 20 New Wharf Road, London N1 9RR
Basingstoke and Oxford
Associated companies throughout the world
www.panmacmillan.com

ISBN 1 4050 4830 1 (HB)
ISBN 1 4050 5232 5 (TPB)

135798642

A CIP catalogue record for this book is available from
the British Library.

Book design by Susan Turner
Printed and bound in Great Britain by
Mackays of Chatham plc, Chatham, Kent

To Jake

CONTENTS

LOOKING
F · O · R
J A K E

LOOKING FOR JAKE

I don't know how I lost you. I remember there was that long time of searching for you, frantic and sick-making . . . I was almost ecstatic with anxiety. And then I found you, so that was alright. Only I lost you again. And I can't make out how it happened.

I'm sitting out here on the flat roof you must remember, looking out over this dangerous city. There is, you remember, a dull view from my roof. There are no parks to break up the urban monotony, no towers worth a damn. Just an endless, featureless crosshatching of brick and concrete, a drab chaos of interlacing backstreets stretching out interminably behind my house. I was disappointed when I first moved here; I didn't see what I had in that view. Not until Bonfire Night.

I just caught a buffet of cold air and the sound of wet cloth in the wind. I saw nothing, of course, but I know that an early riser flew right past me. I can see dusk welling up behind the gas towers.

That night, November the fifth, I climbed up and watched the cheap fireworks roar up all around me. They burst at the level of my eyes, and I traced their routes in reverse to mark all the tiny gardens and balconies from which they flew. There was no way I could keep track; there were just too many. So I sat up there in the midst of all that red and gold and gawped in awe. That washed-out grey city I had ignored for days spewed out all that power, that sheer beautiful energy.

I was seduced then. I never forgot that display, I was never again fooled by the quiescence of the backstreets I saw from my bedroom window. They were dangerous. They remain dangerous.

But of course it's a different kind of dangerous now. Everything's changed. I floundered, I found you, I lost you again, and I'm stuck above these pavements with no one to help me.

I can hear hissing and gentle gibbering on the wind. They're roosting close by, and with the creeping dark they're stirring, and waking.

You never came round enough. There was I with my new flat above the betting shops and cheap hardware stores and grocers of Kilburn High Road. It was cheap and lively. I was a pig in shit. I was happy as Larry. I ate at the local Indian and went to work and self-consciously patronised the poky little independent bookshop, despite its pathetic stock. And we spoke on the phone and you even came by, a few times. Which was always excellent.

I know I never came to you. You lived in fucking Barnet. I'm only human.

What were you up to, anyway? How could I be so close to some-one, love someone so much, and know so little about their life? You wafted into northwest London with your plastic bags, vague about where you'd been, vague about where you were going, who you were seeing, what you were up to. I still don't know how you had the money to indulge your tastes for books and music. I still don't understand what happened with you and that woman you had that fucked-up affair with.

I always liked how little our love-lives impacted on our relationship. We would spend the day playing arcade games and shooting the shit about *x* or *y* film, or comic, or album, or book, and only as an afterthought as you gathered yourself to go, we'd mention the heartache we were suffering, or the blissed-out perfection of our new lovers.

But I had you on tap. We might not speak for weeks, but one phone call was all it would ever need.

That won't work now. I don't dare touch my phone anymore. For a long time there was no dialling tone, only irregular bursts of static, as if my phone were scanning for signals. Or as if it were jamming them.

The last time I picked up the receiver something whispered to me down the wires, asked me a question in a reverential tone, in a language I did not understand, all sibilants and dentals. I put the phone down carefully and have not lifted it since.

So I learnt to see the view from my roof in the garish glow of fireworks, to hold it in the awe it deserved. That view is gone now. It's changed. It has the same topography, it's point for point the same as it ever was, but it's been hollowed out and filled with something new. Those dark thoroughfares are no less beautiful, but everything has changed.

The angle of my window, the height of my roof, hid the tarmac and paving stones from me: I saw the tops of houses and walls and rubble and skips, but I couldn't see ground level, I never saw a single human being walk those streets. And that lifeless panorama I saw *brimmed* with potential energy. The roads might be thronging, there might be a street party or a traffic accident or a riot just out of my sight. It was a very full emptiness I learnt to see, on Bonfire Night, a very charged desolation.

That charge has changed polarity. The desolation remains. Now I can see no one because no one is there. The roads are not thronging, and there are no street parties out there at all, nor could there ever be again.

Sometimes, of course, those streets must snap into sharp focus as a figure strides down them, determined and nervous, as I myself stride down Kilburn High Road when I leave the house. And usually the figure will be lucky, and reach the deserted supermarket without incident, and find food and leave and get home again, as I have been lucky.

Sometimes, though, they will fall through a faultline in the pavement and disappear with a despairing wail, and the street will be empty. Sometimes they will smell something enticing from a cosy-looking house, trip eager into the open front door, and be gone. Sometimes they will pass through glimmering filaments that dangle from the dirty trees, and they will be reeled in.

I imagine some of these things. I don't know how people are disappeared, in these strange days, but hundreds of thousands, millions of souls have gone. London's main streets, like the high road I can see from the front of my house, contain only a few anxious figures—a drunk, maybe, a lost-looking policeman listening to the gibberish from his radio, someone sitting nude in a doorway—everyone avoiding everyone else's eyes.

The backstreets are almost deserted.

What's it like where you are, Jake? Are you still out there in Barnet? Is it full? Has there been a rush to the suburbs?

I doubt it's as dangerous as Kilburn.

Nowhere's as dangerous as Kilburn.

I've found myself living in the Badlands.

This is where it's all at, this is the centre. Only a few stupid shits like me live here now, and we are disappearing one by one. I have not seen the corduroy man for days, and the glowering youth who camped down in the bakery is no longer there.

We shouldn't stay here. We have, after all, been warned.

Kill. Burn.

Why do I stay? I could make my way in reasonable safety southwards, towards the centre. I've done it before; I know what to do. Travel at midday, clutch my *A–Z* like a talisman. I swear it protects me. It's become my grimoire. It would take an hour or so to walk to Marble Arch, and it's a main road all the way. Those are reasonable odds.

I've done it before, walked down Maida Vale, over the canal, full these days of obscure detritus. Past the tower on the Edgware Road with the exoskeleton of red girders that jut into the sky twenty feet above the flat roof. I have heard something padding and snorting in the confines of that high prison, caught a glimpse of glistening muscle and slick fur shaking the metal in agitation.

I think the things that flap drop food into the cage from above.

But get past that and I'm home free, onto Oxford Street, where most of London now lives. I was last there a month ago, and they'd done a decent job of it. Several shops are operating, accepting the absurd hand-scrawled notes that pass for currency, selling what items they can salvage, or make, or find delivered to them inexplicably in the morning.

They can't escape it, of course, what's happening to the city. Signs of it abound.

With so many people gone the city is generating its own rubbish. In the cracks of buildings and the dark spaces under abandoned cars little knots of matter are self-organising into grease-stained chip wrappers, broken toys, cigarette packets, before snapping the tiny umbilicus that anchors them to the ground and drifting out across the streets. Even on Oxford Street every morning sees a fresh crop of litter, each filthy newborn piece marked with a minuscule puckered navel.

Even on Oxford Street, every day without fail in front of the newsagents, the bundles appear: the *Telegraph* and *Lambeth News*. The only papers to survive the quiet cataclysm. They are generated daily, written, published, and delivered by person or persons or forces unseen.

I already crept downstairs today, Jake, to pick up my copy of the *Telegraph* from across the road. The headline is "Autochthonic Masses Howling and Wet-Mouthed." The subhead: "Pearl, Faeces, Broken Machines."

But even with these reminders, Oxford Street is a reassuring place. Here, people get up and go to work, dress in clothes we would recognise from nine months ago, have coffee in the morning, and resolutely ignore the impossibility of what they are doing. So why don't I stay there?

I think it's the invitation from the Gaumont State that keeps me here, Jake.

I can't leave Kilburn behind. There are secrets here I haven't found. Kilburn is the centre of the new city, and the Gaumont State is the centre of Kilburn.

The Gaumont was inspired, preposterously, by New York's Empire State Building. On a miniature scale, perhaps, but its lines and curves are dignified and impassive and easily ignore the low brick-and-dirt camouflage of their surroundings. It was still a cinema when I was a child, and I remember the symmetrical sweep of the twin staircases within, the opulence of chandelier and carpet and marble tracings.

Multiplexes, with their glorified video screens and tatty decor, are unimpressed by cinema. The Gaumont is of an age when film was still a miracle. It was a cathedral.

It closed and grew shabby. And then it opened again, to the electronic chords of slot machines in the vestibule. Outside, two huge neon standards explained the Gaumont's new purpose in vertical script, reading downwards: BINGO.

You were my first thought, as soon as I knew something had happened. I don't remember waking when the train pulled into London. My first memory is stepping off the carriage into the evening cool and feeling afraid.

It was no ESP, no sixth sense that told me something was wrong. It was my eyes.

The platform was full, as you would expect, but the crowd moved like none I had ever seen. There were no tides, no currents moving to and from the indicator board, the ticket counter, the shops. No fractal patterns emerged from this mass. The flap of a butterfly's wing in one corner of the station would create no typhoons, no storms, not a sough of wind anywhere else. The deep order of chaos had broken down.

It looked as I imagine purgatory must. A huge room full of vacant souls milling atomised and pointless, each in personal despair.

I saw a guard, as alone as all the others.

What's happened? I asked him. He was confused, shaking his head. He would not look at me. Something's happened, he said. Something . . . there was a collapse . . . nothing works properly . . . there's been a . . . a breakdown . . .

He was being very inexact. That wasn't his fault. It was a very inexact apocalypse.

Between the time I had closed my eyes on the train and the time I had opened them again, some organising principle had failed.

I've always imagined the occurrence in very literal terms. I have always envisaged a vast impossible building, a spiritual power station with an unstable core shitting out the world's energy and connectivity. I've always envisaged the cogs and wheels of that unthinkable machinery overheating, some critical mass being reached . . . the mechanisms faltering and seizing up as the core explodes soundlessly and spews its poisonous fuel across the city and beyond.

In Bhopal, Union Carbide vomited up a torturing, killing bile. In Chernobyl the fallout was a more insidious cellular terrorism.

And now Kilburn erupts with vague entropy.

I know, Jake, I know, you can't help smiling, can you? From the awesome and terrible to the ridiculous. The walls here are not stacked high with corpses. There is rarely any blood when the inhabitants of London disappear. But the city's winding down, Jake, and Kilburn is the epicentre of the burnout.

I left the guard alone in his confusion.

Got to find Jake, I thought.

You're probably smiling self-deprecatingly when you read that, but I swear to you it's true. You'd been in the city when it happened, you had *seen* it. Think of it, Jake. I was asleep, in transit, neither here nor there. I didn't know this city, I'd never been here before. But you'd watched it being born.

There was no one else in the city for me. You could be my guide, or we could at least be lost together.

The sky was utterly dead. It looked cut out of matte black paper and pasted above the silhouettes of the towers. All the pigeons were gone. We didn't know it then, but the unseen flapping things had burst into existence full-grown and ravenous. In the first few hours they swept the skies quite clean of prey.

The streetlamps were still working, as they are now, but in any case there was nothing profound about the darkness. I wandered nervously, found a telephone box. It didn't seem to want my money but it let me make the call anyway.

Your mother answered.

Hello, she said. She sounded listless and nonplussed.

I paused for far too long. I was groping for new etiquette in this new time. I had no sense of social rules, and I stammered as I wondered whether to say something about the change.

Is Jake there please? I finally said, banal and absurd.

He's gone, she said. He's not here. He went out this morning to shop, and he hasn't come back.

Your brother came on the line then and spoke brusquely. He went to some bookshop, he said, and I knew where you were then.

It was the bookshop we found on the right as you leave Willesden Green station, where the slope of the high road begins to steepen. It is cheap and capricious. We were seduced by the immaculate edition of *Voyage to Arcturus* in the window, and entertained by the juxtaposition of Kierkegaard and Paul Daniels.

If I could have chosen where to be when London wound down, it would be in that zone, where the city first notices the sky, at the summit of a hill, surrounded by low streets that let sound escape into the clouds. Kilburn, ground zero, just over the thin bulwark of backstreets. Perhaps you had a presentiment that morning, Jake, and when the breakdown came you were ready, waiting in that perfect vantage point.

It's dark out here on the roof. It's been dark for some time. But I can see enough to write, from deflected streetlamps and maybe from the moon, too. The air is buffeted more and more by the passage of those hungry, unseen things, but I'm not afraid.

I can hear them fighting and nesting and courting in the Gaumont's tower, jutting over my neighbours' houses and shops. A little while ago there was a dry sputter and crack, and a constant low buzz now underpins the night sounds.

I am attuned to that sound. The murmur of neon.

The Gaumont State is blaring its message to me across the short, deserted distance of pavement.

I am being called to over the organic nonsense of the flyers and the more constant whispers of young rubbish in the wind.

I've heard it all before, I've read it before. I'm taking my own sweet fucking time over this letter. Then I'll see what's being asked of me.

I took the tube to Willesden.

I wince to think of it now, I jerk my mind away. I wasn't to know. It was safer then, anyway, in those early days.

I've crept into the underground stations in the months since, to check the whispered rumours for myself. I've seen the trains go by with the howling faces in all the windows, too fast to see clearly, something like dogs, I've seen trains burning with cold light, long slow trains empty except for one dead-looking woman staring directly into my eyes, en route Jesus Christ knows where.

It was nothing like that back then, not nearly so dramatic. It was too cold and too quiet, I remember. And I am not sure the train had a driver. But it let me go. I came to Willesden and as I stepped out onto that uncovered station I could feel something different about the world. There was a very slow epiphany building up under the skin of the night, oozing out of the city's pores, breaking over me ponderously.

I climbed the stairs out of that underworld.

When Orpheus looked back, Jake, it wasn't stupid. The myths are slanderous. It wasn't the sudden fear that she wasn't there that turned his head. It was the threatening light from above. What if it was not the same, out there? It's so human, to turn and catch the eye of your companion on a return journey, to share a moment's terror that everything you know will have changed.

There was no one I could look back to, and everything I knew had changed. Pushing open the doors onto the street was the bravest thing I have ever done.

I stood on the high railway bridge. I was hit by wind. Across the street before me, emerging from below the bridge, below my feet, the elegant curved gorge containing the tracks stretched away. Steep banks of scrub contained it, squat bushes and weeds that tugged petulantly at the scree.

There was very little sound. I could see only a few stars. I felt as if the whole sky scudded above me.

The shop was dark but the door opened. It was a relief to walk into still air.

We're fucking shut, somebody said. He sounded despairing.

I wound between the piles of strong-smelling books towards

the till. I could see shapes and shades in this halfhearted darkness. An old bald man was slumped on a stool behind the desk.

I don't want to buy anything, I said. I'm looking for someone. I described you.

Look around, mate, he said. Fucking empty. What do you want from me? I ain't seen your friend or no one.

Very fast, I felt hysteria. I swallowed back a desire to run to all the corners of the shop and throw piles of books around, shouting your name, to see where you were hiding. As I fought to speak the old man took some kind of contemptuous pity on me and sighed.

One like the one you said, he's been drifting in and out of here all day. Last here about two hours ago. If he comes in again he can fuck off, I'm closed.

How do you tell the incredible? It seems odd, what strikes us as unbelievable.

I had learnt, very fast, that the rules of the city had imploded, that sense had broken down, that London was a broken and bloodied thing. I accepted that with numbness, only a very little astonished. But I was nearly sick with disbelief and relief to walk out of that shop and see you waiting.

You stood under the eaves of a newsagent's, half in shadow, an unmistakable silhouette.

If I stop for a moment it is all so prosaic, so obvious, that you would wait for me there. When I saw you, though, it was like a miracle.

Did you shudder with relief to see me?

Could you believe your eyes?

It's difficult to remember that, right now, when I am up here on the roof surrounded by the hungry flapping things that I cannot see, without you.

We met in the darkness that dripped off the front of the building's facade. I hugged you tight.

Man . . . I said.

Hey, you said.

We stood like fools, silent for a while.

Do you understand what's happened? I said.

You shook your head, shrugged and waved your arms vaguely to encompass everything around us.

I don't want to go home, you said. I felt it go. I was in the shop and I was looking at this weird little book and I felt something huge just . . . slip away.

I was asleep in a train. I woke up and found it like this.

What happens now?

I thought you could tell me that. Didn't you all get issued . . . rule books or something? I thought I was punished for being asleep, that's why I didn't understand anything.

No, man. You know, loads of people have just . . . disappeared, I swear. When I was in the shop I looked up just before, and there were four other people in there. And then I looked up just after and there was only me and this other guy, and the shopkeeper.

Smiles, I said. The cheerful one.

Yeah.

We stood silent again.

This is the way the world ends, you said.

Not with a bang, I continued, but with a . . .

We thought.

. . . with a long-drawn-out breath? you suggested.

I told you that I was walking home, to Kilburn, just over the way. Come with me, I said. Stay at mine.

You were hesitant.

Stupid, stupid, stupid, I'm sure it was my fault. It was just the old argument, about you not coming to see me enough, not staying longer, translated into the world's new language. Before the fall you would have made despairing noises about having to be somewhere, hint darkly at commitments you could not explain, and disappear. But in this new time those excuses became absurd.

And the energy you put into your evasions was channelled else-where, into the city, which was hungry like a newborn thing, which sucked up your anxiety, assimilated your inchoate desires and fulfilled them.

At least walk with me over to Kilburn, I said. We can work out what we're going to do when we're there.

Yeah, sure man, I just want to . . .

I couldn't make out what it was you wanted to do.

You were distracted, you kept looking over my shoulder at something, and I was looking around quickly, to see what was in-triguing you. There was a sense of interruptions, though the night was as silent as ever, and I kept glancing back at you, and I tugged at you to make you come with me and you said Sure sure man, just one second, I want to see something and you began to cross the road with your eyes fixed on something out of my sight and I was getting angry and then I lost my grip on you because I could hear a sound from over the brow of the railway bridge, from the east. I could hear the sound of hooves.

My arm was still outstretched but I was no longer touching you, and I turned my head towards the sound, I stared at the hill's apex. Time stretched out. The darkness just above the pavement was split by a wicked splinter that grew and grew as something long and thin and sharp appeared over the hill. It sliced the night at an acute angle. A clenched, gloved fist rose below it, clutching it tight. It was a sword, a splendid ceremonial sabre. The sword pulled a man after it, a man in a strange helmet, a long silver spike adorning his head and a white plume streaming out in his wake.

He rode in an insane gallop but I felt no urgency as he burst into view, and I had all the time I needed to see him, to study his clothes, his weapon, his face, to recognise him.

He was one of the horsemen who stands outside the palace . . . Are they called the household cavalry? With the hair draped from their helmet spike in an immaculate cone, their mirrored boots, their bored horses. They are legendary for their immobility. It is a tourist game to stare at them and mock them and stroke their mounts' noses, while no flicker of human emotion defiles their duty.'

As this man's head broke the brow of the hill I saw that his face was creased and cracked into an astonishing warrior's expression, the snarl of an attacking dog, idiot bravery such as must have been painted across the faces of the Light Brigade.

His red jacket was unbuttoned and it flickered around him like a flame. He half stood in his stirrups, crouched low, grasping the reins in his left hand, his right held high with that beautiful blade spitting light into my face. His horse rose into view, its veins huge under its white skin, its eyes rolling in an insane equine leer, drool spurting from behind its bared teeth, its hooves hammering down the deserted tarmac of the Willesden railway bridge.

The soldier was silent, though his mouth was open as if he shouted his valedictory roar. He rode on, holding his sword high, bearing down on some imaginary enemy, pushing his horse on towards Dollis Hill, down past the Japanese restaurant and the record shop and the bike dealer and the vacuum-cleaner repair man.

The soldier swept past me, stunning and stupid and misplaced. He rode between us, Jake, so close that beads of sweat hit me.

I can picture him on duty as the cataclysm fell, sensing the change in the order of things and knowing that the queen he was sworn to protect was gone or irrelevant, that his pomp meant nothing in the decaying city, that he had been trained into absurdity and uselessness, and deciding that he would be a soldier, just once. I see him clicking his heels and cantering through the confused streets of central London, picking up speed as the anger at his redundancy grows, giving the horse its head, letting it run, feeling it shy at the strange new residents of the skies, until it was galloping hard and he draws his weapon to prove that he can fight, and careers off into the flatlands of northwest London, to disappear or die.

I watched his passing, dumbstruck and in awe.

And when I turned back, of course, Jake, when I turned back, you had gone.

. . .

The frantic searches, the shouts and the misery you can imagine for yourself. I have little enough dignity as it is. It went on for a long time, though I had known as I raised my head to your lack that I would not find you.

Eventually I found my way to Kilburn, and as I walked past the Gaumont State I looked up and saw that neon message, garish and banal and terrifying. The message that is there still, the request that tonight, finally, after so many months, I think I will acquiesce to.

I don't know where you went, how you were disappeared. I don't know how I lost you. But after all my searching for a hiding place, that message on the face of the Gaumont cannot be coincidence. Although it might, of course, be misleading. It might be a game. It might be a trap.

But I'm sick of waiting, you know? I'm sick of wondering. So let me tell you what I'm going to do. I'm going to finish this letter, soon now, and I'm going to put it in an envelope with your name on it. I'll put a stamp on it (it can't hurt), and I'll venture out into the street—yes, even in the heart of the night—and I'll put it in the post box.

From there, I don't know what'll happen. I don't know the rules of this place at all. It might be eaten by some presence inside the box, it might be spat back out at me, or reproduced a hundred times and pasted on the windows of all the warehouses in London. I'm hoping that it will find its way to you. Maybe it'll appear in your pocket, or at the door of your place, wherever you are now. If you are anywhere, that is.

It's a forlorn hope. I admit that. Of course I admit that.

But I had you, and I lost you again. I'm marking your passing. And I am marking mine.

Because you see, Jake, then I'm going to walk the short distance up Kilburn High Road to the Gaumont State, and I'm going to read its plea, its command, and this time I think I will obey.

The Gaumont State is a beacon, a lighthouse, a warning we

missed. It jags impassive into the clouds as the city founders on rocks. Its filthy cream walls are daubed with a hundred markings; human, animal, meteorological, and other. In its squat square tower lies the huge nest of rags or bones or hair where the flying things bicker and brood. The Gaumont State exerts its own gravity over the changed city. I suspect all compasses point to it now. I suspect that in the magnificent entrance, framed by those wide stairs, something is waiting. The Gaumont State is the generator of the dirty entropy that has taken London. I suspect there are many fascinating things inside.

I'm going to let it reel me in.

Those two huge pinkish-red signs that heralded the Gaumont's rebirth as a temple of cheap games—they have changed. They are selective. They ignore certain letters, and have done ever since that night. Both now scorn the initial B. The sign on the left illuminates only the second and third letters, that on the right only the fourth and fifth. The signs flicker on and off in antiphase, taking turns to blaze their gaudy challenge.

IN . . .

GO . . .

IN.

GO IN.

GO IN.

Go in.

Alright. OK. I'll go in. I'll tidy up my house and post my letter and stand in front of that edifice, squinting at the now-opaque glass that keeps its secrets, and I will go in.

I don't really believe you're in there, Jake, if you're reading this. I don't really believe that any longer. I know that can't be so. But I can't leave it alone. I can leave no stone unturned.

I'm so fucking lonely.

I'll climb those exquisite stairs, if I get that far. I'll cross the grand corridors, wind through tunnels into the great vast hall that I believe will be glowing very bright. If I get that far.

Could be that I'll find you. I'll find something, something will find me.

I won't be coming home, I'm sure.

I'll go in. The city doesn't need me around while it winds down. I was going to catalogue its secrets, but that was for my benefit, not the city's, and this is just as good.

I'll go in.

See you soon, I hope, Jake. I hope.

All my love,

FOUNDATION

Y ou watch the man who comes and speaks to buildings. He circles the houses, looking up from the sidewalks, from the concrete gardens, looking down at the supports that go into the earth. He enters every room, taps windows and wiggles ill-fitted panes, he prods at plaster, hauls into attics. In the basements he listens to supports, and all the time he whispers.

The buildings whisper back, he says. He works in brown-stones, in tenements, banks and warehouses across the city. They tell him where their faultlines run. When he's done he tells you why the crack is spreading, why the wall is damp, where erosion is, what the cost will be to fix it or to let it rot. He is never wrong.

Is he a surveyor? A structural engineer? He has no framed cer-tificates but a thick portfolio of references, a ten-year reputation. There are cuttings about him from across America. They have called him the house-whisperer. He has been a phenomenon for years.

When he speaks he wears a large and firm smile. He has to push his words past it so they come out misshapen and terse. He fights not to raise his voice over the sounds he knows you cannot hear.

"Yeah no problem but that supporting wall's powdering," he says. If you watch him close you will see that he peeps quickly at the earth, again and again, at the building's sunken base. When he goes below, into the cellar, he is nervy. He talks more quickly. The building speaks loudest to him down there, and when he comes up again he is sweating below his smile.

When he drives he looks to either side of the road with tremendous and unending shock, taking in all the foundations. Past building sites he stares at the earthmovers. He watches their trundling motion as if they are some carnivore.

Every night he dreams he is where air curdles his lungs and the sky is a toxic slurry of black and black-red clouds that the earth vomits and the ground is baked to powder and lost boys wonder and slough off flesh in clots and do not see him or each other though they pass close by howling without words or in a language of collapsing jargon, acronyms and shorthands that once meant something and now are the grunts of pigs.

He lives in a small house in the edges of the city, where once he started to build an extra room, till the foundations screamed too loud. A decade later there is only a hole through striae of earth, past pipes, a pit, waiting for walls. He will not fill it. He stopped digging when a dark, thick and staining liquid welled up from below his suburban plot, clinging to his spade, cloying, unseen by any but him. The foundation spoke to him then.

In his dream he hears the foundation speak to him in its multiple voice, its muttering. And when at last he sees it, the foundation in the tight-packed hot earth, he wakes retching and it takes moments before he knows he is in his bed, in his home, and that the foundation is still speaking.

—we stay

—we are hungry

.   .   .

Each morning he kisses good-bye the photograph of his family. They left years ago, frightened by him. He sets his face while the foundation tells him secrets.

In a midcity apartment block the residents want to know about the crack through two of their floors. The man measures it and presses his ear to the wall. He hears echoes of voices from below, travelling, rising through the building's bones. When he cannot put it off anymore, he descends to the basement.

The walls are grey and wet-stained, painted with a little graffiti. The foundation is speaking clearly to him. It tells him it is hungry and hollow. Its voice is the voice of many, in time, desiccated.

He sees the foundation. He sees through the concrete floor and the earth to where girders are embedded and past them to the foundation.

A stock of dead men. An underpinning, a structure of entangled bodies and their parts, pushed tight, packed together and become architecture, their bones broken to make them fit, wedged in contorted repose, burnt skins and the tatters of their clothes pressed as if against glass at the limits of their cut, running below the building's walls, six feet deep below the ground, a perfect runnel full of humans poured like concrete and bracing the stays and the walls.

The foundation looks at him with all its eyes, and the men speak in time.

—we cannot breathe

There is no panic in their voices, nothing but the hopeless patience of the dead.

—we cannot breathe and we shore you up and we eat only sand

He whispers to them so no one else can hear.

"Listen," he says. They eye him through the earth. "Tell me," he says. "Tell me about the wall. It's built on you. It's weighing down on you. Tell me how it feels."

—it is heavy, they say, and we eat only sand, but at last the man coaxes the dead out of their solipsism for a few moments and they look up, and close their eyes, all in time, and hum, and tell him, it is old, this wall built on us, and there is rot halfway up its flank and there is a break that will spread and the sides will settle.

The foundation tells him everything about the wall and for a moment the man's eyes widen, but then he understands that no, there is no danger. Untreated, this wall will only slump and make the house more ugly. Nothing will collapse. Hearing that he relaxes and stands, and backs away from the foundation which watches him go.

"You don't have to worry about it," he tells the residents' committee. "Maybe just fix it up, smooth it down, that's all you have to do."

And in a suburban mall there is nothing to stop expansion onto waste ground, and in the character house the stairs are beyond repair, and the clocktower has been built using substandard bolts, and the apartment's ceiling needs damp-proofing. The buried wall of dead tells him all these things.

Every home is built on them. It is all one foundation, that underpins his city. Every wall weighs down upon the corpses that whisper to him with the same voice, the same faces, ripped-up cloth and long-dried blood and bodies torn up and their components used to fill gaps between bodies, limbs and heads stowed tidily between men bloated by gas and spilling dust from their cavities, the whole and partial dead concatenated.

Every house in every street. He listens to the buildings, to the foundation that unites them.

In his dream he tramps through land that swallows his feet. Missing men shuffle in endless, anxious circles and he passes them by. Syrupy-thick liquid laps at him from just below the dust. He hears the foundation. He turns and there is the foundation. It is taller. It has breached the ground. A wall of dead-men bricks as high as his thighs, its edges and its top quite smooth. It is embedded with thousands of eyes and mouths that work as he approaches, spilling rheum and skin and sand.

—we do not end, we are hungry and hot and alone

Something is being built upon the foundation.

There have been years of petty construction, the small schemes of developers, the eagerness of people to improve their homes. Doggedly he makes the foundation tell him. Where there is no problem he passes that on, or where there is a small concern. Where problems are so great that building will be halted early on he tells that, too.

It is nearly a decade that he has been listening to buildings. It is a long time till he finds what he has been looking for.

The block is several storeys high, built thirty years before from shoddy concrete and cheap steel by contractors and politicians who got rich on the deficiencies. The fossils of such corruption are everywhere. Mostly their foundering is gradual, doors sticking, elevators failing, subsidence, over years. Listening to the foundation, the man knows something here is different.

He grows alarmed. His breath is short. He murmurs to the buried wall of dead, begging them to be sure.

The foundation is in swampland—the dead men can feel the ooze rising. The basement walls are crumbling. The supports are veined, infinitesimally, with water. It will not be long. The building will fall.

"Are you sure?" he whispers again, and the foundation looks at him with its countless dust-thick and haemorrhaged eyes and says yes. Trembling, he stands and turns to the caretaker, the housing manager.

"These old things," he says. "They ain't pretty, and they weren't well built, and yeah you're going to get damp, but you've got nothing to worry about. No problem. These walls are solid."

He slaps the pillar beside him and feels vibrations through to the water below it, through the honeycomb of its eroded base, into the foundation where the dead men mutter.

In the nightmare he kneels before the wall of torn-up flesh. It is chest-high now. The foundation is growing. It is nothing without a wall, a temple.

He wakes crying and stumbles into his basement. The foundation whispers to him and it is above the ground now; it stretches into his walls.

The man has weeks to wait. The foundation grows. It is slow, but it grows. It grows up into the walls and down, too, extending into the earth, spreading its base, underpinning more and more.

Three months after he visited the high-rise he sees it on the local news. It looks like someone who has suffered a stroke; its side is slack, tremulous. Its southern corner has slumped and sandwiched on itself, opening up its flesh to forlorn half-rooms that teeter at the edge of the air. Men and women are hauled out on stretchers.

Figures flutter across the screen. Many dead. Six are children. The man turns the volume up to drown out the whispers of the foundation. He begins to cry and then is sobbing. He hugs himself, croons his sadness; he holds his face in his hands.

"This is what you wanted," he says. "I paid you back. Please, leave me alone. It's done."

In the basement he lies down and weeps on the earth, the foundation beneath him. It looks up from its random gargoyle poses. It blinks dust out of its dead eyes and watches. Its stare burns him.

"There's something for you to eat," he whispers. "God, please. It's done, it's done. Leave me alone. You have something to eat. I've paid it back. I've given you something."

. . .

In the smogged dream he keeps walking and hears the static calls of lost and lonely comrades. The foundation stretches out across flattened dunes. It whispers in its choked voice as it has since that first day.

He helped build the foundation. A long way away. Between two foreign countries, while borders were in chaos. He had come through. First Infantry (Mechanized). In the last days of February, ten years ago. The conscripted opposition, hunkered down in trenches in the desert, their tools poking out through wire, sounding off and firing.

The man and his brigade came. They patted down the components vigorously, mixed up the cement with a half-hour pounding, howitzers and rockets commingling grit and everything else stacked in the sunken gutters of men like pestles and mortars, pasting everything into a good thick red base. The tanks came with their toylike motion, gunstalks rotating but silent. They did their job with other means. Plows mounted at their fronts, they traced along the lines dug in the dirt. With humdrum efficiency they shunted the hot sand into the trenches, pouring it over the contents, the mulch and ragged soup and the men who ran and tried to fire or to surrender or to scream until the desert dust gushed in and encased them and did its job, funnelling into them so their sounds were choked and they became frantic, then sluggish and still, packed the thousands down together with their friends and the segments of their friends, in their holes and miles of dugout lines.

Behind the tanks with their tractor-attachments M2 Bradleys straddled the lines of newly piled-up sand where protrusions showed the construction unfinished, the arms and legs of men beneath, some still twitching like insects. The Bradleys hosed the building site with their 7.62 mms, making sure to shove down all the material at the top, anything that might get out, making it patted down.

And then he had come behind, with the ACEs. Armored Combat Earthmovers, dozers with the last of the small-arms pinging against their skins. He had finished off the job. With his scoop, he had smoothed everything away. All the untidy detritus of the building work, the sticks and bits of wood, the sand-clogged rifles like sticks, the arms and legs like sticks, the sand-blasted heads that had tumbled slowly with the motion of the earth and now protruded. He flattened all the projections from the ground, smeared them across the dirt and smeared more dirt across them to tidy them away.

On the 25th of February in 1991, he had helped build the foundation. And as he looked out across the spread-out, flattened acres, the desert made neat, wiped clean for those hours, he had heard dreadful sounds. He had seen suddenly and terribly through the hot and red-set sand and earth to the dead, in their orderly trenches that angled like walls, and intersected and fanned out, that stretched for miles, like the plans not of a house or a palace but a city. He had seen the men made into mortar, and he had seen them looking at him.

The foundation stretched below everything. It spoke to him. It would not be quiet. In his dream or out.

He thought he would leave it behind him in the desert, in that unnatural flat zone. He thought the whispering would dissipate across the thousands of miles. He had come home. And then his dream had started. His purgatory of well fires and bloody sky and dunes, where his dead comrades were lost, made feral by loneliness. The others, the foundation, the other dead, were thousands strong. They were endless.

—morning of goodness, they whispered to him in their baked dead voices. morning of light

—praise be to god

—you built us so

—we are hot and alone. we are hungry. we eat only sand. we are full of it. we are full but hungry. we eat only sand

He had heard them nightly and tried to forget them, tried to forget what he had seen. But then he dug a pit in his yard, to put down a foundation for his house, and he had found one waiting. His wife had heard him screaming, had run out to see him scrabbling in the hole, bloodying his fingers to get out. Dig deep enough, he told her later, though she did not understand, it's there already.

A year after he had built it and first seen it, he had reached the foundation again. The city around him was built on that buried wall of dead. Bone-filled trenches stretched under the sea and linked his home to the desert.

He would do anything not to hear them. He begged the dead, met their gaze. He prayed for their silence. They waited. He thought of the weight on them, heard their hunger, at last decided what they must want.

"Here's something for you," he shouts, and cries again, after the years of searching. He pictures the families in the apartment tumbling down to rest among the foundation. "There's something for you; it can be over. Stop now. Oh, leave me alone."

He sleeps where he lies, on the cellar floor, walked across by spiders. He goes to his dream desert. He walks his sand. He hears the howling of lost soldiers. The foundation stretches up for countless thousands of yards, for miles. It has become a tower in the charred sky. It is all the same material, the dead, only their eyes and mouths moving. Little clouds of sand sputter as they speak. He stands in the shadow of the tower he was made to build, its walls of shredded khaki, flesh and ochre skin, tufted with black and dark red hair. From the sand around it oozes the same dark liquid he saw in his own yard. Blood or oil. The tower is like a minaret in hell, some inverted Babel that reaches the sky and speaks only one language. All its voices still saying the same, the words he has heard for years.

The man wakes. He listens. For a long time he is motionless. Everything waits.

When he cries out it starts slow and builds, growing louder for long seconds. He hears himself. He is like the lost American soldiers in his dream.

He does not stop. Because it is day, the day after his offering, after he gave the foundation what he thought it hankered for, after he paid it back. But he can still see it. He can still hear it, and the dead are still saying the same things.

They watch him. The man is alone with the foundation, and he knows that they will not leave.

He cries for those in the apartment that fell, who died for nothing at all. The foundation wants nothing from him. His offering means nothing to the dead in their trenches, crisscrossing the world. They are not there to taunt or punish or teach him, or to exact revenge or blood-price, they are not enraged or restless. They are the foundation of everything around him. Without them it would crumble. They have seen him, and taught him to see them, and they want nothing from him.

All the buildings are saying the same things. The foundation runs below them all, fractured and made of the dead, and it is saying the same things.

—we are hungry. we are alone. we are hot. we are full but hungry

—you built us, and you are built on us, and below us is only sand

THE
BALL
ROOM

THE BALL ROOM

I'm not employed by the store. They don't pay my wages. I'm with a security firm, but we've had a contract here for a long time, and I've been here for most of it. This is where I know people. I've been a guard in other places—still am, occasionally, on short notice—and until recently I would have said this was the best place I'd been. It's nice to work somewhere people are happy to go. Until recently, if anyone asked me what I did for a living, I'd just tell them I worked for the store.

It's on the outskirts of town, a huge metal warehouse. Full of a hundred little fake rooms, with a single path running through them, and all the furniture we sell made up and laid out so you can see how it should look. Then the same products, disassembled, packed flat and stacked high in the warehouse for people to buy. They're cheap.

Mostly I know I'm just there for show. I wander around in my uniform, hands behind my back, making people feel safe, making the merchandise feel protected. It's not really the kind of stuff you can shoplift. I almost never have to intervene.

The last time I did was in the ball room.

On weekends this place is just crazy. So full it's hard to walk: all couples and young families. We try to make things easier for people. We have a cheap café and free parking, and most important of all we have a crèche. It's at the top of the stairs when you first come in. And right next to it, opening out from it, is the ball room.

The walls of the ball room are almost all glass, so people in the store can look inside. All the shoppers love watching the children: there are always people outside, staring in with big dumb smiles. I keep an eye on the ones that don't look like parents.

It's not very big, the ball room. Just an annexe really. It's been here for years. There's a climbing frame all knotted up around itself, and a net made of rope to catch you, and a Wendy house, and pictures on the walls. And it's full of colour. The whole room is two feet deep in shiny plastic balls.

When the children fall, the balls cushion them. The balls come up to their waists, so they wade through the room like people in a flood. The children scoop up the balls and splash them all over each other. They're about the size of tennis balls, hollow and light so they can't hurt. They make little *pudda-thudda* noises bouncing off the walls and the kids' heads, making them laugh.

I don't know why they laugh so hard. I don't know what it is about the balls that makes it so much better than a normal playroom, but they *love* it in there. Only six of them are allowed at a time, and they queue up for ages to get in. They get twenty minutes inside. You can see they'd give anything to stay longer. Sometimes, when it's time to go, they howl, and the friends they've made cry, too, at the sight of them leaving.

I was on my break, reading, when I was called to the ball room.

I could hear shouting and crying from around the corner, and as I turned it I saw a crowd of people outside the big window. A man was clutching his son and yelling at the childcare assistant and the store manager. The little boy was about five, only just old enough to go in. He was clinging to his dad's trouser leg, sobbing.

The assistant, Sandra, was trying not to cry. She's only nineteen herself.

The man was shouting that she couldn't do her bloody job, that there were way too many kids in the place and they were completely out of control. He was very worked up and he was gesticulating exaggeratedly, like in a silent movie. If his son hadn't anchored his leg he would have been pacing around.

The manager was trying to hold her ground without being confrontational. I moved in behind her, in case it got nasty, but she was calming the man down. She's good at her job.

"Sir, as I said, we emptied the room as soon as your son was hurt, and we've had words with the other children—"

"You don't even know which one did it. If you'd been keeping an *eye* on them, which I imagine is your bloody *job*, then you might be a bit less . . . *sodding* ineffectual."

That seemed to bring him to a halt and he quieted down, finally, as did his son, who was looking up at him with a confused kind of respect.

The manager told him how sorry she was, and offered his son an ice cream. Things were easing down, but as I started to leave I saw Sandra crying. The man looked a bit guilty and tried to apologise to her, but she was too upset to respond.

The boy had been playing behind the climbing frame, in the corner by the Wendy house, Sandra told me later. He was burrowing down into the balls till he was totally covered, the way some children like to. Sandra kept an eye on the boy but she could see the balls bouncing as he moved, so she knew he was okay. Until he came lurching up, screaming.

The store is full of children. The little ones, the toddlers, spend their time in the main crèche. The older ones, eight or nine or ten, they normally walk around the store with their parents, choosing their own bedclothes or curtains, or a little desk with drawers or whatever. But if they're in between, they come back for the ball room.

They're so funny, moving over the climbing frame, concentrating hard. Laughing all the time. They make each other cry, of course, but usually they stop in seconds. It always gets me how they do that: bawling, then suddenly getting distracted and running off happily.

Sometimes they play in groups, but it seems like there's always one who's alone. Quite content, pouring balls onto balls, dropping them through the holes of the climbing frame, dipping into them like a duck. Happy but playing alone.

Sandra left. It was nearly two weeks after that argument, but she was still upset. I couldn't believe it. I started talking to her about it, and I could see her fill up again. I was trying to say that the man had been out of line, that it wasn't her fault, but she wouldn't listen.

"It wasn't him," she said. "You don't understand. I can't be *in* there anymore."

I felt sorry for her, but she was overreacting. It was out of all proportion. She told me that since the day that little boy got upset, she couldn't relax in the ball room at all. She kept trying to watch all the children at once, all the time. She became obsessed with double-checking the numbers.

"It always seems like there's too many," she said. "I count them and there's six, and I count them again and there's six, but it always seems there's too many."

Maybe she could have asked to stay on and only done duty in the main crèche, managing name tags, checking the kids in and out, changing the tapes in the video, but she didn't even want to do that. The children loved that ball room. They went on and on about it, she said. They would never have stopped badgering her to be let in.

. . .

They're little kids, and sometimes they have accidents. When that happens, someone has to shovel all the balls aside to clean the floor, then dunk the balls themselves in water with a bit of bleach.

This was a bad time for that. Almost every day, some kid or other seemed to pee themselves. We kept having to empty the room to sort out little puddles.

"I had every bloody one of them over playing with me, every second, just so we'd have no problems," one of the nursery workers told me. "Then after they left . . . you could smell it. Right by the bloody Wendy house, where I'd have sworn none of the little buggers had got to."

His name was Matthew. He left a month after Sandra. I was amazed. I mean, you can see how much they love the children, people like them. Even having to wipe up dribble and sick and all that. Seeing them go was proof of what a tough job it was. Matthew looked really sick by the time he quit, really grey.

I asked him what was up, but he couldn't tell me. I'm not sure he even knew.

You have to watch those kids all the time. I couldn't do that job. Couldn't take the stress. The children are so unruly, and so tiny. I'd be terrified all the time, of losing them, of hurting them.

There was a bad mood to the place after that. We'd lost two people. The main store turns over staff like a motor, of course, but the crèche normally does a bit better. You have to be qualified, to work in the crèche, or the ball room. The departures felt like a bad sign.

I was conscious of wanting to look after the kids in the store. When I did my walks I felt like they were all around me. I felt like I had to be ready to leap in and save them any moment. Everywhere I looked, I saw children. And they were as happy as ever, running through the fake rooms and jumping on the bunkbeds, sitting at the desks that had been laid out ready. But now the way they ran around made me wince, and all our furniture, which meets or exceeds the most rigorous international standards for safety, looked like it was lying in wait to injure them. I saw head wounds in every coffee-table corner, burns in every lamp.

I went past the ball room more than usual. Inside was always some harassed-looking young woman or man trying to herd the children, and them running through a tide of bright plastic that thudded every way as they dived into the Wendy house and piled up balls on its roof. The children would spin around to make themselves dizzy, laughing.

It wasn't good for them. They loved it when they were in there, but they emerged so tired and crotchety and teary. They did that droning children's cry. They pulled themselves into their parents' jumpers, sobbing, when it was time to go. They didn't want to leave their friends.

Some children were coming back week after week. It seemed to me their parents ran out of things to buy. After a while they'd make some token purchase like tea lights and just sit in the café, drinking tea and staring out of the window at the grey flyovers while their kids got their dose of the room. There didn't look like much that was happy to these visits.

The mood infected us. There wasn't a good feeling in the store. Some people said it was too much trouble, and we should close the ball room. But the management made it clear that wouldn't happen.

You can't avoid night shifts.

There were three of us on that night, and we took different sections. Periodically we'd each of us wander through our patch, and between times we'd sit together in the staffroom or the unlit café and chat and play cards, with all sorts of rubbish flashing on the mute TV.

My route took me outside, into the front car lot, flashing my torch up and down the tarmac, the giant store behind me, with shrubbery around it black and whispery, and beyond the barriers the roads and night cars, moving away from me.

Inside again and through bedrooms, past all the pine frames and the fake walls. It was dim. Half-lights in all the big chambers full of beds never slept in and sinks without plumbing. I could stand still and there was nothing, no movement and no noise.

One time, I made arrangements with the other guards on duty, and I brought my girlfriend to the store. We wandered hand in hand through all the pretend rooms like stage sets, trailing torchlight. We played house like children, acting out little moments—her stepping out of the shower to my proffered towel, dividing the paper at the breakfast bar. Then we found the biggest and most expensive bed, with a special mattress that you can see nearby cut in cross-section.

After a while, she told me to stop. I asked her what the matter was, but she seemed angry and wouldn't say. I led her out through the locked doors with my swipe card and walked her to her car, alone in the lot, and I watched her drive away. There's a long one-way system of ramps and roundabouts to leave the store, which she followed, unnecessarily, so it took a long time before she was gone. We don't see each other anymore.

In the warehouse, I walked between metal shelf units thirty feet high. My footsteps sounded to me like a prison guard's. I imagined the flat-packed furniture assembling itself around me.

I came back through kitchens, following the path towards the café, up the stairs into the unlit hallway. My mates weren't back: there was no light shining off the big window that fronted the silent ball room.

It was absolutely dark. I put my face up close to the glass and stared at the black shape I knew was the climbing frame; the Wendy house, a little square of paler shadow, was adrift in plastic balls. I turned on my torch and shone it into the room. Where the beam touched them, the balls leapt into clown colours, and then the light moved and they went back to being black.

In the main crèche, I sat on the assistant's chair, with a little half-circle of baby chairs in front of me. I sat like that in the dark, and listened to no noise. There was a little bit of lamplight, orangey through the windows, and once every few seconds a car would pass, just audible, way out on the other side of the parking lot.

I picked up the book by the side of the chair and opened it in torchlight. Fairy tales. Sleeping Beauty, and Cinderella.

There was a sound.

A little soft thump.

I heard it again.

Balls in the ball room, falling onto each other.

I was standing instantly, staring through the glass into the darkness of the ball room. *Pudda-thudda,* it came again. It took me seconds to move, but I came close up to the window with my torch raised. I was holding my breath, and my skin felt much too tight.

My torch beam swayed over the climbing frame and out the window on the other side, sending shadows into the corridors. I directed it down into those bouncy balls, and just before the beam hit them, while they were still in darkness, they shivered and slid away from each other in a tiny little trail. As if something was burrowing underneath.

My teeth were clenched. The light was on the balls now, and nothing was moving.

I kept that little room lit for a long time, until the torchlight stopped trembling. I moved it carefully up and down the walls, over every part, until I let out a big dumb hiss of relief because I saw that there were balls on the top of the climbing frame, right on its edge, and I realised that one or two of them must have fallen off, bouncing softly among the others.

I shook my head and my hand swung down, the torchlight going with it, and the ball room went back into darkness. And as it did, in the moment when the shadows rushed back in, I felt a brutal cold, and I stared at the little girl in the Wendy house, and she stared up at me.

The other two guys couldn't calm me down.

They found me in the ball room, yelling for help. I'd opened both doors and I was hurling balls out into the crèche and the corridors, where they rolled and bounced in all directions, down the stairs to the entrance, under the tables in the café.

At first I'd forced myself to be slow. I knew that the most important thing was not to scare the girl any more than she must have been already. I'd croaked out some daft, would-be cheerful greeting, come inside, shining the torch gradually towards the Wendy house, so I wouldn't dazzle her, and I'd kept talking, whatever nonsense I could muster.

When I realised she'd sunk down again beneath the balls, I became all jokey, trying to pretend we were playing hide-and-seek. I was horribly aware of how I might seem to her, with my build and my uniform, and my accent.

But when I got to the Wendy house, there was nothing there.

"She's been left behind!" I kept screaming, and when they understood they dived in with me and scooped up handfuls of the balls and threw them aside, but the two of them stopped long before me. When I turned to throw more of the balls away, I realised they were just watching me.

They wouldn't believe she'd been in there, or that she'd got out. They told me they would have seen her, that she'd have had to come past them. They kept telling me I was being crazy, but they didn't try to stop me, and eventually I cleared the room of all the balls, while they stood and waited for the police I'd made them call.

The ball room was empty. There was a damp patch under the Wendy house, which the assistants must have missed.

. . .

For a few days, I was in no state to come in to work. I was fevered. I kept thinking about her.

I'd only seen her for a moment, till the darkness covered her. She was five or six years old. She looked washed out, grubby and bleached of colour, and cold, as if I saw her through water. She wore a stained T-shirt, with the picture of a cartoon princess on it.

She'd stared at me with her eyes wide, her face clamped shut. Her grey, fat little fingers had gripped the edge of the Wendy house.

The police had found no one. They'd helped us clear up the balls and put them back in the ball room, and then they'd taken me home.

I can't stop wondering if it would have made any difference to how things turned out, if anyone had believed me. I can't see how it would. When I came back to work, days later, everything had already happened.

After you've been in this job a while, there are two kinds of situations you dread.

The first one is when you arrive to find a mass of people, tense and excited, arguing and yelling and trying to push each other out of the way and calm each other down. You can't see past them, but you know they're reacting ineptly to something bad.

The second one is when there's a crowd of people you can't see past, but they're hardly moving, and nearly silent. That's rarer, and invariably worse.

The woman and her daughter had already been taken away. I saw the whole thing later on security tape.

It had been the little girl's second time in the ball room in a matter of hours. Like the first time, she'd sat alone, perfectly happy, singing and talking to herself. Her minutes were up, her mother had loaded her new garden furniture into the car and come to take her home. She'd knocked on the glass and smiled, and the little girl had waded over happily enough, until she realised that she was being summoned.

On the tape you can see her whole body language change. She starts sulking and moaning, then suddenly turns and runs back to the Wendy house, plonking herself among the balls. Her mother looks fairly patient, standing at the door and calling for her, while the assistant stands with her. You can see them chatting.

The little girl sits by herself, talking into the empty doorway of the Wendy house, with her back to the adults, playing some obstinate, solitary final game. The other kids carry on doing their thing. Some are watching to see what happens.

Eventually, her mother yells at her to come. The girl stands and turns round, facing her across the sea of balls. She has one in each hand, her arms down by her sides, and she brings them up and stares at them, and at her mother. *I won't*, she's saying, I heard later. *I want to stay. We're playing.*

She backs into the Wendy house. Her mother strides over to her and bends in the doorway for a moment. She has to get down on all fours to get inside. Her feet stick out.

There's no sound on the tape. It's when you see all the children jerk, and the assistant run, that you know the woman has started to scream.

The assistant later told me that when she tried to rush forward, it seemed as if she couldn't get through the balls, as if they'd become heavy. The children were all getting in her way. It was bizarrely, stupidly difficult to cross the few feet to the Wendy house, with other adults in her wake.

They couldn't get the mother out of the way, so between them they lifted the house into the air over her, tearing its toy walls apart.

The child was choking.

Of course, of course the balls are designed to be too big for anything like this to happen, but somehow she had shoved one far inside her mouth. It should have been impossible. It was too far, wedged too hard to prise out. The little girl's eyes were huge, and her feet and knees kept turning inward towards each other.

You see her mother lift her up and beat her upon the back, very hard. The children are lined against the wall, watching.

One of the men manages to get the mother aside, and raises the girl for the Heimlich manoeuvre. You can't see her face too clearly on the tape, but you can tell that it is very dark now, the colour of a bruise, and her head is lolling.

Just as he has his arms about her, something happens at the man's feet, and he slips on the balls, still hugging her to him. They sink together.

They got the children into another room. Word went through the store, of course, and all the absent parents came running. When the first arrived she found the man who had intervened screaming at the children while the assistant tried desperately to quiet him. He was demanding they tell him where the other little girl was, who'd come close and chattered to him as he tried to help, who'd been getting in his way.

That's one of the reasons we had to keep going over the tape, to see where this girl had come from, and gone. But there was no sign of her.

Of course, I tried to get transferred, but it wasn't a good time in the industry, or in any industry. It was made pretty clear to me that the best way of holding on to my job was to stay put.

The ball room was closed, initially during the inquest, then for "renovation," and then for longer while discussions went on about its future. The closure became unofficially indefinite, and then officially so.

Those adults who knew what had happened (and it always surprised me, how few did) strode past the room with their toddlers strapped into pushchairs and their eyes grimly on the showroom trail, but their children still missed the room. You could see it when they came up the stairs with their parents. They'd think they were going to the ball room, and they'd start talking about it, and shouting about the climbing frame and the colours, and when they realised it was closed, the big window covered in brown paper, there were always tears.

Like most adults I turned the locked-up room into a blind spot. Even on night shifts when it was still marked on my route I'd turn away. It was sealed up, so why would I check it? Particularly when it still felt so terrible in there, a bad atmosphere as tenacious as stink. There are little card swipe units we have to use to show that we've covered each area, and I'd do the one by the ball room door without looking, staring at the stacks of new catalogues at the top of the stairs. Sometimes I'd imagine I could hear noises behind me, soft little *pudda-thuddas*, but I knew it was impossible so there was no point even checking.

It was strange to think of the ball room closed for good. To think that those were the last kids who'd ever get to play there.

One day I was offered a big bonus to stay on late. The store manager introduced me to Mr. Gainsburg from head office. It turned out she didn't just mean the UK operation, but the corporate parent. Mr. Gainsburg wanted to work late in the store that night, and he needed someone to look after him.

He didn't reappear until well past eleven, just as I was beginning to assume that he'd given in to jet lag and I was in for an easy night. He was tanned and well dressed. He kept using my Christian name while he lectured me about the company. A couple of times I wanted to tell him what my profession had been where I come from, but I could see he wasn't trying to patronise me. In any case I needed the job.

He asked me to take him to the ball room.

"Got to sort out problems as early as you can," he said. "It's the number one thing I've learned, John, and I've been doing this a while. One problem will always create another. If you leave one little thing, think you can just *ride* it out, then before you know it you've got two. And so on.

"You've been here a while, right John? You saw this place before it closed. These crazy little rooms are a fantastic hit with kids. We have them in all our stores now. You'd think it would be an extra, right? A nice-to-have. But I tell you, John, kids love these places, and kids . . . well, kids are really, really important to this company."

The doors were propped open by now and he had me help him carry a portable desk from the show floor into the ball room.

"Kids *make* us, John. Nearly forty percent of our customers have young children, and most of those cite the kid-friendliness of our stores as one of the top two or three reasons they come here. Above quality of product. Above *price*. You drive here, you eat, it's a day out for the family.

"Okay, so that's one thing. Plus, it turns out that people who are shopping for their kids are much more aware of issues like safety and quality. They spend way more per item, on average, than singles and childless couples, because they want to know they've done the best for their kids. And our margins on the big-ticket items are way healthier than on entry-level product. Even low-income couples, John, the proportion of their income that goes on furniture and household goods just rockets up at pregnancy."

He was looking around him at the balls, bright in the ceiling lights that hadn't been on for months, at the ruined skeleton of the Wendy house.

"So what's the first thing we look at when a store begins to go wrong? The facilities. The crèche, the childcare. Okay, tick. But the results here have been badly off-kilter recently. All the stores have shown a dip, of course, but this one, I don't know if you've noticed, it's not just revenues are down, but traffic has sunk in a way that's completely out of line. Usually, traffic is actually surprisingly resilient in a downturn. People buy less, but they keep coming. Sometimes, John, we even see numbers go *up*.

"But here? Visits are down overall. Proportionally, traffic from couples with children is down even more. And *repeat* traffic from couples with children has dropped through the floor. That's what's unusual with this store.

"So why aren't they coming back as often? What's different here? What's changed?" He gave a little smile and looked ostentatiously around, then back at me. "Okay? Parents can still leave their kids in the crèche, but the kids aren't asking their parents for repeat visits like they used to. Something's missing. Ergo. Therefore. We need it back."

He laid his briefcase on the desk and gave me a wry smile.

"You know how it is. You tell them and tell them to fix things as they happen, but do they listen? Because it isn't them who have to patch it up, right? So then you end up with not one problem but two. Twice as much trouble to bring under control." He shook his head ruefully. He was looking around the room, into all the corners, narrowing his eyes. He took a couple of deep breaths.

"Okay, John, listen, thanks for all your help. I'm going to need a few minutes here. Why don't you go watch some TV, get yourself a coffee or something? I'll come find you in a while."

I told him I'd be in the staff room. I turned away and heard him open his case. As I left I peered through the glass wall and tried to see what he was laying out on the desk. A candle, a flask, a dark book. A little bell.

Visitor numbers are back up. We're weathering the recession remarkably well. We've dropped some of the deluxe product and introduced a back-to-basic raw pine range. The store has actually taken on more staff recently than it's let go.

The kids are happy again. Their obsession with the ball room refuses to die. There's a little arrow outside it, a bit more than three feet off the ground, which is the maximum height you can be to come in. I've seen children come tearing up the stairs to get in and find out that they've grown in the months since their last visit, that they're too big to come in and play. I've seen them *raging* that they'll never be allowed in again, that they've had their lot, forever. You know they'd give anything at all, right then, to go back. And the other children watching them, those who are just a little bit smaller, would do anything to stop and stay as they are.

Something in the way they play makes me think that Mr. Gainsburg's intervention may not have had the exact effect everyone was hoping for. Seeing how eager they are to rejoin their friends in the ball room, I wonder sometimes if it was intended to.

To the children, the ball room is the best place in the world. You can see that they think about it when they're not there, that they dream about it. It's where they want to stay. If they ever got lost, it's the place they'd want to find their way back to. To play in the Wendy house and on the climbing frame, and to fall all soft and safe on the plastic balls, to scoop them up over each other, without hurting, to play in the ball room forever, like in a fairy tale, alone, or with a friend.

REPORTS OF CERTAIN EVENTS IN LONDON

REPORTS OF CERTAIN EVENTS IN LONDON

On the 27th of November 2000, a package was delivered to my house. This happens all the time — since becoming a professional writer the amount of mail I get has increased enormously. The flap of the envelope had been torn open a strip, allowing someone to look inside. This also isn't unusual: because, I think, of my political life (I am a varyingly active member of a left-wing group, and once stood in an election for the Socialist Alliance), I regularly find, to my continuing outrage, that my mail has been peered into.

I mention this to explain why it was that I opened something not addressed to me. I, China Miéville, live on —ley Road. This package was addressed to a Charles Melville, of the same house-number —ford Road. No postcode was given, and it had found its way, slowly, to me. Seeing a large packet torn half-open by some cavalier spy, I simply assumed it was mine and opened it.

It took me a good few minutes to realise my mistake: the covering note contained no greeting by name to alert me. I read it along with the first few of the enclosed papers with growing bewilderment, convinced (absurd as this must sound) that this was to do with some project or other I had got involved with and then forgotten. When finally I looked again at the name on the envelope, I was wholly surprised.

That was the point at which I was morally culpable, rather than simply foolish. By then I was too fascinated by what I had read to stop.

I've reproduced the content of the papers below, with explanatory notes. Unless otherwise stated they're photocopies, some stapled together, some attached with paper clips, many with pages missing. I've tried to keep them in the order they came in; they are not always chronological. Before I had a sense of what was in front of me, I was casual about how I put the papers down. I can't vouch that this was how they were originally organised.

――――◆◆◆◆――――

[*Cover note. This is written on a postcard, in a dark blue ink, a cursive hand. The photograph is of a wet kitten emerging from a sink full of water and suds. The kitten wears a comedic expression of anxiety.*]

Where are you? Here as requested. What do you want this for anyway? I scribbled thoughts on some. Can't find half the stuff. I don't think anyone's noticed me rummaging through the archives, and I managed to get into your old place for the rest (thank god you file) but come to next meeting. You can get people on your side but be clever. In haste. Are you taking sides? Talk soon. Will you get this? Come to next meeting. More as I find it.

――――◆◆◆――――

[*This page was originally produced on an old manual typewriter.*]

BWVF Meeting, 6 September 1976

Agenda.
1. Minutes of the last meeting.
2. Nomenclature.
3. Funds.
4. Research notes.
5. Field reports.
6. AOB.

1. Last minutes:
Motion to approve JH, Second FR. Vote: unani-
mous.

2. Nomenclature:
FR proposes namechange. 'BWVF' dated. CT reminds
FR of tradition. FR insists 'BWVF' exclusive,
proposes 'S (Society) WVF' or 'G (Gathering)
WVF'. CT remonstrates. EN suggests 'C (Coven)
WVF', to laughter. Meeting growing impatient. FR
moves to vote on change, DY seconds. Vote: 4
for, 13 against. Motion denied.
[*Someone has added by hand:* 'Again! Silly Cow.']

3. Funds/Treasury report.
EN reports this quarter several payments made,
totalling £—. [*The sum is effaced with black ink.*] Agreed
to keep this up-to-date to avoid repeat of
Gouldy-Statten debacle. Subscriptions are
mostly current and with

[*This is the end of a page and the last I have of these minutes.*]

—◆••◆—

[*The next piece is a single sheet that looks word-processed.*]

1 September 1992

M E M O

Members are kindly asked to show more care when handling items in the collection. Standards have become unacceptably lax. Despite their vigilant presence, curators have reported various soilings, including: fingerprints on recovered wood and glass; ink spots on cornices; caliper marks on guttering and ironwork; waxy residue on keys.

Of course research necessitates handling but if members cannot respect these unique items conditions of access may have to become even more stringent.

Before entering, remember:

•Be careful with your instruments.

•Always wash your hands.

[*The next page is numbered '2' and begins halfway through a paragraph. Luckily it contains a header.*]

BWVF PAPERS, NO. 223. JULY 1981.

uncertain, but there is little reason to doubt his veracity. Both specimens tested exactly as one would expect for V$\underline{D}$, suggesting no difference between VD and VF at even a molecular level. Any distinction must presumably be at the level of gross morphology, which defies our attempts at comparison, or of a noncorporeal essence thus-far beyond our capacity to measure.

Whatever the reality, the fact that the two specimens of VF mortar can be added to the BWVF collection is cause for celebration.

This research should be ready to present by the end of this year.

REPORT ON WORK IN PROGRESS:
VF and Hermeneutics
by B. Bath.

Problems of knowledge and the problematic of Knowing. Considerations of VF as urban scripture. Kabbala considered as interpretive model. Investigation of VF as patterns of interference. Research currently ongoing, ETA of finished article uncertain.

REPORT ON WORK IN PROGRESS:
Recent changes in VF Behaviour
by E. Nugen.

Tracking the movements of VF is notoriously difficult. [*Inserted here is a scrawl — 'No bloody kidding. What do you think we're all bloody doing here?*] Reconstructing these patterns over the longue durée [*the accent is added by hand*] is perforce a matter of plumbing a historical record that is, by its nature and definitionally, partial, anecdotal and uncertain. As most of my readers know it has long been my aim to extract from the annals of our society evidence for long-term cycles (See Working Paper 19, Once More on the Statten Curve), an aim on which I have not been entirely unsuccessful.

I have collated the evidence from the major verified London sightings of the last three decades (two of those sightings my own) and can conclusively state that the time between VF arrival at and departure from a locus has decreased by a factor of 0.7. VF are moving more quickly.

In addition, tracking their movements after each appearance has become more complicated and (even) less certain. In 1940, application of the Deschaine Matrix with regard to a given VF's arrival time and duration on-site would result in a 23% chance of predicting reappearance parameters (within two months and two miles): today that same process nets only a 16% chance. VF are less predictable than they have ever been (barring, perhaps, the Lost Decade of 1876–86).

The shift in this behaviour is not linear but punctuated, sudden bursts of change over the years: once between 1952 and '53, again in late 1961, again in '72 and '76. The causes and consequences are not yet known. Each of these pivotal moments has resulted in an increased pace of change. The anecdotal evidence we have all heard, that VF have recently become more skittish and agitated, appears to be correct.

I intend to present this work in full within 18 months. I wish to thank CM for help with the research. [*This CM is presumably Charles Melville, to whom the package was addressed. Clipped to the BWVF papers is this handwritten note:*

Yes, Edgar is a pompous arse but he is on to something big.

What is it Edgar N. is onto? Of course I wondered, and still wonder, though now I think perhaps I know.]

———◆•••◆———

[*Then there is a document unlike the others so far. It is a booklet, a few pages long. It was when I started to read this that I stopped, frowned, looked again at the envelope, realised my inadvertent intrusion, and decided almost instantly that I would not stop reading. 'Decided' doesn't really get the sense of the urgency with which I continued, as if I had no choice. But then if I say that, I absolve myself of wrongdoing which I won't do, so let's say I 'decided', though I'm unsure that I did. In any case, I continued reading. This document is printed on both sides like a flyer. The first sentence below is in large red font, and constitutes the booklet's front cover.*]

URGENT: *Report of a Sighting.*

Principal witness: FR.

Secondary: EN.

On Thursday 11th February 1988, so far as it is possible to tell between 3:00 a.m. and 5:17 a.m., a little way south of Plumstead High Street SE18, Varmin Way occurred.

Even somewhat foreshortened from its last known appearance (Battersea 1983 — see the VF Concordance), Varmin Way is in a buckled configuration due to the constraints of space. One end adjoins Purrett Road between numbers 44 and 46, approximately forty feet north of Saunders Road: Varmin Way then appears to describe a tight S-curve, emerging halfway up Rippolson Road between numbers 30 and 32 (see attached map). [*There is no map.*]

Two previously terraced dwellings on each of the intersected streets have now been separated by Varmin Way. One on Rippolson is deserted: surreptitious enquiries have been made of inhabitants of each of the others, but none have remarked with anything other than indifference to the newcomer. Eg: in response to FR's query of one man if he knew the name of 'that alley', he glanced at the street now abutting his house, shrugged and told her he was 'buggered if he knew'. This response is of course typical of VF occurrence-environs (See B. Harman, 'On the Non-Noticing', BWVF Working Papers no. 5).

A partial exception is one thirty-five-year-old Purrett Road man, resident in the brick dwelling newly on Varmin Way's north bank. Observed on his way toward Saunders Road, crossing Varmin Way, he tripped on the new kerb. He looked down at the asphalt and up at brick corners of the junction, paced back and forward five times with a quizzical expression, peering down the street's length, without entering it, before continuing on his journey, looking back twice.

[*This is the end of the middle page of the leaflet. Folded and inserted inside is a handwritten letter. I have therefore decided to reproduce it here in the middle of the leaflet text. It reads:*]

Charles,

In haste. So sorry I could not reach you sooner – obviously phone not an option. I <u>told</u> you I could work this out: Tiona was only on-site because of me, but I modestly listed her as principal for politics' sake. Charles, we're about to go in and I'm telling you even from where I'm standing I can see the evidence, this is the real thing. Next time, next time. Or get down here! I'm sending this first class (of course!) so when you get it rush down here. But you know Varmin Way's reputation – it's restless, will probably be gone. But come find me! I'll be here at least.

Edgar

At the end of this note is appended, in the same handwriting as that of the package's introductory note:

What a bastard! I take it this was when you and he stopped seeing eye to eye? Why did he cut you out like that, and why so coyly?

The leaflet then continues:]

Initial investigation shows that the new Varmin Way–overlooking walls of the houses now separated on Purrett Road are flat concrete. Those of Rippolson Road, though, are of similar brick to their fronts, bearing the usual sigil of the VF's identity, and are broken by small windows at the very top, through the net curtains of which nothing can be seen. (See 'On Neomural Variety', by H. Burke, WBVF Working Papers no. 8)

Those innards of Varmin Way which can be seen from its adjoining streets bear all the usual signs of VF morphology (are, in other words, apparently unremarkable), and are in accordance with earlier documented descriptions of the subject. In this occurrence, it being short, FR and EN were able to conduct the Bowery Resonance Experiment, stationing themselves at either end of the VF and shouting to each other down its lengths (until forced to stop by externalities). [*Here in Edgar's hand has been inserted* 'Some local thuggee threatening to do me in if I didn't shut up!'] Each could clearly hear the other, past the kinks in this configuration of Varmin Way.

More experiments are to follow.

--------◆•••◆--------

[*When I reached this point I was trembling. I had to stop, leave the room, drink some water, force myself to breathe slowly. I'm tempted to add more about this, about the sudden and threatened speculations these documents raised in me, but I think I should stay out of it.*

Immediately after the report of the sighting was another, similarly produced pamphlet.]

URGENT: *Report of an Aborted Investigation.*

Present: FR, EN, BH.

[*Added here is another new comment in Charles's nameless contact's hand. It reads:* 'Dread to think how gutted you were to be replaced by

Bryn as new favourite. What exactly did you <u>do</u> to get Edgar so pissed off?']

At 11:20 p.m. on Saturday 13 February 1988, from its end on Rippolson Road, an initial examination was made of Varmin Way. Photographs were taken establishing the VF's identity (figure 1). [*Figure 1 is a surprisingly good-quality reproduction of a shot, showing a street sign by a wall, standing at leg-height on two little metal or wooden posts. The image is at a peculiar angle, which I think is the result of the photograph not being taken straight on, but from Rippolson Road, beyond. In an unusual old serif font, the sign reads* Varmin Way.]

As the party prepared for the expedition, certain events took place or were insinuated which led to a postponement and quick regrouping at a late-night café on Plumstead High Street. [*What were those 'certain events'? The pointed imprecision suggested to me something deliberately not committed to paper, something that the readers of this report, or perhaps a subgroup of them, would understand. These writings are a strange mix of the scientifically exact and the imprecise — even the failure to specify the café is surprising. But it is the baleful vagueness of the certain events that will not stop worrying at me.*] When the group returned to Rippolson Road at 11:53 p.m., to their great frustration, Varmin Way had unoccurred.

[*Two monochrome pictures end the piece. They have no explanatory notes or legend. They are both taken in daylight. On the left is a photograph of two houses, on either side of a small street of low century-old houses which curves sharply to the right, it looks like, quickly unclear with distance. The right-hand picture is the two facades again, but this time the houses — recognisably the same from a window's crack, from a smear of paint below a sash, from the scrawny front gardens and the distinct unkempt buddleia bush — are closed up together. They are no longer semi-detached. There is no street between them.*]

[So.

I stopped for a bit. I had to stop. And then I had to read on again.

A single sheet of paper. Typewritten again apart from the name, now on an electronic machine.]

Could you see it, Charles? The damage, halfway down Varmin Way? It's there, it's visible in the picture in that report. [*This must mean the picture on the left. I stared at it hard, with the naked eye and through a magnifying glass. I couldn't make out anything.*] It's like the slates from Scry Pass, the ones I showed you in the collection. <u>You</u> could see it in the striae and the marks, even if none of the bloody curators did. Varmin Way wasn't just passing through, it was <u>resting</u>, it was <u>recovering</u>, it had been attacked. I am right.

Edgar

[I kept reading.

Though it's not signed, judging by the font, what follows are a couple of pages of another typed letter from Edgar.]

earliest occurrence I can find of it is in the early 1700s (you'll hear 1790 or '91 or something — nonsense, that's just the official position based on the archives — this one isn't verified but be-lieve me it's correct). Only a handful of years after the Glorious Revolution we find Antonia Chesterfield referring in her diaries to 'a right rat of a street, ascamper betwixt Waterloo and the Mall, a veritable Vermin, in name as well as kind. Beware — Touch a rat and he will bite, as others have found, of our own and of the Vermin's vagrant tribe'. That's a reference to Varmin Way — Mrs Chesterfield was in the Brotherhood's precursor (and you'd not have heard her complaining about that name either — Fiona take note!).

You see what she's getting at, and I think she was the first. I don't know, Charles, correlation is so terribly hard, but look at some of the other candidates. Shuck Road; Caul Street; Stang Street; Teratologue Avenue (this last I think is fairly voracious); et al. So far as I can work it out, Varmin Way and Stang Street were highly antagonistic at that stage, but now they're almost certainly noncombative. No surprise: Sole Den Road is the big enemy these days — remember 1987?

(Incidentally, talking of that first Varmin occurrence, did you ever read all the early cryptolit I sent you?

The Clerk entered into a Snickelway
That then was gone again by close of day

Fourteenth century, imagine. I'll bet you a pound there are letters from disgruntled Britannic procurators complaining about errant alleyways around the Temple of Mithras. But there's not much discussion of the hostilities until Mrs Chesterfield.)

Anyway, you see my point. It's the only way one can make sense of it all, of all this that I've been going on about for so long. The Viae are fighting, and I think they always have.

And there's no idiot nationalism here either, as

[And here is the end of the page. And there is another message added, clearly referring to this letter, from CM's nameless interlocutor. 'I believe it', he says, or she says, but I think of it as a man's handwriting though

that's a problematic assumption. 'It took me a while, but I believe Edgar's bellum theory. But I know you, Charles, "pure research" be buggered as far as you're concerned. I know what Edgar's doing, but I cannot see where you are going with this.']

————◆••◆————

URGENT: *Report of a Traveller.*

Wednesday June 17th 1992.

We are receiving repeated reports, which we are attempting to verify, of an international visit. Somewhere between Willesden Green and Dollis Hill (details are unclear), Ulica Nerwowosc has arrived. This visitor from Krakow has been characterised by our comrades in the Kolektyw as a mercurial mediaeval alleyway, very difficult to predict. Though it has proved impossible to photograph, initial reports correlate with the Kolektyw's description of the Via. Efforts are ongoing to capture an image of this elusive newcomer, and even to plan a Walk, if the risks are not too great.

No London street has sojourned elsewhere for some time (perhaps not unfortunate — a visit from Bunker Crescent was, notoriously, responsible for the schism in the BWVF Chicago Chapter in 1956), but the last ten years have seen six other documented visitations to London from foreign Viae Ferae. See table.

DATES	VISITOR	USUAL RESIDENCE	NOTES
6/9/82– 8/9/82	Rue de la Fascination	Paris	Spent three days in Neasden, motionless from arrival to departure, jutting south of Prout Grove NW10.
3/1/84– 4/1/84	West Fifth Street	New York	Appeared restless, settling for only up to two hours at a time, moving among various locations in Camberwell and Highgate.
11/2/84	Heulstrasse	Berlin	A relatively wide thoroughfare, the empty shopfronts of Heulstrasse cut north of the East London Crematorium in Bow for half a day, relocating late that night to Sydenham, and moving for three hours in backstreets, always just evading investigators.
22/10/87, 24/10/87	Unthinker Road	Glasgow	This tiny cobbled lane, seemingly only a chance gap between the backs of houses, occurred on the Thursday morning jutting off Old Compton Street W1, spent a day occurring with stealthy movements further and further into Soho, unoccurred on the Friday, recurring on Saturday only to cut sharply south toward Piccadilly Circus and disappear.
15/4/90?	Boulevard de la Gare Intrinsèque	Paris	Uniquely, this Via Fera was not witnessed by an investigator, but by a rare noticing civilian whose enquiries about a French-named street of impressive dimensions and architecture in the heart of Catford came to the Brotherhood's attention.
29/11/91– 1/12/91	Chup Shawpno Lane	Calcutta	The pale clay of C.S. Lane, its hard earth road cut by tram tracks, were exhaustively documented by TY and FD during its meanderings through Camden and Kentish Town.

[There is a thick card receipt, stamped with some obscure sign, its left-hand columns rendered in crude typeface, those on the right filled out in black ink.]

BWVF collection.

Date: 7/8/1992

Name: C. Melville

Curator present: G. Benedict

Requested: Item 117: a half-slate recovered
                    from Scry Pass, 7/11/1958.
                    Item 34: a splinter of glass recovered
                    from Caul Street, 8/2/1986.
                    Item 67: an iron ring and key recovered
                    from Stang Street, 6/5/1936.

———◆•••◆———

[This next letter is on headed paper, beautifully printed.]

SOCIÉTÉ POUR
L'ÉTUDE DES RUES SAUVAGES

20 June 1992

Dear Mr Melville,

Thank you for your message and congratulations for have this visitor. We in Paris were fortunate to have this pretty Polish street rest with us in 1988 but I did not see it.

I confirm that you are correct. Boulevard de la Gare Intrinsèque and the Rue de la Fascination have both stories about them. We call him le jockey, a man who is supposed to live on streets like these and to make them move for him, but these are only stories for the children. There are no people on these *rues sauvages*, in Paris, and I think there are none in London too. No one knows why the streets have gone to London that time, like no one knows why your Importune Avenue moved around the area where is now the Arc de la Défence twelve years ago.

Yours truly,

Claudette Santier

<hr>

[*There is a handwritten letter.*]

My Dear Charles,

I'm quite aware that you feel ill-used. I apologise for that. There is no point, I think, rehearsing our disagreements, let alone the unpleasant contretemps they have led to. I cannot see that you are going anywhere with these investigations, though, and I simply do not have enough years left to indulge your ideas, nor enough courage (were I younger... Ah but were I younger what would I not do?).

I have performed three Walks in my time, and have seen the evidence of the wounds the Viae leave on each other. I have tracked the combatants and shifting loyalties. Where, in contrast, is the evidence behind your claims? Why, on the basis of your intuition, should anyone discard the cautions that may have kept us alive? It is not as if what we do is safe, Charles. There are reasons for the strictures you are so keen to overturn.

Of course yes I have heard all the stories that you have: of the streets that occur with lights ashine and men at home! of the antique costermongers' cries still heard over the walls of Dandle Way! of the street-riders! I do not say I don't believe them, any more than I don't – or do – believe the stories that Potash Street and Luckless Road courted and mated and that that's how Varmin Way was born, or the stories of where the Viae Ferae go when they unoccur. I have no way of judging. This mythic company of inhabitants and street-tamers may be true, but so long as it is also a myth, you have nothing. I am content to observe, Charles, not to become involved.

Good God, who knows what the agenda of the streets might be? Would you really, would you _really_, Charles, risk attempting ingress? Even if you could? After everything you've read and heard? Would you risk taking sides?

Regretfully and fondly,

Edgar

———◄••••►———

[_This is another handwritten note. I think it is in Edgar's hand, but it is hard to be sure._]

Saturday 27th November 1999.

Varmin Way's back.

———◄••••►———

[_We are near the end of the papers now. What came out of the package next looks like one of the pamphlet-style reports of sightings. It is marked with a black band in one corner of the front cover._]

URGENT: _Report of a Walk._

Walkers: FR, EN, BH (author).

At 11:20 p.m. on Sunday 28th November 1999, a Walk was made the length of Varmin Way. As well as its tragic conclusion, most members will be aware of the extraordinary circumstances surrounding this investigation — since records began, there is no evidence in the archives of a Via Fera returning to the site of an earlier occurrence. Varmin Way's reappearance, then, at precisely the same location in Plumstead, between Purrett and Rippolson Road, as that it inhabited in February 1988, was profoundly shocking, and necessitated this perhaps too-quickly-planned Walk.

FR operated as base, remaining stationed on Rippolson Road (the front yard of the still-deserted number 32 acting as camp). Carrying toolbags and wearing Council overalls over their harnesses and belay kits, BH and EN set out. Their safety rope was attached to a fencepost close to FR. The Walkers remained in contact with FR throughout their three-hour journey, by radio.

In this occurrence of Varmin Way, the street is a little more than 100 metres long. [*An amendment here:* 'Can you imagine Edgar going metric? What kind of a homage is this?'] We proceeded slowly. [*Here another insertion:* 'Ugh. Change of person.' *By now I was increasingly irritated with these interruptions. I never felt I could ignore them, but they broke the flow of my reading. There was something vaguely passive-aggressive in their cheer, and I felt as if Charles Melville would have been similarly angered by them. In an effort to retain the flow I'll start this sentence again.*]

We proceeded slowly. We walked along the unpainted tar in the middle of Varmin Way, equidistant from the rows of streetlamps. These lamps are indistinguishable from those in the neighbouring streets. There are houses to either side, all of them with all their windows unlit, looking like low workers' cottages of Victorian vintage (though the earliest documented reports of Varmin Way date from 1792 — this apparent aging of form gives credence

[*To my intense frustration, several pages are missing, and this is where the report therefore ends. There are, however, several photographs in an envelope, stuffed in among the pages. There are four. They are dreadful shots, taken with a flash too close or too far, so that their subject is either effaced by light or peering out from a cowl of dark. Nonetheless they can just be made out.*]

The first is a wall of crumbling brick, the mortar fallen away in scabs. Askew across the print, taken from above, is a street sign. Varmin Way, it says, in an antiquated iron font. Written in biro on the photograph's back is: The Sigil.

The second is a shot along the length of the street. Almost nothing is visible in this, except perspective lines sketched in dark on dark. None of the houses has a front garden: their doors open directly onto the pavement. They are implacably closed, whether for centuries or only moments it is of course impossible to tell. The lack of a no-man's-land between house and Walker makes the doors loom. Written on the back of this image is: The Way.

The third is of the front of one of the houses. It is damaged. Its dark windows are broken, its brick stained, crumbling where the roof is fallen in. On the back is written: The Wound.

The last picture is of an end of rope and a climbing buckle, held in a young man's hands. The rope is frayed and splayed: the metal clip bent in a strange corkscrew. On the back of the photograph is nothing.]

[And then comes the last piece in the envelope. It is undated. It is in a different hand to the others.]

What did you do? How did you do it? What did you do, you bastard?

I saw what happened. Edgar was right, I saw where Varmin Way had been hurt. But you know that, don't you?

What did you do to Varmin Way to make it do that? What did you do to Edgar?

Do you think you'll get away with it?

That was everything. When I'd finished, I was frantic to find Charles Melville.

I think the ban on telephone conversations must extend to email and web pages. I searched online, of course, for BWVF, 'wild streets', 'feral streets', 'Viae Ferae', and so on. I got nothing. BWVF got references to cars or technical parts. I tried 'Brotherhood of Witnesses to/Watchers of the Viae Ferae' without any luck. 'Wild streets' of course got thousands: articles about New Orleans Mardi Gras, hard-boiled ramblings, references to an old computer game, and an article about the Cold War. Nothing relevant.

I visited each of the sites described in the scraps of literature, the places where all the occurrences occurred. For several weekends I wandered in scraggy arse-end streets in north or south London, or sometimes in sedate avenues, even once (following Unthinker Road) walking through the centre of Soho. Inevitably, I suppose, I kept returning to Plumstead.

I would hold the before-and-after pictures up and look at the same houses of Rippolson Road, all closed up, an unbroken terrace.

Why did I not repackage all this stuff and send it on to Charles Melville, or take it to his house in person? The envelope wrongly sent to —ley Road was addressed to —ford Road. But there is no —ford Road in London. I have no idea how to find Charles.

The other reason I hesitated was that Charles had begun to frighten me.

The first few times I went walking, took photos secretively, I still thought as if I was witnessing some Oedipal drama. Reading and rereading the material, though, I realised that what Charles had done to Edgar was not the most important thing here. What was important was how he had done it.

I have eaten and drunk at all the cafés on Plumstead High Street. Most are unremarkable, one or two are extremely bad, one or two very good. In each establishment I asked, after finishing my tea, whether the owner knew anyone called Charles Melville. I asked if they'd mind me putting up a little notice I'd written.

'Looking for CM', it read. 'I've some documents you mislaid — maps of the area etc. Complicated streets! Please contact:' and then an anonymous email address I'd set up. I heard nothing.

I'm finding it hard to work. These days I am very conscious of corners. I fix my eyes on an edge of brick (or concrete or stone), where another road meets the one I'm walking, and I try to remember if I've ever noticed it before. I look up suddenly as I pass, to catch out anything hurriedly occurring. I keep seeing furtive motions and snapping up my head at only a tree in wind or an opened window. My anxiety — perhaps I should honestly call it foreboding — remains.

And if I ever did see anything more, what could I do? Probably we're irrelevant to them. Most of us. Their motivations are unimaginable, as opaque as brickwork sphinxes'. If they consider us at all, I doubt they care what's in our interests: I think it's that indifference that breeds these fears I cannot calm, and makes me wonder what Charles has done.

I say I heard nothing, after I put up my posters. That's not quite accurate. In fact, on the 4th of April 2001, five months after that first package, a letter arrived for Charles Melville. Of course I opened it immediately.

It was one page, handwritten, undated. I am looking at it now. It reads:

Dear Charles,

Where are you Charles?

I don't know if you know by now — I suspect you do — that you've been excommunicated. No one's saying that you're responsible for what happened to Edgar — no one can say that, it would be to admit far too much about what you've been doing — so they've got you on non-payment of subscriptions. Ridiculous, I know.

I believe you've done it. I never thought you could — I never thought anyone could. Are there others there? Are you alone?

Please, if ever you can, tell me. I want to know.

Your friend.

It was not the content of this letter but the envelope that so upset me. The letter, stamped and postmarked and delivered to my house, was addressed to 'Charles Melville, Varmin Way'.

This time, it's hard to pretend the delivery is coincidence. Either the Royal Mail is showing unprecedented consistency in misdirection, or I am being targeted. And if the latter, I do not know by whom or what: by pranksters, the witnesses, their renegade, or their subjects. I am at the mercy of the senders, whether the letter came to me hand-delivered or by stranger ways.

That is why I have published this material. I have no idea what my correspondents want from me. Maybe this is a test, and I've failed: maybe I was about to get a tap on the shoulder and a whispered invitation to join, maybe all this is the newcomer's manual, but I don't think so. I don't know why I've been shown these things, what part I am of another's plan, and that makes me afraid. So as an unwilling party to secrets, I want to disseminate them as widely as I can. I want to protect myself, and this is the only way I can think to do so. (The other possibility, that this was what I was required to do, hasn't passed me by.)

I can't say he owes me an explanation for all this, but I'd like a chance to persuade Charles Melville that I deserve one. I have his documents — if there is anyone reading this who knows how I can reach him, to return them, please let me know. You can contact me through the publisher of this book.

As I say, there is no —ford Road in London. I have visited all the other alternatives. I have knocked at the relevant number in —fast and —land and —nail Streets, and —ner and —hold Roads, and —den Close, and a few even less likely. No one has heard of Charles Melville. In fact, number such-and-such —fast Street isn't there anymore: it's been demolished; the street is being reshaped. That got me thinking. You can believe that got me thinking.

'What's happening to —fast Street?' I wondered. 'Where's it going?'

I can't know whether Charles Melville has broken Varmin Way, has tamed it, is riding it like a bronco through the city and beyond. I can't know if he's taken sides, is intervening in the unending savage war among the wild streets of London. Perhaps he and Edgar were wrong, perhaps there's no such fight, and the Viae Ferae are peaceful nomads, and Charles has just got tired and gone away. Perhaps there are no such untamed roads.

There's no way of knowing. Nonetheless I find myself thinking, wondering what's happening round that corner, and that one. At the bottom of my street, of —ley Road, there are some works going on. Men in hard hats and scaffolding are finishing the job time started of removing tumbledown walls, of sprucing up some little lane so small as to be nameless, nothing but a cat's-run full of rubbish and the smell of piss. They're reshaping it, is what it looks like. I think they're going to demolish an abandoned house and widen the alleyway.

We are in new times. Perhaps the Viae Ferae have grown clever, and stealthy. Maybe this is how they will occur now, sneaking in plain sight, arriving not suddenly but so slowly, ushered in by us, armoured in girders, pelted in new cement and paving. I think on the idea that Charles Melville is sending Varmin Way to come for me, and that it will creep up on me with a growl of mixers and drills. I think on another idea that this is not an occurrence but an unoccurrence, that Charles has woken —ley Road my home out of its domesticity, and that it is yawning, and that soon it will shake itself off like a fox and sniff the air and go wherever the feral streets go when they are not resting, I and my neighbours tossed on its back like fleas, and that in some months' time the main street it abuts will suddenly be seamless between the Irish bookie and the funeral parlour, and that —ley Road will be savaged by and savaging Sole Den Road, breaking its windows and walls and being broken in turn and coming back sometimes to rest.

FAMILIAR

A witch needed to impress his client. His middleman, who had arranged the appointment, told him that the woman was very old—"hundred at least"—and intimidating in a way he could not specify. The witch intuited something unusual, money or power. He made careful and arduous preparations. He insisted that he meet her a month later than the agent had planned.

His workshop was a hut, a garden shed in the shared allotments of north London. The woman edged past plots of runner beans, tomatoes, failing root vegetables and trellises, past the witch's neighbours, men decades younger than her but still old, who tended bonfires and courteously did not watch her.

The witch was ready. Behind blacked-out windows his little wooden room was washed. Boxes stowed in a tidy pile. The herbs and organic accoutrements of his work were out of the way but left visible—claws, skins like macabre facecloths, bottles stopped up, and careful piles of dust and objects. The old woman looked them over. She stared at a clubfooted pigeon chained by its good leg to a perch.

"My familiar."

The woman said nothing. The pigeon sounded and shat.

"Don't meet his eye, he'll steal your soul out of you." The witch hung a black rag in front of the bird. He would not look his client clear on. "He's basilisk, but you're safe now. He's hidden."

From the ceiling was a chandelier of unshaped coat hangers and pieces of china, on which three candles scabbed with dripping were lit. Little pyramids of wax lay on the wooden table beneath them. In their guttering the witch began his consultation, manipulating scobs of gris-gris—on the photographs his client provided he sprinkled leaf flakes, dirt, and grated remnants of plastic with a herb shaker from a pizzeria.

The effects came quickly so that even the cold old woman showed interest. Air dried up and expanded until the shed was stuffy as an aeroplane. There were noises from the shelves: mummied detritus moved anxious. It was much more than happened at most consultations, but the witch was still waiting.

In the heat the candles were moist. Strings of molten wax descended. They coated each other and drip-dripped in instantly frozen splashes. The stalactites extended, bearding the bottom of the candelabrum. The candles burnt too fast, pouring off wax, until the wire was trimmed with finger-thick extrusions.

They built up matter unevenly, curling out away from the table, and then they sputtered and seemed not to be dripping grease but drooling it from mouths that stretched open stringy within the wax. Fluttering tongues emerged and colourless eyes from behind nictitating membranes. For moments the things were random sculptures and then they were suddenly and definitively organic. At their ends, the melted candles' runoff was a fringe of little milk-white snakes. They were a few inches of flesh. Their bodies merged, anchored, with wax. They swayed with dim predatory intent and whispered.

The old woman screamed and so did the witch. He turned his cry though into a declamation and wavered slightly in his chair, so that the nest of dangling wax snakes turned their attention to him.

The pigeon behind its dark screen called in distress. The snakes stretched vainly from the candles and tried to strike the witch. Their toxin dribbled onto the powder of his hex, mixed it into wet grime under which the woman's photographs began to change.

It was an intercession, a series of manipulations even the witch found tawdry and immoral: but the pay was very good, and he knew that for his standing he must impress. The ceremony lasted less than an hour, the grease-snakes leaking noise and fluid, the pigeon ceaselessly frightened. At the end the witch rose weakly, his profuse sweat making him gleam like the wet wax. Moving with strange speed, too fast to be struck, he cut the snakes off where their bodies became candle, and they dropped onto the table and squirmed in death, bleeding thick pale blood.

His client stood and smiled, taking the corpses of the half-snakes and her photographs, carefully leaving them soiled. She was clear-eyed and happy and she did not wince at light as the witch did when he opened the door to her and gave her instructions for when to return. He watched her go through the kitchen gardens and only closed his shed door again when she was out of sight.

The witch drew back the screen from before the terrified pigeon and was about to kill it, but he stared at the stubs of wax where the snakes had been and instead he opened a window and let the bird out. He sat at the table and breathed heavily, watching the boxes at the back of the hut. The air settled. The witch could hear scratching. It came from inside a plastic toolbox, where he had stashed his real familiar.

He had called a familiar. He had been considering it for a long time. He had had a rough understanding that it would give him a conduit to a fecundity, and that had bolstered him through the pain and distaste of what the conjuration had needed. Listening to the curious scritch-scritch he fingered the scabs on his thighs and chest. They would scar.

The information he had found on the technique was vague—passed-on vagrants' hedge-magic, notepad palimpsests, marginalia in phone books. The mechanics of the operation had never been clear. The witch consoled himself that the misunderstanding was not his fault. He had hoped that the familiar, when it came, would fit his urban practice. He had hoped for a rat, big and dirty-furred, or a fox, or a pigeon such as the one he had displayed. He had thought that the flesh he provided was a sacrifice. He had not known it was substance.

With the lid off, the toolbox was a playpen, and the familiar investigated it. The witch looked at it, queasy. It had coated its body in the dust, so it no longer left wetness. Like a sea slug, ungainly, flanged with outgrowths of its own matter. Heavy as an apple, it was an amalgam of the witch's scraps of fat and flesh, coagulated with his sputum, cum, and hoodoo. It coiled, rolled itself busy into corners of its prison. It clutched towards the light, convulsing its pulp.

Even in its container, out of sight, the witch had felt it. He had felt it groping in the darkness behind him, and as he did with a welling up like blood he had made the snakes come, which he could not have done before. The familiar disgusted him. It made his stomach spasm, it left him ill and confounded, and he was not sure why. He had flensed animals for his calling, alive sometimes, and was inured to that. He had eaten shit and roadkill when liturgy demanded. But that little rag of his own flesh gave him a kind of passionate nausea.

When the thing had first moved he had screamed, realising what his familiar would be, and spewed till he was empty. And still it was almost beyond him to watch it, but he made himself, to try to know what it was that revolted him.

The witch could feel the familiar's enthusiasm. A feral fascination for things held it together, and every time it tensed and moved by peristalsis around its plastic cell the contractions of its dumb and hungry interest passed through the witch and bent him double. It was stupid: wordless and searingly curious. The witch could feel it make sense of the dust, now that it had rolled in it, randomly then deliberately, using it for something.

He wanted the strength to do again what he had done for the woman, though making the snakes had exhausted him. His familiar manipulated things, was a channel for manipulation; it lived to change, use, and know. The witch very much wanted that power it had given him, and he closed his eyes and made himself sure he could, he could steel himself. But looking at the nosing dusted red thing he was suddenly weak and uncertain. He could feel its mindless mind. To have his own effluvia maggot through him with every experience, he could not bear it, even with what it gave him. It made him a sewer. Every few seconds in his familiar's presence he was swallowing his own bile. He felt its constant eager interest like foulness, God knew why. It was not worth it. The witch decided.

It could not be killed, or if it could he did not know how. The witch took a knife to it but it investigated the blade avidly, only parting and re-forming under his efforts. It tried to grip the metal.

When he bludgeoned it with a flatiron it recoiled and regrouped its matter, moved over and around the weapon, soiling it with itself, and making the iron into a skate on which it tried to move. Fire only discomfited it, and it sat tranquil in acid. It studied every danger as it had dust, trying to use it, and the echo of that study turned the witch's gut.

He tipped the noisome thing into a sack. He could feel it shove itself at the fabric's pores, and he moved quickly. The witch drove, hessian fumbling in the toolbox beside him (he could not put it behind him, where he could not see it, where it might get out and conduct its investigations near his skin).

It was almost night when he stopped by the Grand Union Canal. In the municipal gardens of west London, between beat-up graffitied bridges, in earshot of the last punk children in the skate park, the witch tried to drown his familiar. He was not so stupid as to think it would work, but to drop the thing, weighted with rocks and tied up, into the cool and dirty water, was a relief so great he moaned. To see it drunk up by the canal. It was gone from him. He ran.

Cosseted by mud, the familiar tried to learn. It sent out temporary limbs to make sense of things. It strained without fear against the sack.

It compared everything it found to everything it knew. Its power was change. It was tool-using; it had no way of knowing except to put to use. The world was infinite tools. By now the familiar understood dust well, and had a little knowledge of knives and irons. It felt the water and the fibrous weave of the bag, and did things with them to learn that they were not what it had used before.

Out of the sack, in muddy dark, it swam ugly and inefficient, learning scraps of rubbish and little life. There were hardy fish even in so grubby a channel, and it was not long before it found them. It took a few carefully apart, and learned to use them.

The familiar plucked their eyes. It rubbed them together, dangled them from their fibres. It sent out microscopic filaments that tickled into the blood-gelled nerve stalks. The familiar's life was contagious. It sucked the eyes into itself and suddenly as visual signals reached it for the first time, though there was no light (it was burrowing in the mud) it *knew* that it was in darkness. It rolled into shallows, and with its new vitreous machines it saw streetlamp light cut the black water.

It found the corpses of the fish again (using sight, now, to help it). It unthreaded them. It greased itself with the slime on their skins. One by one it broke off the ribs like components of a model kit. It embedded them in its skin (its minute and random blood vessels and muscle fibres insinuating into the bone). It used them to walk, with the sedate pick-picking motion of an urchin.

The familiar was tireless. Over hours it learned the canal bed. Each thing it found it used, some in several ways. Some it used in conjunction with other pieces. Some it discarded after a while. With each use, each manipulation (and only with that manipulation, that change) it read meanings. The familiar accumulated brute erudition, forgetting nothing, and with each insight the next came easier, as its context grew. Dust had been the first and hardest thing to know.

When the familiar emerged from the water with the dawn, it was poured into a milk-bottle carapace. Its clutch of eyes poked from the bottleneck. It nibbled with a nail clipper. With precise little bullets of stone it had punctured holes in its glass sides, from which legs of waterlogged twig-wood and broken pens emerged. To stop it sinking into wet earth its feet were coins and flat stones. They looked insecurely attached. The familiar dragged the brown sack that had contained it. Though it had not found a use for it, and though it had no words for the emotion, it felt something like sentiment for the hessian.

All its limbs were permanently reconfigured. Even those it tired of and kicked off were wormed with organic ruts for its juices. Minuscule muscles and tendons the thickness of spider-silk but vastly stronger rooted through the components of its bric-a-brac body, anchoring them together. The flesh at its centre had grown.

The familiar investigated grass, and watched the birds with its inadequate eyes. It trouped industrious as a beetle on variegated legs.

Through that day and night the familiar learned. It crossed paths with small mammals. It found a nest of mice and examined their parts. Their tails it took for prehensile tentacles; their whiskers bristled it; it upgraded its eyes and learned to use ears. It compared what it found to dust, blades, water, twigs, fish ribs, and sodden rubbish: it learned mouse.

It learned its new ears, with focused fascination. Young Londoners played in the gardens, and the familiar stayed hidden and listened to their slang. It heard patterns in their sequenced barks.

There were predators in the gardens. The familiar was the size of a cat, and foxes and dogs sometimes went for it. It was now too big for the bottle-armour, had burst it, but had learned instead to fight. It raked with shards of china, nails, and screws—not with anger, but with its unchanging beatific interest. It was impossibly sure-footed on its numerous rubbish legs. If an attacker did not run fast enough, the familiar would learn it. It would be used. The familiar had brittle fingertips, made of dogs' teeth.

The familiar moved away from the gardens. It followed the canal bank to a graveyard, to an industrial sidings, to a dump. It gave itself a shape with wheels, plunging its veins and tissue into the remnants of a trolley. When later it discarded them, pulling them out, the wheels bled.

Sometimes it used its tools like their original owners, as when it took its legs from birds (scampering over burnt-out cars like a rock rabbit on four or six avian feet). It could change them. In sun, the familiar shaded its eyes with flanges of skin that had been cats' ears.

It had learned to eat. Its hunger, its feeding was a tool like dust had been: the familiar did not need to take in nourishment but doing so gave it satisfaction, and that was enough. It made itself a tongue from strips of wet towel, and made a mouth full of interlocking cogs. These teeth rotated in its jaw, chewing, driving food scraps back towards the throat.

In the small hours of morning, in a waste lot stained by chemical spill, the familiar finally made a tool of the sack that had delivered it. It found two broken umbrellas, one skeletal, the other ragged, and it busied itself with them, holding them tight with hair-grip hands, manipulating them with rat tails. It secured the sackcloth to them with its organic roots. After hours of calculated tinkering, during which it spoke English words in the mind it had built itself, the reshaped umbrellas spasmed open and shut on analogues of shoulders, and with a great gust the familiar flew.

Its umbrellas beat like scooping bat wings, and the greased hessian held it. It flew random as a butterfly, staring at the moon with cats' and dogs' eyes, its numerous limbs splayed. It hunted with urban bramble, thorned stalks that whipped and pinioned prey from the air and the ground. It scoured the scrubland of cats. It spasmed between tower blocks, each wing contraction jerking it through the air. It shouted the words it had learned, without sound.

There were only two nights that it could fly, before it was too large, and it loved them. It was aware of its pleasure. It used it as it grew. The summer became unusually hot. The familiar hid in the sudden masses of buddleia. It found passages through the city. It lived in wrecking yards and sewers, growing, changing, and using.

Though it replaced them regularly, the familiar kept its old eyes, moving them down itself so that its sight deteriorated along its back. It had learned caution. It was educated: two streets might be empty, but not identically so, it knew. It parsed the grammar of brick and neglected industry. It listened at doors, cupping the cones of card, the plastic funnels with which it extended its ears. Its vocabulary increased. It was a Londoner.

Every house it passed it marked like a dog: the familiar pissed out its territory with glands made from plastic bottles. Sniffing with a nose taken from a badger, it sprayed a liquid of rubbish-tip juices and the witch's blood in a rough circle across the flattened zones of the north city, where the tube trains emerged from underground. The familiar claimed the terraced landscape.

It seemed a ritual. But it had watched the little mammals of the landfills and understood that territory was a tool, and it used it and learned it, or thought it did until the night it was tracing its limits into suburban spaces, and it smelt another's trail.

The familiar raged. It was maddened. It thrashed in a yard that reeked of alien spoor, chewing tires and spitting out their rags. Eventually, it hunkered down to the intruder's track. It licked it. It bristled throughout its body of witch flesh and patchwork trash. The new scent was sharper than its own, admixed with different blood. The familiar hunted.

The trail ran across back gardens, separated by fences that the familiar vaulted easily, trickled across toys and drying grass, over flowerbeds and rockeries. The prey was old and tough: it told in the piss. The familiar used the smell to track, and learned it, and understood that it was the newcomer here.

In the sprawl of the outer city the stench became narcotic. The familiar stalked silently on rocks like hooves. The night was warm and overcast. Behind empty civic halls, tags, and the detritus of vandalism. It ended there. The smell was so strong, it was a fight-drug. It blistered the familiar's innards. Cavities opened in it, rudimentary lungs like bellows: it made itself breathe, so that it could pant to murder.

Corrugated iron and barbed wire surrounds. The witch's familiar was the intruder. There were no stars, no lamplight. The familiar stood without motion. It breathed out a challenge. The breath drifted across the little arena. Something enormous stood. Debris moved. Debris rose and turned and opened its mouth and caught the exhalation. It sucked it in out of all the air, filled its belly. It learned it.

Dark expanded. The familiar blinked its eyelids of rain-wet leather offcuts. It watched its enemy unfold.

This was an old thing, an old familiar, the bull, the alpha. It had escaped or been banished or lost its witch long ago. It was broken bodies, wood and plastic, stone and ribbed metal, a constellation of clutter exploding from a mass of skinless muscle the size of a horse. Beside its wet bloody eyes were embedded cameras, extending their lenses, powered by organic current. The mammoth shape clapped some of its hand-things.

The young familiar had not known until then that it had thought itself alone. Without words, it wondered what else was in the city—how many other outcasts, familiars too foul to use. But it could not think for long as the monstrous old potentate came at it.

The thing ran on table legs and gripped with pincers that were human jaws. They clenched on the little challenger and tore at its accrued limbs.

Early in its life the familiar had learned pain, and this attack gave it agony. It felt itself lessen as the attacker ingested gulps of its flesh. The familiar understood in shock that it might cease.

Its cousin taught it that with its new mass it could bruise. The familiar could not retreat. Even bleeding and with arms, legs gone, with eyes crushed and leaking and something three times its size opening mouths and shears and raising flukes that were shovels, the intoxicant reek of a competitor's musk forced it to fight.

More pain and the loss of more self. The little insurgent was diminishing. It was awash in rival stink. A notion came to it. It pissed up in its adversary's eyes, spraying all the bloody muck left in it and rolling away from the liquid's arc. The hulking thing clamoured silently. Briefly blinded, it put its mouth to the ground and followed its tongue.

Behind it, the familiar was motionless. It made tools of shadows and silence, keeping dark and quiet stitched to it as the giant tracked its false trail. The little familiar sent fibres into the ground, to pipework inches below. It connected to the plastic with tentacles quickly as thick as viscera, made the pipe a limb and organ, shoving and snapping it a foot below its crouching opponent. It drove the ragged end up out of the earth, its plastic jags spurs. It ground it into the controlling mass of the old familiar, into the dead centre of meat, and as the wounded thing tried to pull itself free, the guileful young familiar sucked through the broken tube.

It ballooned cavities in itself, gaping vacuums at the ends of its new pipe intestine. The suction pinioned its enemy, and tore chunks of bloody matter from it. The familiar drew them through the buried duct, up into its own body. Like a glutton it swigged them.

The trapped old one tried to raise itself but its wood and metal limbs had no purchase. It could not pull itself free, and the pipe was too braced in earth to tear away. It tried to thread its own veins into the tubing and vie for it, to make its own oesophagus and drink down its attacker, but the vessels of the young familiar riddled the plastic, and the dying thing could not push them aside, and with all the tissue it had lost to the usurper, they were now equal in mass, and now the newcomer was bigger, and now bigger still.

Tissue passed in fat pellets into the swelling young familiar sitting anchored by impromptu guts. Venting grave little breaths, the ancient one shrivelled and broke apart, sucked into a plughole. The cobweb of its veins dried up from all its borrowed limbs and members, and they disaggregated, nothing but hubcaps again, and butcher's remnants, a dead television, tools, mechanical debris, all brittled and sucked clean of life. The limbs were arranged around clean ground, from which jagged a shard of piping.

All the next day, the familiar lay still. When it moved, after dark, it limped though it replaced its broken limbs: it was damaged internally, it ached with every step it took, or if it oozed or crawled. All but a few of its eyes were gone, and for nights it was too weak to catch and use any animals to fix that. It took none of its opponent's tools, except one of the human jaws that had been pincers. It was not a trophy, but something to consider.

It metabolised much of the flesh-matter it had ingested, burnt it away (and the older familiar's memories, of self-constitution on Victorian slag-heaps, troubled it like indigestion). But it was still severely bloated. It pierced its distended body with broken glass to let out pressure, but all that oozed out of it was its new self.

The familiar still grew. It had been enlarging ever since it emerged from the canal. With its painful victory came a sudden increase in its size, but it knew it would have reached that mass anyway.

Its enemy's trails were drying up. The familiar felt interest at that, rather than triumph. It lay for days in a car-wrecking yard, using new tools, building itself a new shape, listening to the men and the clatter of machines, feeling its energy and attention grow, but slowly. That was where it was when the witch found it.

An old lady came before it. In the noon heat the familiar sat loose as a doll. Over the warehouse and office roofs, it could hear church bells. The old lady stepped into its view and it looked up at her.

She was glowing, with more, it seemed, than the light behind her. Her skin was burning. She looked incomplete. She was at the edge of something. The familiar did not recognise her but it remembered her. She caught its eye and nodded forcefully, moved out of sight. The familiar was tired.

"There you are."

Wearily the familiar raised its head again. The witch stood before it.

"Wondered where you got to. Buggering off like that."

In the long silence the familiar looked the man up and down. It remembered him, too.

"Need you to get back to things. Job to finish."

The familiar's interest wandered. It picked at a stone, looked down at it, sent out veins and made it a nail. It forgot the man was there, until his voice surprised it.

"Could feel you all the time, you know." The witch laughed without pleasure. "How we found you, isn't it?" Glanced back at the woman out of the familiar's sight. "Like following me nose. Me gut."

Sun baked them all.

"Looking well."

The familiar watched him. It was inquisitive. It felt things. The witch moved back. There was a purr of summer insects. The woman was at the edge of the clearing of cars.

"Looking well," the witch said again.

The familiar had made itself the shape of a man. Its flesh centre was several stone of spread-out muscle. Its feet were boulders again, its hands bones on bricks. It would stand eight feet tall. There was too much stuff in it and on it to itemise. On its head were books, grafted in spine-first, their pages constantly riffling as if in wind. Blood vessels saturated their pages, and engorged to let out heat. The books sweated. The familiar's dog eyes focused on the witch, then the gently cooking wrecks.

"Oh Jesus."

The witch was staring at the bottom of the familiar's face, half pointing.

"Oh Jesus what you *do?*"

The familiar opened and closed the man-jaw it had taken from its opponent and made its own mouth. It grinned with third-hand teeth.

"What you fucking *do* Jesus *Christ*. Oh shit man. Oh no."

The familiar cooled itself with its page-hair.

"You got to come back. We need you again." Pointing vaguely at the woman, who was motionless and still shining. "Ain't done. She ain't finished. You got to come back.

"I can't *do it* on my own. Ain't got it. She ain't paying me no more. She's fucking *ruining me.*" That last he screamed in anger directed backwards, but the woman did not flinch. She reached out her hand to the familiar, waved a clutch of mouldering dead snakes. "Come back," said the witch.

The familiar noticed the man again and remembered him. It smiled.

The man waited. "Come *back,*" he said. "Got to come *back,* fucking *back*." He was crying. The familiar was fascinated. "Come *back*." The witch tore off his shirt. "You been *growing*. You been fucking *growing* you won't stop, and I can't do nothing without you now and you're *killing* me."

The woman with the snakes glowed. The familiar could see her through the witch's chest. The man's body was faded away in random holes. There was no blood. Two handspans of sternum, inches of belly, slivers of arm-meat all faded to nothing, as if the flesh had given up existing. Entropic wounds. The familiar looked in interest at the gaps. He saw into the witch's stomach, where hoops of gut ended where they met the hole, where the spine became hard to notice and did not exist for a space of several vertebrae. The man took off his trousers. His thighs were punctuated by the voids, his scrotum gone.

"You got to come back," he whispered. "I can't do nothing without you, and you're killing me. Bring me back."

The familiar touched itself. It pointed at the man with a chicken-bone finger, and smiled again.

"Come *back*," the witch said. "She wants you; I need you. You fucking *have* to come back. Have to *help* me." He stood cruciform. The sun shone through the cavities in him, breaking up his shadow with light.

The familiar looked down at black ants labouring by a cigarette end, up at the man's creased face, at the impassive old woman holding her dead snakes like a bouquet. It smiled without cruelty.

"Then *finish*," the witch screamed at it. "If you ain't going to come back then fucking *finish*." He stamped and spat at the familiar, too afraid to touch but raging. "You *fucker*. I can't stand this. Finish it for me you *fucker*." The witch beat his fists against his naked holed sides. He reached into a space below his heart. He wailed with pain and his face spasmed, but he fingered the inside of his body. His wound did not bleed, but when he drew out his shaking hand it was wet and red where it had touched his innards.

He cried out again and shook blood into the familiar's face. "That what you *want*? That do you? You fucker. Come *back* or make it stop. Do *something* to *finish*."

From the familiar's neck darted a web of threads, which fanned out and into the corona of insects that surrounded it. Each fibre snaked into a tiny body and retracted. Flies and wasps and fat bees, a crawling handful of chitin was reeled in to the base of the familiar's throat, below its human jaw. The hair-thin tendrils scored through the tumour of living insects and took them over, used them, made them a tool. They hummed their wings loudly in time, clamped to the familiar's skin.

The vibrations resonated through its boccal cavity. It moved its mouth as it had seen others do. The insectile voice box echoed through it and made sound, which it shaped with lips.

"Sun," it said. Its droning speech intrigued it. It pointed into the sky, over the nude and fading witch's shoulder, up way beyond the old woman. It closed its eyes. It moved its mouth again and listened closely to its own quiet words. Rays bounced from car to battered car, and the familiar used them as tools to warm its skin.

ENTRY TAKEN FROM A MEDICAL ENCYCLOPAEDIA

NAME: *Buscard's Murrain,* or *Wormword*

COUNTRY OF ORIGIN: Slovenia (probably).

FIRST KNOWN CASE: Primoz Jansa, a reader for a blind priest in the town of Bled in what is now northern Slovenia. In 1771 at the age of thirty-six Jansa left Bled for London. The first record of his presence there (and the first description of Buscard's Murrain) is in a letter from Ignatius Sancho to Margaret Cocksedge dated 4th February 1774.[1]

SYMPTOMS: The disease incubates for up to three years, during which time the infected patient suffers violent headaches. After

---

[1] "I doubt not that you have heard of Mister *Jansa*—a fellow of lamentable aspect—who is daily seen around the squares of his adopted city where his intense bearing entices crowds of the curious; when surrounded the fellow excoriates 'em in obscure tongues such as would shame the most *pious* and ecstatic of quakers. Those gathered mock the afflicted with mummery. But horrors! A number of those who have mimicked poor Jansa have fallen to his brain-fever, and are now partners in his *unorthodox ministry*." (Kate Vinegar [ed], *The London Letters of Ignatius Sancho* [Providence 1954], p. 337.)

this, full-blown Buscard's Murrain is manifested in slowly failing mental faculties and severe mood swings between three conditions: near full lucidity; a feverish seeking out of the largest audience possible; and a state of loud, hysterical glossolalia. Samuel Buscard infamously denoted these states *torpid*, *prefatory* and *grandiloquent* respectively, thereby appearing to take the side of the disease.

After between three and twelve years, the patient enters the terminal phase of the disease. The so-far gradual mental collapse speeds up markedly, leaving him or her in a permanent vegetative state within months.

Those present during the nonsensical "grandiloquence" of a murrain sufferer report that one particular word—the worm-word—is repeated often, followed by a pause as the sufferer waits for a response. If any of those listening repeats the word, the sufferer's satisfaction is obvious.

Later, it is from among these mimics that the next batch of the infected will be found.

HISTORY: At the insistence of the respected Dr. William Haygarth, all murrain sufferers were released into the care of Dr. Samuel Buscard in 1775.[2] During postmortem investigations on the brains of infected victims Buscard discovered what he thought were parasitic worms, which he named after himself. When a committee of aetiologists examined his evidence, they found that the vermiform specimens were made of cerebral matter itself. Buscard was denounced amid claims that he had made the "worms" himself by perforating the brains with a cheese-screw.

---

[2] There is no record of Haygarth fraternising with or even mentioning Dr. Buscard before or after this time, and the reasons behind his 1775 recommendation are opaque. In his diaries, Haygarth's assistant William Fin noted "a disparity between Dr. H's *words* and his *tone* when he claimed Dr. Buscard as his *very good friend*" (quoted in Marcus Gadd's *A Buscardology Primer* [London 1972], p.iii). De Selby, in his unpublished "Notes on Buscard," claims that Buscard was blackmailing Haygarth. What incriminating material he might have held on his more esteemed colleague remains unknown.

The committee renamed the disease "gibbering fever," and half-heartedly claimed it to be the result of "bad air."

Samuel Buscard was ordered to surrender Jansa to the committee, but he produced papers showing that his patient had succumbed and been buried. The disgraced doctor then disappeared from public view and died in 1777.

His research was continued by his son Jacob, also a doctor. In 1782 Jacob Buscard astounded the medical establishment with the publication of his famous pamphlet proving that the brain-tissue "worms" were capable of independent motion in the head, and that the cerebrums of sufferers were riddled with convoluted tunnels. "The first Dr. Buscard was thus correct," he wrote. "Not *bad air* but a voracious parasite—a *murrain*—afflicts the gibberers."

> There is a word, which when spoken inveigles its way into the mind of the speaker and manifests itself in his flesh. It forces its bearer to speak itself again and again, in the company of others, that they might be tempted to echo it. With each utterance another wormword is born, until the brain is tunnelled quite through: and when those listening repeat what they have heard, in curiosity or mockery, if their utterance is just so, a wormword is hatched in their heads. Not quite the parasite envisaged by my wronged father, but a parasite nonetheless.[3]

Jacob Buscard's pamphlet dates his revelation to 1780, during one of his numerous interrogations of Jansa in his "torpid" state. Jansa told Buscard that his illness had started one day while he was reading to his master in Bled. Between the pages of the book he had found a slip of paper on which was written two words. Jansa read the first word aloud, and thus started the earliest known outbreak of wormword. His ensuing headache caused him to drop the paper, which was subsequently lost. "With the translation of

---

[3] *A Posthumous Vindication of Dr. Samuel Buscard: Proof That "Gibbering Fever" Is Indeed Buscard's Murrain.* (London 1782), p. 17.

those few letters into sound," Jacob Buscard wrote, "the wretched Jansa became midwife and host to the wormword."[4]

The younger Buscard's breakthrough won him a tremendous reputation, marred by his admissions that he and his father had forged Jansa's death certificate and kept him alive and imprisoned as an experimental subject for the past seven years. Jansa was found in the Buscard basement in the advanced stages of his disease and taken to a madhouse, where he died two months later. Jacob Buscard escaped prosecution for kidnapping, torture, and accessory to forgery by fleeing to Munich, where he disappeared.[5]

London suffered periodic outbreaks of Buscard's murrain until the passage of the Gibbering Act of 1810 legalised the incarceration of the infected in soundproof sanatoria.[6] The era of mass infection was over, and only occasional isolated cases have been recorded since.

It took the late twentieth century and the work of Jacob Buscard's great-great-great-great-great granddaughter Dr. Mariella Buscard conclusively to dispel the superstitious notions about "evil words" that have clouded even scholarly discussions of the disease. In her seminal 1995 *Lancet* article "It's the Synapses, Stupid!", the latest Dr. Buscard proves the murrain to be simply an unpleasant (though admittedly unusual) biochemical reaction.

She points out that with every action of the human body, including speech, a unique configuration of thousands of minute chemical reactions occurs in the brain. Dr. Buscard shows that when the wormword is spoken with a precise inflection, the concomitant synaptic firing has the unfortunate property of reconfig-

---

[4] Ibid., p. 25.

[5] His last known letter (to his son Matthew) is dated January 1783, and contains a hint as to his plans. Jacob complains "I have not even the money to finish this. Carriage to Bled is a scandalous expense!" (Quoted in Ali Khamrein's *Medical Letters* [New York 1966], p. 232.)

[6] These notorious "Buscard Shacks" loom large in popular culture of the time. See for example the ballad "Rather the Poorhouse than a Buscard Shack" (reproduced in Cecily Fetchpaw's *Hanoverian Street Songs: Populism and Resistance* [Pennsylvania 1988], p. 677).

uring nerve-fibres into discrete self-organising clusters. The tiny chemical reactions, in other words, turn nerves into parasites. Boring through the brain and using their own newly independent bodies to reroute neural messages, these marauding lengths of brain matter periodically take control of their host. They particularly affect his or her speech, in an attempt to fullfil their instincts to reproduce.

Following the format established in Jacob Buscard's pamphlet, the wormword is traditionally rendered *yGudluh*. This is recorded with some trepidation: the main vector for the transmission of Buscard's murrain over the last two centuries has been the literature about it.[7]

CURES: Randolph Johnson's claims about bergamot oil in *Confessions of a Disease Junkie* are spurious: there is no known cure for Buscard's murrain.[8] There is, however, persistent speculation that the second word on Jansa's lost paper, if spoken, might engender some cure in the brain: perhaps a predatory "hunter" synapse to devour the wormwords. Several "Jansa's papers" have appeared over the decades, all forgeries.[9] Despite numerous careful searches, Jansa's paper remains lost.[10]

---

[7] Contrary to the impression given by the media after the 1986 Statten-Dogger incident, *deliberate* exposure to the risks of wormword is neither common nor new. Ully Statten was (no doubt unwittingly) continuing a tradition established in the late eighteenth century. In what could be considered a late Georgian extreme sport, London's young rakes and coffeehouse dandies would take turns reading the word aloud, each risking correct pronounciation and thereby infection.

[8] This will come as no surprise to those familiar with Johnson's work. The man is a liar, a fraud, and a bad writer (whose brother is Britain's third-largest importer of bergamot oil).

[9] There is a comprehensive list in Gadd, op. cit., p. 74.

[10] "Years of Violent Ransacking Leave Slovenia's Historic Churches in Ruins," *Financial Times*, 3/7/85.

DETAILS

When the boy upstairs got hold of a pellet gun and fired snips of potato at passing cars, I took a turn. I was part of everything. I wasn't an outsider. But I wouldn't join in when my friends went to the yellow house to scribble on the bricks and listen at the windows.

One girl teased me about it, but everyone else told her to shut up. They defended me, even though they didn't understand why I wouldn't come.

I don't remember a time before I visited the yellow house for my mother.

On Wednesday mornings at about nine o'clock I would open the front door of the decrepit building with a key from the bunch my mother had given me. Inside there was a hall and two doors, one broken and leading to the splintering stairs. I would unlock the other and enter the dark flat. The corridor inside was unlit and smelt of old wet air. I never walked even two steps down that hallway. Rot and shadows merged, and it looked as if the passage disappeared a few yards from me. The door to Mrs. Miller's room was right in front of me. I would lean forward and knock.

Quite often there were signs that someone else had been there recently. Scuffed dust and bits of litter. Sometimes I was not alone. There were two other children I sometimes saw slipping in or out of the house. There were a handful of adults who visited Mrs. Miller.

I might find one or other of them in the hallway outside the door to her flat, or even sometimes in the flat itself, slouching in the crumbling dark hallway. They would be slumped over or reading some cheap-looking book or swearing loudly as they waited.

There was a young Asian woman who wore a lot of makeup and smoked obsessively. She ignored me totally. There were two drunks who came sometimes. One would greet me boisterously and incomprehensibly, raising his arms as if he wanted to hug me into his stinking, stinking jumper. I would grin and wave nervously, walk past him. The other seemed alternately melancholic and angry. Occasionally I'd meet him by the door to Mrs. Miller's room, swearing in a strong cockney accent. I remember the first time I saw him, he was standing there, his red face contorted, slurring and moaning loudly.

"Come on, you old slag," he wailed, "you fucking old *slag*. Come on, please, you cunt."

His words scared me but his tone was wheedling, and I realised I could hear her voice, Mrs. Miller's voice, from inside the room, answering him back. She did not sound frightened or angry.

I hung back, not sure what to do, and she kept speaking, and eventually the drunken man shambled miserably away. And then I could continue as usual.

I asked my mother once if I could have some of Mrs. Miller's food. She laughed very hard and shook her head. In all the Wednesdays of bringing the food over, I never even dipped my finger in to suck it.

My mum spent an hour every Tuesday night making the stuff

up. She dissolved a bit of gelatine or cornflower with some milk, threw in a load of sugar or flavourings, and crushed a clutch of vitamin pills into the mess. She would stir it until it thickened and let it set in a plain white plastic bowl. In the morning it would be a kind of strong-smelling custard that my mother put a dishcloth over and gave me, along with a list of any questions or requests for Mrs. Miller, and sometimes a plastic bucket full of white paint.

So I would stand in front of Mrs. Miller's door, knocking, with a bowl at my feet. I would hear a shifting and then her voice from close by the door.

"Hello," she would call, and then she would say my name a couple of times. "Have you my breakfast? Are you ready?"

I would creep up close to the door and hold the food ready. I would tell her I was.

Mrs. Miller would slowly count to three. On three, the door would swing open a snatch, just a foot or two, and I would thrust the bowl into the gap. She would grab it and slam the door quickly in my face.

I couldn't see very much inside the room. The door was open for less than a second. My strongest impression was of the whiteness of the walls. Mrs. Miller's sleeves were white too, and made of plastic. I never got much of a glimpse at her face, but what I saw was unmemorable. A middle-aged woman's eager face.

If I had a bucket full of paint, we would run through the routine again. Then I would sit cross-legged in front of her door and listen to her eat.

"How's your mother?" she would shout.

At that I would unfold my mother's careful queries. She's ok, I'd say, she's fine. She says she has some questions for you.

I'd read my mother's strange questions in my careful child monotone, and Mrs. Miller would pause and make interested sounds, and clear her throat and think out loud. Sometimes she would take ages to come to an answer, and sometimes it would be almost immediate.

"Tell your mother she can't tell if a man's good or bad from that," she'd say. "Tell her to remember the problems she had with your father." Or: "Yes, she can take the heart of it out. Only she has to paint it with the special oil I told her about." "Tell your mother seven. But only four of them concern her, and three of them used to be dead."

"I can't help her with that," she told me once, quietly. "Tell her to go to a doctor, quickly." And my mother did, and she got well again.

"What do you not want to do when you grow up?" Mrs. Miller asked me one day.

That morning when I had come to the house the sad cockney vagrant had been banging on the door of her room again, the keys to the flat flailing in his hand.

"He's begging you, you fucking old tart, please, you owe him, he's so fucking angry," he'd been shouting. "Only it ain't you gets the fucking sharp end, is it? *Please,* you cow, you fucking cow, I'm on me knees . . ."

"My door knows you, man," Mrs. Miller had declared from within. "It knows you and so do I. You know it won't open to you. I didn't take out my eyes, and I'm not giving in now. Go home."

I had waited nervously as the man gathered himself and staggered away, and then, looking behind me, I had knocked on her door and announced myself. It was after I'd given her her food that she asked her question.

"What do you not want to do when you grow up?"

If I had been a few years older her inversion of the cliché would have annoyed me: it would have seemed mannered and contrived. But I was only a young child, and I was quite delighted.

I don't want to be a lawyer, I told her carefully. I spoke out of loyalty to my mother, who periodically received crisp letters which made her cry or smoke fiercely, and swear at fucking lawyers, fucking smart-arse lawyers.

Mrs. Miller was delighted.

"Good boy!" She snorted. "We know all about lawyers. Bastards, right? With the small print! Never be tricked by the small print! It's right there in front of you, *right there in front of you,* and you can't even *see* it, and then suddenly it *makes you notice it!* And I tell you, once you seen it it's got you!" She laughed excitedly. "Don't let the small print get you. I tell you a secret." I waited quietly, and my head slipped nearer the door.

"The devil's in the details!" She laughed again. "You ask your mother if that's not true. The devil is in the details!"

I'd wait the twenty minutes or so until Mrs. Miller had finished eating, and then we'd reverse our previous procedure and she'd quickly hand me out an empty bowl. I would return home with the empty container and tell my mother the various answers to her various questions. Usually she would nod and make notes. Occasionally she would cry.

After I told Mrs. Miller that I did not want to be a lawyer she started asking me to read to her. She made me tell my mother, and told me to bring a newspaper or one of a number of books. My mother nodded at the message and packed me a sandwich the next Wednesday, along with *The Mirror.* She told me to be polite and do what Mrs. Miller asked, and that she'd see me in the afternoon.

I wasn't afraid. Mrs. Miller had never treated me badly from behind her door. I was resigned, and only a little bit nervous.

Mrs. Miller made me read stories to her from specific pages that she shouted out. She made me recite them again and again, very carefully. Afterwards she would talk to me. Usually she started with a joke about lawyers, and about small print.

"There's three ways not to see what you don't want to," she told me. "One is the coward's way and too painful. The other is to close your eyes forever, which is the same as the first, when it comes to it. The third is the hardest and the best: you have to make sure *only the things you can afford to see* come before you."

. . .

One morning when I arrived the stylish Asian woman was whispering fiercely through the wood of the door, and I could hear Mrs. Miller responding with shouts of amused disapproval. Eventually the young woman swept past me, leaving me cowed by her perfume.

Mrs. Miller was laughing, and she was talkative when she had eaten.

"She's heading for trouble, messing with the wrong family! You have to be careful with all of them," she told me. "Every single *one* of them on that other side of things is a tricksy bastard who'll kill you soon as *look* at you, given half a chance.

"There's the gnarly throat-tipped one . . . and there's old hasty, who I think had best remain nameless," she said wryly. "All old bastards, all of them. You *can't trust them* at all, that's what I say. I should know, eh? Shouldn't I?" She laughed. "Trust me, trust me on this: it's too easy to get on the wrong side of them.

"What's it like out today?" she asked me. I told her that it was cloudy.

"You want to be careful with that," she said. "All sorts of faces in the clouds, aren't there? Can't help noticing, can you?" She was whispering now. "Do me a favour when you go home to your mum: don't look up. There's a boy. Don't look up at all."

When I left her, however, the day had changed. The sky was hot, and quite blue.

The two drunk men were squabbling in the front hall, and I edged past them to her door. They continued bickering in a depressing, garbled murmur throughout my visit.

"D'you know, I can't even really remember what it was all *about,* now!" Mrs. Miller said when I had finished reading to her. "I can't remember! That's a terrible thing. But you don't forget the basics. The exact question escapes me, and to be honest I think maybe I was just being nosy or showing off . . . I can't say I'm proud of it, but it could have been that. It could. But whatever the question, it was all about a way of seeing an answer.

"There's a way of looking that lets you read things. If you look at a pattern of tar on a wall, or a crumbling mound of brick or somesuch . . . there's a way of unpicking it. And if you know how, you can trace it and read it out and see the things hidden *right there in front of you*—the things you've been seeing but not noticing, all along. But you have to learn how." She laughed. It was a high-pitched, unpleasant sound. "Someone has to teach you. So you have to make certain friends.

"But you can't make friends without making enemies.

"You have to open it all up for you to see inside. You make what you see into a window, and you see what you want through it. You make what you see a sort of a *door*."

She was silent for a long time. Then: "Is it cloudy again?" she asked suddenly. She went on before I answered.

"If you look up, you look into the clouds for long enough, and you'll see a face. Or in a tree. Look in a tree, look in the branches, and soon you'll see them just so, and there's a face or a running man, or a bat or whatever. You'll see it all suddenly, a picture in the pattern of the branches, and you won't have *chosen* to see it. And you can't *unsee* it.

"That's what you have to learn to do, to read the details like that and see what's what and learn things. But you've to be damn careful. You've to be careful not to disturb anything." Her voice was absolutely cold, and I was suddenly very frightened.

"Open up that window, you'd better be damn careful that what's in the details doesn't look back and see you."

The next time I went, the maudlin drunk was there again wailing obscenities at her through her door. She shouted at me to come back later, that she didn't need her food right now. She sounded resigned and irritated, and she went back to scolding her visitor before I had backed out of earshot.

He was screaming at her that she'd gone too far, that she'd pissed about too long, that things were coming to a head, that there was going to be hell to pay, that she couldn't avoid it forever, that it was her own fault.

When I came back he was asleep, snoring loudly, curled up a few feet into the mildewing passage. Mrs. Miller took her food and ate it quickly, returned it without speaking.

When I returned the following week, she began to whisper to me as soon as I'd knocked on the door, hissing urgently as she opened it briefly and grabbed the bowl.

"It was an accident, you know," she said, as if responding to something I'd said. "I mean of *course* you know in *theory* that anything might happen. You get *warned*, don't you? But oh my . . . oh my *God* it took the breath out of me and made me cold to realise what had happened."

I waited. I could not leave, because she had not returned the bowl. She had not said I could go. She spoke again, very slowly.

"It was a new day." Her voice was distant and breathy. "Can you even imagine? Can you see what I was ready to do? I was poised . . . to change . . . to see everything that's hidden. The best place to hide a book is in a library. The best place to hide secret things is there, in the visible angles, in our view, in plain sight.

"I had studied and sought, and learnt, finally, to see. It was time to learn truths.

"I opened my eyes fully, for the first time.

"I had chosen an old wall. I was looking for the answer to some question that I told you I can't even *remember* now, but the question wasn't the main thing. That was the opening of my eyes.

"I stared at the whole mass of the bricks. I took another glance, relaxed my sight. At first I couldn't stop seeing the bricks as bricks, the divisions as layers of cement, but after a time they became pure vision. And as the whole broke down into lines and shapes and shades, I held my breath as I began to see.

"Alternatives appeared to me. Messages written in the pockmarks. Insinuations in the forms. Secrets unraveling. It was bliss.

"And then without warning my heart went tight, as I saw something. I made sense of the pattern.

"It was a mess of cracks and lines and crumbling cement, and as I looked at it, I saw a pattern in the wall.

"I saw a clutch of lines that looked just like something . . . terrible—something old and predatory and utterly terrible—staring right back at me.

"And then I saw it move."

"You have to understand me," she said. "Nothing changed. See? All the time I was looking I saw the wall. But that first moment, it was like when you see a face in the cloud. I just noticed in the pattern in the brick, I just noticed something, looking at me. Something angry.

"And then in the very next moment, I just . . . I just noticed another load of lines—cracks that had always been there, you understand? Patterns in broken brick that I'd seen only a second before—that looked exactly like that same thing, a little closer to me. And in the next moment a third picture in the brick, a picture of the thing closer still.

"Reaching for me."

"I broke free then," she whispered. "I ran away from there in terror, with my hands in front of my eyes, and I was *screaming*. I ran and ran.

"And when I stopped and opened my eyes again, I had run to the edges of a park, and I took my hands slowly down and dared to look behind me, and saw that there was nothing coming from the alley where I'd been. So I turned to the little snatch of scrub and grass and trees.

"And I saw the thing again."

Mrs. Miller's voice was stretched out as if she were dreaming. My mouth was open, and I huddled closer to the door.

"I saw it in the leaves," she said forlornly. "As I turned I saw the leaves in such a way . . . Just a chance conjuncture, you understand? I noticed a pattern. I *couldn't not.* You don't choose whether to see faces in the clouds. I saw the monstrous thing again and it still reached for me, and I shrieked and all the mothers and fathers and children in that park turned and gazed at me, and I turned my eyes from that tree and whirled on my feet to face a little family in my way.

"And the thing was there in the same pose. I saw it in the outlines of the father's coat and the spokes of the baby's pushchair, and the tangles of the mother's hair. It was just another mess of lines, you see? But you don't choose what you notice. And I couldn't help but notice just the right lines out of the whole, just the lines out of all the lines there, just the ones to see the thing again, a little closer, looking at me.

"And I turned and saw it closer still in the clouds, and I turned again and it was clutching for me in the rippling weeds in the pond, and as I closed my eyes I swear I felt something touch my dress.

"You understand me? You understand?"

I didn't know if I understood or not. Of course now I know that I did not.

"It lives in the details," she said. "It travels in that . . . in that perception. It moves through those chance meetings of lines. Maybe you glimpse it sometimes when you stare at clouds, and then maybe it might catch a glimpse of you, too.

"But it saw me *full on.* It's jealous of its place, and there was I peering through without permission, like a nosy neighbour through a hole in the fence. I know what it is. I know what happened.

"It lurks before us, in the everyday. It's the boss of *all the things* hidden in plain sight. Terrible things, they are. Appalling things. Just almost in reach. Brazen and invisible.

"It caught my glances. It can move through whatever I see.

"For most people it's just chance, isn't it? What shapes they see in a tangle of wire. There's a thousand pictures there, and when you look, some of them just appear. But now . . . the thing in the lines chooses the pictures for me. It can thrust itself forward. It makes me see it. It's found its way through. To me. Through what I see. I opened a door into my perception."

She sounded frozen with terror. I was not equipped for that kind of adult fear, and my mouth worked silently for something to say.

"That was a long, long journey home. Every time I peeked through the cracks in my fingers, I saw that thing crawling for me.

"It waited ready to pounce, and when I opened my eyes even a crack I opened the door again. I saw the back of a woman's jumper, and in the details of the fabric the thing leapt for me. I glimpsed a yard of broken paving and I noticed just the lines that showed me the thing . . . *baying*.

"I had to shut my eyes quick. I *groped* my way home.

"And then I taped my eyes shut and I tried to think about things."

There was silence for a time.

"See, there was always the easy way, that scared me rotten, because I was never one for blood and pain," she said suddenly, and her voice was harder. "I held the scissors in front of my eyes a couple of times, but even bandaged blind as I was I couldn't bear it. I suppose I could've gone to a doctor. I can pull strings, I could pull in a few favours, have them do the job without pain.

"But you know I never . . . really . . . reckoned . . . that's what I'd do," she said thoughtfully. "What if you found a way to close the door? Eh? And you'd already put out your eyes? You'd feel such a fool, wouldn't you?

"And you know it wouldn't be good enough to wear pads and eyepatches and all. I tried. You catch glimpses. You see the glimmers of light and maybe a few of your own hairs, and that's the doorway right there, when the hairs cross in the corner of your eye so that if you notice just a few of them in just the right way, they look like something coming for you. That's a doorway.

"It's . . . unbearable . . . having sight, but trapping it like that.

"I'm not giving up. See . . ." Her voice lowered, and she spoke conspiratorially. "*I still think I can close the door.* I learnt to see. I can unlearn. I'm looking for ways. I want to see a wall as bricks again. Nothing more. That's why you read for me," she said. "Research. Can't look at it myself, of course—too many edges and lines and so on on a printed page—so you do it for me. And you're a good boy to do it."

I've thought about what she said many times, and still it makes no sense to me. The books I read to Mrs. Miller were school textbooks, old and dull village histories, the occasional romantic novel. I think that she must have been talking of some of her other visitors, who perhaps read her more esoteric stuff than I did. Either that, or the information she sought was buried very cleverly in the banal prose I faltered through.

"In the meantime, there's another way of surviving," she said. "Leave the eyes where they are, but don't give them any details.

"That thing can force me to notice its shape, but only in what's there. That's how it travels. You imagine if I saw a field of wheat. Doesn't even bear thinking about! A million million little *edges,* a million lines. You could make pictures of damn anything out of them, couldn't you? It wouldn't take any effort at all for the damn thing to make me notice it. The damn *lurker.* Or in a gravel drive or, or a building site, or a lawn . . .

"But I can outsmart it." The note of cunning in her voice made her sound deranged. "Keep it away till I work out how to close it off.

"I had to prepare this blind, with the wrappings round my

head. Took me a while, but here I am now. Safe. I'm safe in my little cold room. I keep the walls *flat white.* I covered the windows
and painted them too. I made my cloak out of plastic, so's I can't
catch a glimpse of cotton weave or anything when I wake up.

"I keep my place nice and . . . simple. When it was all done, I
unwrapped the bandages from my head, and I blinked slowly . . .
and I was alright. Clean walls, no cracks, no features. I don't look
at my hands often or for long. Too many creases. Your mother
makes me a good healthy soup looks like cream, so if I accidentally
look in the bowl, there's no broccoli or rice or tangled-up
spaghetti to make *lines and edges.*

"I open and shut the door so damned quick because I can only
afford a moment. That thing is ready to pounce. It wouldn't take a
second for it to leap up at me out of the sight of your hair or your
books or whatever."

Her voice ebbed out. I waited a minute for her to resume, but
she did not do so. Eventually I knocked nervously on the door and
called her name. There was no answer. I put my ear to the door. I
could hear her crying, quietly.

I went home without the bowl. My mother pursed her lips a
little but said nothing. I didn't tell her any of what Mrs. Miller had
said.

The next time I delivered Mrs. Miller's food, in a new container, she whispered harshly to me: "It preys on my eyes, all the
white. Nothing to see. Can't look out the window, can't read, can't
gaze at my nails. Preys on my mind.

"Not even my memories are left," she said. "It's colonising
them. I remember things . . . happy times . . . and the thing's waiting in the texture of my dress, or in the crumbs of my birthday
cake. I didn't notice it then. But I can see it now. My memories
aren't mine anymore. Not even my imaginings. Last night I
thought about going to the seaside, and the thing was there in the
foam on the waves."

. . .

She spoke very little the next few times I visited her. I read the chapters she demanded, and she grunted curtly in response. She ate quickly.

Her other visitors were there more often now, as the spring came in. I saw them in new combinations and situations: the glamourous young woman arguing with the friendly drunk; an old man sobbing at the far end of the hall. The aggressive man was often there, cajoling and moaning, and occasionally talking conversationally through the door, being answered like an equal. Other times he screamed at her as usual.

I arrived on a chilly day to find the drunken cockney sleeping a few feet from the door, snoring gutturally. I gave Mrs. Miller her food and then sat on my coat and read to her from a women's magazine as she ate.

When she had finished her food I waited with my arms outstretched, ready to snatch the bowl from her. I remember that I was very uneasy, that I sensed something wrong. I was looking around me anxiously, but everything seemed normal. I looked down at my coat and the crumpled magazine, at the man who still sprawled comatose in the hall.

As I heard Mrs. Miller's hands on the door, I realised what had changed. The drunken man was not snoring. He was holding his breath.

For a tiny moment I thought he had died, but I could see his body trembling, and my eyes began to open wide and I stretched my mouth to scream a warning, but the door had already begun to swing in its arc, and before I could even exhale the stinking man pushed himself up faster than I would have thought him capable and bore down on me with bloodshot eyes.

I managed to keen as he reached me, and the door faltered for an instant as Mrs. Miller heard my voice. But the man grabbed hold of me in a terrifying fug of alcohol. He reached down and snatched my coat from the floor, tugged at the jumper I had tied around my waist with his other hand, and hurled me hard at the door.

It flew open, smacking Mrs. Miller aside. I was screaming and crying. My eyes hurt at the sudden burst of cold white light from all the walls. I saw Mrs. Miller rubbing her head in the corner, struggling to her senses. The staggering, drunken man hurled my checked coat and my patterned jumper in front of her, reached down and snatched my feet, tugged me out of the room in an agony of splinters. I wailed snottily with fear.

Behind me, Mrs. Miller began to scream and curse, but I could not hear her well because the man had clutched me to him and pulled my head to his chest. I fought and cried and felt myself lurch as he leaned forward and slammed the door closed. He held it shut.

When I fought myself free of him I heard him shouting.

"I told you, you slapper," he wailed. "I fucking told you, you silly old whore. I fucking warned you it was time . . ." Behind his voice I could hear shrieks from the room. Both of them kept shouting and crying and screaming, and the floorboards pounded, and the door shook, and I heard something else as well.

As if the notes of all the different noises in the house fell into a chance meeting, and sounded like more than dissonance. The shouts and bangs and cries of fear combined in a sudden audible illusion like another presence.

Like a snarling voice. A lingering, hungry exhalation.

I ran then, screaming and terrified, my skin freezing in my T-shirt. I was sobbing and retching with fear, little bleats bursting from me. I stumbled home and was sick in my mother's room, and kept crying and crying as she grabbed hold of me and I tried to tell her what had happened, until I was drowsy and confused and I fell into silence.

My mother said nothing about Mrs. Miller. The next Wednesday we got up early and went to the zoo, the two of us, and at the time

I would usually be knocking on Mrs. Miller's door I was laughing at camels. The Wednesday after that I was taken to see a film, and the one after that my mother stayed in bed and sent me to fetch cigarettes and bread from the local shop, and I made our breakfast and ate it in her room.

My friends could tell that something had changed in the yellow house, but they did not speak to me about it, and it quickly became uninteresting to them.

I saw the Asian woman once more, smoking with her friends in the park several weeks later, and to my amazement she nodded to me and came over, interrupting her companions' conversation.

"Are you alright?" she asked me peremptorily. "How you doing?"

I nodded shyly back and told her that I was fine, thank you, and how was she?

She nodded and walked away.

I never saw the drunken, violent man again.

There were people I could probably have gone to to understand more about what had happened to Mrs. Miller. There was a story that I could chase, if I wanted to. People I had never seen before came to my house and spoke quietly to my mother, and looked at me with what I suppose was pity or concern. I could have asked them. But I was thinking more and more about my own life. I didn't want to know Mrs. Miller's details.

I went back to the yellow house once, nearly a year after that awful morning. It was winter. I remembered the last time I spoke to Mrs. Miller and I felt so much older it was almost giddying. It seemed such a vastly long time ago.

I crept up to the house one evening, trying the keys I still had, which to my surprise worked. The hallway was freezing, dark, and stinking more strongly than ever. I hesitated, then pushed open Mrs. Miller's door.

It opened easily, without a sound. The occasional muffled noise from the street seemed so distant it was like a memory. I entered.

She had covered the windows very carefully, and still no light made its way through from outside. It was extremely dark. I waited until I could see better in the ambient glow from the outside hallway.

I was alone.

My old coat and jumper lay spread-eagled in the corner of the room. I shivered to see them, went over and fingered them softly. They were damp and mildewing, covered in wet dust.

The white paint was crumbling off the wall in scabs. It looked as if it had been left untended for several years. I could not believe the extent of the decay.

I turned slowly around and gazed at each wall in turn. I took in the chaotic, intricate patterns of crumbling paint and damp plaster. They looked like maps, like a rocky landscape.

I looked for a long time at the wall farthest from my jacket. I was very cold. After a long time I saw a shape in the ruined paint. I moved closer with a dumb curiosity far stronger than any fear.

In the crumbling texture of the wall was a spreading anatomy of cracks that—seen from a certain angle, caught just right in the scraps of light—looked in outline something like a woman. As I stared at it it took shape, and I stopped noticing the extraneous lines, and focused without effort or decision on the relevant ones. I saw a woman looking out at me.

I could make out the suggestion of her face. The patch of rot which constituted it made it look as if she was screaming.

One of her arms was flung back away from her body, which seemed to strain against it, as if she was being pulled away by her hand and was fighting to escape, and was failing. At the end of her crack-arm, in the space where her captor would be, the paint had fallen away in a great slab, uncovering a huge patch of wet, stained, textured cement.

And in that dark infinity of markings, I could make out any shape I wanted.

GO BETWEEN

Something was in the bread. Morley was cutting, and on the fourth strike of the knife, the metal braked.

Behind him his friends talked over their food. Morley prised the dough apart and touched something smooth. He had marked it with a scratch. Morley could see the thing's colour, a drab charcoal. He frowned. It had been a long time since this had happened.

"What's up?" someone said to him, and when he turned his face was relaxed.

"It's gone mouldy."

He put the bread in the rubbish, where he could reach it again.

When the others were gone Morley took the bread out and pulled it apart. From its crumbs he drew a tube, a grey baton that fit thickly in his hand. The line of a seal was just visible at one end. Morley did not open it. He turned it over. There were instructions on it, in small type, embossed as if punched out from within.

CONCEAL BY RUBBISH BIN AT EASTERNMOST EXIT ST. JAMES PARK, it said. ASAP. YWBC.

Morley turned it over. He felt the crack of its opening and the larger more ragged mark he had made. The mar made him anxious.

He packaged it tightly in a hard cardboard tube. Walking to the park, he clutched the cylinder, until he realised how he must look, and he turned slowly and he hoped seemingly idly to see who if anyone was watching him, and he relaxed his grip on the tube until he thought perhaps it was too much and that someone might now be able to snatch it. He reached the gate with relief and paused, fussed ostentatiously with his newspaper, put down the tube and tucked it up to the bin with his foot before walking away.

The next day he completed the evaluations he was working on. Morley ate lunch out, and when he headed for home he stopped and bought two new hardbacks, started to read one on the train. (He opened it with a moment's frisson, but it was all there.) He had ice cream in a cinema café until the next showing of a film that he sat through until the end of the final credits. He ate at a pizzeria, sitting outside, reading his book, but nothing did any good.

Through it all he never stopped waiting. He imagined the park wardens, the dustmen and -women becoming intrigued by the cardboard tube, looking to see that they were not watched and taking it from the piles they collected. He imagined them opening his package, unscrewing that grey rod and drawing out whatever it was he had been charged to deliver. He should be calmer, he knew, but it had been so many months since he had last had to do this. Finally, two days later, when he thought it must have arrived wherever it was going, he felt relief.

He pushed his life back into its usual shape, quickly. Though he could not think that this was the last of it, he was pleased that he had not obsessed as he sometimes did, that he had lost only two days to his duty. Early on it had been more. He was so successful that when he at last received another instruction it came as a shock.

. . .

October, and Morley was enjoying London's autumn smell. In a newsagent's he picked up a copy of the *Standard*, and hesitated by the chocolate, looking at the low-fat version he had trained himself to pretend he liked but suddenly hungry for a real bar, which with guilty devil-may-care he took and paid for. He unwrapped it as he walked. The first bite he swallowed: it was on the second that his teeth touched something hard and he gasped and came halting, and stared into the wet and melting sweet at something much darker and more cold inside.

He stared at the chocolate and thought *but I was about to take the other one*. It was a long time since he had dwelled on that phenomenon. He had thought himself inured to his instructors' unerring knowledge of what he would pick.

In the first months he had been constantly aghast at the fact, had imagined unseen cadres watching him, gauging what he was about to buy, somehow pushing their messages into things just before he touched them, but that was impossible. The inserts were there already, waiting for him.

Morley, always knowing that it was useless, had attempted to trick those who contacted him. In shops he would hover for many seconds, his hand over a specific item; he would pick it up, walk on, then suddenly return and grab a replacement.

It made no difference. For weeks and months at a time his shopping was untouched, but when they wanted to pass on a command, he could not evade them. Twice, obscurely shaped, opaque containers were delivered in products he knew he had taken quickly and at random: in a jar of mayonnaise; threaded through a pack of dustbin liners.

Once Morley had spent days living only off translucent products, holding each glass or plastic container up to the light to see it was uncontaminated by commands before buying it, but he had been too hungry to continue like that for long.

. . .

The chocolate contained something like a fat pen-lid. Thankfully Morley had not bitten it.

LEAVE ON YOUR SEAT ON THE LAST SOUTHBOUND VICTORIA LINE TRAIN BETWEEN PIMLICO AND VAUXHALL, it said. ASAP. YWBC.

Morley stared at the order, and hated it.

This time, when he obeyed it, he did not try to distract himself. With something between resentment and self-indulgence he let himself think only of his task, of what might go wrong. From the station at Vauxhall he went straight home and drew a chart of all the places the little package might be intercepted. He ranked them, in order of potential danger.

The next day and the day after that he called in sick and spent the day watching news. Police intercepted a bomb in Syria; Greek doctors saved the lives of twins; a strike by baggage handlers in Paris was averted; a serial sex offender caught in Berlin. It might be any of these, Morley thought, and he stared at the screen at these and other stories, and tried to read some secret nod to him in the reporters' words, in the facts of each case.

Of course his actions might have their effects in the work of hidden agencies, which measured their successes precisely in stories that no one would ever hear. Morley knew that. He knew he could not know, that he might be wasting his time.

He knew also that what he forwarded might have no effect at all, on anything: he did not believe it, but he knew it might be.

This must be important work. He had long ago decided that was the only thing that made sense. It was what had first changed his opinion of his tasks, had turned his paranoia, his fear, into something like pride.

The truth was that it was not just the tedium of clear soups and water or white wine that had aborted his experiment with see-through goods: it was also a growing sense of anxiety, a fear that he was succeeding, that he *was* missing messages, and that he must not, that important things depended on him doing the duty given him.

He had never believed that the insertions were everywhere, that everyone received them randomly but that no one said a word. He had been chosen, for opaque reasons, to be the middle-man. Whoever was contacting him must need anonymity, certainty that they were not traced. Hence this subterfuge, entrusting their deliveries to a stranger.

Morley had been watched for years, since he was a boy. It was the only thing that made sense. They must have had to make sure he was suitable, that he would not fail, that his curiosity would not goad him to open the little containers and let their contents get into the wrong hands, into his hands.

A few days on there was another grey baton in his bread. CONCEAL BY RUBBISH BIN AT EASTERNMOST EXIT ST. JAMES PARK, it said again. ASAP. YWBC. Morley was horrified. He had never had an instruction repeated before. He winced at its corrective tone. Thankfully this time he had not cut the insert.

There was the bread-knife mark, twice my teeth dented the thing, there was that one I dropped and chipped. They must know it's a risk, he thought, reiterating arguments he had had with himself many times. *They wouldn't put it where it could be scratched like that if it mattered. Probably this is nothing to do with that.* Still he imagined whoever had received it examining the first tubular casing, touching the blemish, throwing it away unopened, unsure that they could trust it. The thing, the key it contained, might not be used, and that might be what lost the battle.

He obeyed quickly, but out of that reawakened anxiety came others. Watching the news stories, wondering in which braveries or tragedies he had played a tiny part, Morley felt a resurgence of another fear, for the first time in years, that those messages he had missed, if he had missed any, in the years he had tried to escape the instructions, had been crucial to a long-term plan. That everything he did now was too late, and that deserted in a landfill, discarded years ago by some confused consumer in his place, was the small dark box embossed with instructions which he Morley had been supposed to obey, a box that had been key to all these other, later packages, which were now pointless.

Throughout his life as an occasional courier of messages in his milk, his vegetables, his CDs, in hollows cut in the pages of his books, squeezed from toothpaste tubes, though he had wondered often about his unseen superiors, Morley had not speculated much on the hidden items themselves. For much of the time he had just assumed, vaguely, that they must be instructions, messages that could not be trusted to phone lines or email, rolled in protective carapaces. He could not fail to notice, though, that the small hard thing in his chocolate had resembled nothing so much as a bullet.

He thought of that as he watched footage of an assassination, the death of a strongman president in an ex-Soviet republic, shot once by a sniper. The murdered man was huge and did not look quite human. It may have taken a special weapon to end him. Morley tried to make sense of the politics of the place: he could not tell if the dead man had been a good or a bad thing, which at first made him think that the bullet he had passed on (if it had been a bullet) could not have been used for this job, because there was no obvious heroism here. But of course he was in no position to say: perhaps even if this had been an evil, the good that it also did necessitated it.

Morley knew where these thoughts were going. He had been on this route many times, back when he had rebelled against his unseen commanders. He knew what he would think next, and though he did not want to, though he had had this out with himself many times and thought the argument done, he could not stop.

He wondered again if perhaps his actions were on behalf of some body whose agenda he would not share, something malignant.

· · ·

There was an explosion on an oil rig; an attack on Kurdish villages; rapes in Mexico City. A jockey tested positive for drugs, there was a bloodless coup, a bloody intervention. Morley saw the little bullet or bullet-shaped thing or tightly folded instructions in a bulletlike case held in the hand of the horse rider or the doctor whose test discredited him, in the pocket of the African general who took power promising peace, in the gun belt of the mercenary whose forces invaded the capital.

He knew also that these items and the others that preceded them might be nowhere he would ever see. They could be hidden, with the orders they must have contained for those higher up than he.

Did I do that? Morley thought as he watched the successful docking of a shuttle with Mir. *Did I do that?* A child-smuggling ring broken. *That?* The torture and murder of a Russian antiracist. A company excelled. The end of a conflict came, and a new conflict.

Morley went to sleep an unsung hero but woke in the night, horrified at the knowledge that he was a dupe of criminal stupidity. He became a champion again and then a pawn and then an irrelevance.

At work, Morley thought of the men and women who issued him his real orders, in their white room, or their cave. Their satellite.

"You know all this stuff in Chechnya?" someone said to him in the pub, and he started. Yes, he knew about it, he watched the news, and now he thought about the death squads, the resistance fighters.

The person who had spoken was saying something like "they're all as bad as each other," and distractedly Morley was glad to hear that others were intervening and disagreeing, but he was not paying close attention. He hoped that when next he was issued commands, they concerned the Chechnyans. Or the South Sudanese.

"If you could do something about it," someone was saying, but Morley was ahead of her. *I can*, he thought.

Every time he bought anything he felt his stomach sink in case there was an instruction, but he was almost eager. He was afraid that enthusiasm or anxiety would count against him. He was careful to display no expectation. He picked products from shop shelves firmly, without hesitation.

Of course nothing came. For many days nothing came and he thought often of his duty and how he would like to do it. A tanker was lost in the North Sea. Livestock was bled dry in Mexico by some goatsucker, nothing came, crop circles returned, diseases took thousands, corruption brought down banks, nothing came.

When it did, in the end, the instruction was larger than any he had received before. He suspected, before he had unwrapped his carton. He hefted it. "Deep Pan Vegetable Feast," he read, and eyed its thickness.

Inside it was a disk, almost an inch thick, the diameter of a small frisbee, that had been only just covered in dough and cheese. It was the same dark grey that most of the others had been, perhaps a little lighter or darker. Morley shook it but it made no sound. There was a line just visible bisecting it, where it could be prised apart.

FORWARD TO, he read on it, and then a post-office-box number. ASAP, it said. *They want me to send it?* Morley thought, bewildered, as he kept reading. *They've never—* He stopped hard as he reached the next, last, line: THANK YOU FOR YOUR COOPERATION. YOUR WORK IS DONE.

You will be contacted.

Yesterday was bad comparison, yellow wears bad conscience, yule wary basket-case: of course not, of course not. You will be complicit; connected; collected; conniving; coopted; collated;

concerned. Of course not. *You will be contacted.* Morley had understood very early what YWBC meant, letters he had read on every insert with which he had ever been entrusted, until now.

He put the discus-thing on the table, stared at it. For minutes, Morley stared at it, until he knew what it was that he felt: horrified, and bereft.

He should be happy. There was no hint of displeasure in the message. It seemed they were choosing a major task with which to finish his service. The job was done. That was the implication, it wasn't that *his* work was done, but that his *work* was done, that things were irrevocable now. He supposed he had helped bring in a better world.

As he wrapped the canister and put it in a box, though, he thought suddenly, *I've been replaced,* and became so enraged that he slammed the thing down. *Why've they replaced me? What did I do wrong?*

In the post office, in the long, long queue, he could not stop staring at a woman three people in front of him.

She held a large padded envelope close to her. Abruptly she let it drop and held it loosely, while she looked round, taking in everyone. She drew her hands up again, slowly, the package creeping back towards her chest, and she tried to put it down again and walked briskly and with relief to the service window when it opened.

Morley was still. The queue became restive but he did not move. Behind him an elderly Rastafarian gripped a poster tube in two hands. A young mother fussed with the cardboard box she had put beside her baby in its pushchair. A teenager was picking with what looked like great nervousness at the large wrapped case he held.

"Excuse me, mate, are you going to—" someone was saying, but Morley ignored him, stared at the parcels in the line.

I'm surrounded by colleagues, he thought, and then almost instantly, *I'm surrounded by enemies.*

Men and women from his own organisation, or from *splinters* from that organisation, renegades, or opponents dedicated to destroying him, those who would make things far worse for Chechnya, for the economy, those whom he must stop. *None of them know,* he thought. He was the only one who knew that there, in that post office, ignoring each other and filtering out the tiny mutter of a Walkman, glancing at the clock, fidgeting, they were all at war. There must be civilians among them, and they were in danger too. Innocent people could get hurt.

Careful now.

Be careful. Morley swallowed. He closed his eyes. *I'm losing it.* "Mate, excuse me, but the queue's moving—"

"Go on mate—"

What am I doing?

It was sudden, a landslide of certainty. Seeing all his hidden enemies or comrades or random strangers, Morley could not believe he had been taken in, that he had been suckered by the implied do-gooding of his overseers, these skulking contaminators. He was aghast. He thought of the years he had done their work and of each message or item or weapon or computer code he had passed on. As rage grew in him and disgust for his foolishness, a fervour came too, to fix the bad he had done. He could hardly imagine what he must have been party to, but he made himself, he was unflinching. The flies on corpses, the slumps that wiped economies away and left people raging in the streets.

"Mate—"

But Morley was out and running, pushing through the lines, holding his terrible package close, as if he would shield everyone else from it.

No, he thought. *No.*

He held the disc over the waters of the canal, he held it by a skip full of rubbish, by a bonfire on the allotments, but at last he took it back to his house and placed it on his table, a baleful centre-piece.

I won't be part of it anymore, Morley thought. *Fuck you,* he thought, staring at the container. He put a potted plant on it. He tried to make it banal.

That night when his phone rang, Morley was horrified but not so surprised to hear the curt message, the voice so clipped he could not even tell the sex or age of the speaker.

"Is this . . ." it said, and then a gasp, a contained sound, and then, "You're just bloody *asking* for trouble," and there was laughing and the line cut.

Morley did not leave his house for days. He picked up a knife whenever the phone or the doorbell rang, but that one call seemed to be the end of it. *I knew it,* he thought and most or much of the time believed. *I was right about them, they wouldn't* threaten *me if they were . . . on my, on our side.*

Nothing came for him. He watched the disc. It sat below the china pot through the weeks of winter, into spring.

Morley carefully watered the plant. For a time he flinched when he shopped, and then he stopped, and he found nothing in his products. He watched what happened in the world, and was as sure as he could be that he was not to blame. He was more and more certain that he had done the right thing.

By March he had almost stopped worrying. When he came back to his flat one day to find his window broken and his home trashed, his video and stereo taken, his books thrown to the floor, he even fleetingly thought that it was just a burglary. But it did not take him long to trace the footsteps of the intruder, see how they had hurried from room to room, how they had been looking for something.

They had been interrupted, it seemed, had not spent long in the kitchen. The disc was untouched, fringed by the leaves that now half hid it. They would not have expected it to be there. Morley felt the raised instructions again and sat on the floor.

The police were sympathetic. They made it clear that he should not expect too much.

I expect nothing, he thought. *You can't track the likes of these. You're no good to me at all. They want me.*

"Is there . . . is it . . . Is it like most other break-ins?" he could not restrain himself from asking, and the liaison officer nodded and watched him carefully.

"Yes. It's . . ." He moved his lips. "Sometimes people find this sort of thing very upsetting. Would you like me to . . . I can put you in touch with someone to chat to about it. A counsellor . . ." Morley almost laughed at the man's misdirected kindness.

You can't help me, he thought. *No one can.* He wondered what would happen, what the penalty was for renegacy. *I don't regret it,* he thought fiercely. *I'd do it again. I won't courier for them no more, no matter what they do to me.*

When the policeman phoned him, some days later, it took Morley several seconds to understand what he was saying, the message was so unexpected.

"We've got him."

Morley could not understand how the operatives could have been so careless. A botched job, a rush, the incompetence of some new agent; he could not understand it. "They were caught selling the stuff?" he kept saying.

"Yeah," the officer said. They sat in the police-station canteen. "Junkies, they know they should use a fence and all that, but, you know . . ." He waggled his eyebrows to indicate that it was difficult to care when you were high.

Morley wanted to see him, the so-called junkie they had caught, but he was not allowed even to peer through the grille of the cell. His heart was hard in his throat. He thought of the man in that little room. Impassive, in nondescript, forgettable clothes. Waiting for the police to receive a message from some astonishing lawyer, or government minister, and to let him go; or for a midnight visitor to free him in some effortlessly daring raid. Morley imagined him a big man but not so big he was slow, with a face that showed no emotion at all, nor his purpose. Morley did not know if he could bear to see the face of his designated punisher.

Why did you get caught?

It did not take much to find out the supposed name of the man the police were holding. A word to a few of the officers he had dealt with, and he learnt when the suspect would be released— soon to be rearrested, he was assured, immediately they could find a fingerprint or DNA (they'd be coming to dust again). Morley wasn't to worry, they assured him.

Morley could still not well believe what he was going to do. But he could not live this way anymore. He waited as the day went, and grew more and more frightened. He did not give the thought words, but he knew that this might be when he died.

How will I recognise him? he thought, and remembered the photograph the desk clerk had shown him. *Those things aren't accurate. That made him look, I don't know . . .*

He considered the way the man would walk: ignorable, invisible, forgettable, and all full of power. *Have to be very careful . . .* Morley thought again.

I'm going to see one of them, he thought. *Any minute.* He could have retched.

When the man left the police station, Morley felt as if he could not breathe.

It was late. He tracked the man quietly toward estates that sprawled and seemed empty. The man's disguise was consummate: his furtive movements, his anxious little tics perfect. Morley hung back, but as he saw his target stop by a stairwell, in the shadows of some industrial bins, lighting a cigarette, he was overcome.

He had thought he was only there to track, but now he ran forward in fear and anger and wondered as he came if this had always been going to happen. Morley was sobbing as he attacked. He knew he could not give his target a moment.

"Who are you?" he whispered through the scarf around his face. "You leave me alone." He gasped, he sucked in breath, gripped the man's throat and barrelled him down. His hands were shaking very hard. "Who the fuck are you?"

The man he held was whining like a child. Morley pushed his face into concrete. "Shut up, shut up, you're fooling *no one,* you understand?" He jabbed. "*Tell* me, tell me, what do you *want* from me?" He stretched out his arms hard, trying to keep distance.

The burglar was crying. Desperately, Morley kicked him. "Tell me," he said.

"Is it you I done?" the man whimpered. "It didn't mean nothing, it didn't mean nothing, don't cut me . . ." Urgently Morley watched his arms, his legs, ready for an attack. His quarry was thin, and his face was scabbed. It was hard to make sense of his expression. For one moment, Morley saw a calculation on the man's face, and he opened his own eyes aghast, but the expression was gone, and he was unsure.

"Who are you?" Morley said again, and the man, the young man, flapped his hand at the blood on him.

"I ain't nothing," he gasped, and Morley watched him and suddenly understood and came in close.

"What did they tell you?" he said urgently. "I'll make sure you're safe. Whatever they threatened you with, I can, we, the police can protect you. Who were they, the ones told you to break in? *What did they want?*"

But though he shook him and hurt him again, badly, Morley could not make the man talk. He would only cry, holding his arms limp, and Morley had at last to throw him down and run, leaving the young burglar howling and tearing himself from tension and frustration. The man was a flawless actor; or was well-chosen by the hidden agency, for ignorance and expendability; or was too terrified to tell the truth; or the police had the wrong man.

Morley cleaned his flat, took the plant off the disc. He heard no more from the police. When he heard about the poison gas attack, he sat staring at the heavy circle, the evidence of his mutiny.

On the screen, rescuers in chemical suits dragged young men and women out of the subway. Most were dead; some were still dying, noisily drowning on their own deliquescent lungs. Morley watched. Their families mobbed the site, broke through the cordons, were held back by the police and by gusts of gas, braved them, reached their dead lovers and family with their eyes streaming from more than grief. Some succumbed.

Simultaneous attacks in other parts of the city, and Morley heard what the journalists heard, the screams and foreign entreaties. In places of worship, in the offices of giant companies, and in that modern subway, gas made hells. Several devices were found and defused before they were triggered: even more had been supposed to die than the hundreds who did.

A coalition of armies was amassed. There was an onslaught on the poisoners' refuge. Morley watched the conflict.

When his prime minister appeared, came onto his screen to ask for Morley's and his compatriots' support, Morley could focus only on the bookshelves behind the leader. Amid the spines were tasteful statuettes, a couple of plaques, and there at the prime minister's right hand an empty space, what looked like a deliberate gap, what looked like a stand for something, something circular, something the size of the pallet that had propped up Morley's flowers.

Morley felt as if he were choking. *It's a message,* he thought. *They're saying, 'See what we're missing?'*

If I'd sent it on, they would have had it, and they might have stopped this.

It was too late to send it now. Morley was stricken.

He saw photographs of the hideouts from which the master-minds of the attack had fled, and in an alcove in the wall were two saucer-shaped things, covered with writing, and a space for a third, that was not there. *It could have been even worse,* Morley thought then, and his heart surged and misery lifted. *Oh thank God, that was it, it would have been even worse, if I'd not held this back from them.* He stared again at his container, but did not re-main convinced. He could not.

Is it too late?

I'll send it. I'll send it. But he did not want to make things worse.

It was murderous, it was going on, people were dying, and *he had started it,* or possibly perhaps had softened it and made it bet-ter. Morley felt that the guilt would destroy him. If it weren't for the great pride he felt at other times, he was sure he could not have survived.

The battles did not stop, and he stared and stared at the ad-dress on the container. Once he took a knife to it, to open it, but he stopped, in time, when all he had done was score scratches on the surface. He could not risk making things worse.

"I might make it better," he whispered, and nearly prised it apart again, but did not.

Your work is done, it said to him, every time he looked at it. Your work is done, but it was not, and it never would be.

You never had any work, he heard, but ignored, inside himself. Your work meant nothing.

He could send it and the fighting would end and the right side triumph. He would send it, he would end the killing, he decided, except that he could not risk the catastrophe he would or might let loose if he did.

Perhaps it was too late, anyway. It might make no difference. *If I send it and it makes no difference, that's why, it'll be because I left it too late, like a fool.* His burden bent him.

There is no burden, he heard and ignored. You have no work to do. Your work was always done.

Outside moved many people carrying parcels. Morley held the disc and watched the war that he had started or contained or had no effect on at all.

DIFFERENT
SKIES

DIFFERENT SKIES

2 October

Seventy-one and melancholy.

I suppose it should be no surprise. It was not like this last year, though. End of my biblical quotient, should have been hugely traumatic, but the big not-very-secret shindig Charlie et al. organised for me rather took the sting out of it. I didn't think much about the age itself until later. This year, though, I woke up and straightaway felt as old and dry as kindling.

Physically I'm weak but no weaker than yesterday. I still feel as if this fatigue were some interloper. It doesn't bother me as much as it might because I cannot take it seriously. It is so *absurd* that I should be out of breath after a flight of stairs that I feel I *must* be victim to some trick. It is not so much the effect as the simple fact of being past seventy that sticks in my craw. It frightens me. I do not believe it.

No visitors this year, and no great welter of presents. Last year must have exhausted budgets and indulgences. I am down to a couple of handsome books from Charlie (there are other trinkets, of course, but not worth mentioning). People my age have no money, and I think the younger ones resent buying something which will be ownerless again so soon.

I am being morbid. I am hardly at the end. I know that if I were frail, or made a great deal out of birthdays, or were lonely, that I would have visitors. But as I am not and do not, I have subsisted—happily enough—on cards and telephone calls.

I had an extended lunch with Sam at the café, that he gave me gratis when he learnt it was my birthday. Then I came home to supervise the installation of my present to myself.

It is a whimsical thing, which has been a monumental faddle to organise, but as I sit here looking at it, I really can't say I regret it.

I've bought myself a window.

I saw it a fortnight ago at Portobello Market. It was in one of the antiques shops up near the top, by Notting Hill. I can't say why it appeals—it's hardly fine art. But there is something about it which is awfully compelling.

It's about a foot and a half high by two wide. In the centre is a lozenge of deep red glass. Surrounding it in radial sections like slices of pie are eight triangles of what I think was intended to be more-or-less clear glass—to my spoilt late-twentieth-century eyes it looks green or blue, dirty and discoloured. The segments are held together and separated by a framework of thin black lead.

It is a rude piece. Each pane is streaked with knotholes that warp the world behind them. Little scabs of clotted glass. The colours are not pure, and the paint on the pane is at the point of flaking. But still, there is something in it I can't ignore.

The second time I saw it, I realised I was relieved it was still there. So I thought, "This is ridiculous, I don't have to wait for my pocket money," and I bought it. It sat around for a week without being unwrapped. Today I paid a man from the hardware centre to pop round, remove the top central pane from my study window, and replace it with my new—old—window.

I'm sitting at my desk as I write, and I can see it above me. It is fractionally smaller than the other panes, and the man made some wooden frame to fit it tight in the space. He's smoothed the edges down until the frame is totally unobtrusive. He's warned me not to touch the glass for a few days until the putty dries.

It sticks out, I suppose, surrounded by five other, cleaner panes—one to either side and the three below which can be swung open a crack. They are probably half its age, and consequently much purer, flatter glass. But I like the look of the odd thing.

It is at about head height. From up here on the fifth floor, my view over west London is enviable, over half an acre of grassland and then the ranks of lower houses. When I sit at the desk the old window rises to hang suspended over the roofs beyond like a heavy star.

The evening light comes right through the middle piece, the red lump. I suppose it is a sun itself, rising or setting. It is an odd colour for the sun, that dark scarlet. It sends extraordinary coloured rays onto the wall behind me. It is like a fat glass spider in a metal web.

I will resist the temptation to write forlornly "Happy Birthday to me." I do not know what is coming over me. I am going to bed, where I will read one of Charlie's books. A nice day, really. I must put a lid on this mawkish forlorn-old-man thing that I seem to have going.

4 October

I have finished one book and moved on to the other. I phoned Charlie today to tell him how much I was enjoying them (a small lie, as regards the second book—it is not nearly so good). He was pleased but slightly bemused to hear from me, I think. After all, we spoke only three days ago.

This morning I went for a walk long enough to make me ache (not a Herculean feat, of course). I had a chat with Sam on the way back, then got home to this armchair. I will admit to being slightly aghast at the relief it was to sit down.

That was when I spoke to Charlie, and I must admit that it was not the best conversation. Nothing was *wrong*, of course. I am not angry and nor was he. I was just made aware (not deliberately— he was raised too well for that, I like to think) that he does not know what to make of me these days.

I am in a halfway house. We have never been close as friends are close; we do not trade intimacies (his choice, and one I have respected since he was a lad). He is much too old to need me, and I am not yet old enough to need him.

Perhaps he is biding his time until then. Then our affection can come into its own; then roles will become clear, and he can wipe up my drool and cut up my supper for me and wheel me over to the window to enjoy the view.

Since that phone conversation I have sat dumb for a fair old while.

I found myself—I sort of *came to,* I suppose—gazing at the window over my desk.

It is a splendid thing. It is very good to stare at.

I was thinking of it while I walked. All the obvious, idle thoughts: Who could have made it? When? Why? Over what did it look? And so on and on. When I walk into the little study into its light, those questions do not dissipate but return in strength. When I look at that strange glass it makes me think of all the other old windows that have been lost.

It comes to life at this time, in the gloaming. When the light deepens and seems to send spears directly at it.

Although . . . it is not right to say that it comes to life. That is not right. "Life" has never, I think, been its attraction. It is too still for that.

I know it very well, by now. I have spent some time over the last days looking at the eight evenly spaced triangles around the central stone. Each is stained with its own impurities; each is a unique colour. Counting clockwise from the top, my favourite is the sixth, the slice between west and southwest. It is a little bluer than the others, and the ruby at its apex makes that blue shine.

I have reread the words above with amusement and discomfort. For goodness' sake, am I turning into some sort of mystic? I knew I was smitten with the thing—I cannot remember being so thrilled with *ownership* of anything material. But I am perturbed by what I have written: I sound like an obsessive.

The fact is, I have read today, and walked and chatted and all of that, but I have been thinking always of my window.

All manner of whimsies enter my head. The sun has gone, now. The darkening sky is moiling pointlessly with cloud cover. Perhaps the window is not a sun but an asterisk, interrupting the grammar of the sky, with me sitting below it like a footnote.

This is not healthy at all. The low(ish) spirits that settled on me on my birthday must have taken deeper root than I had thought. I think I must be lonely. I will make some phone calls. I think I will go out tonight.

Later

Well how terribly deflating.

My good intentions to snap out of this reverie have been stymied. I do not know anyone who is alive, local, and up for a meal, a drink, or anything else. Flicking through my address book was depressing and led to a meagre list—a pathetic list—of possibilities. And none of them wanted to come out to play.

It is night, now, very quiet, and I feel awfully bloody deserted.

5 October

I was not going to write today, as nothing of any note had happened by the evening (I will not dutifully record the tedium of shopping and television and more bloody reading). But then the oddest thing happened.

It is late, and my sitting room is cold and dark. I am still trembling slightly, nearly half an hour after the event.

I came into the study at about 10 p.m. to fetch a book. I did not bother with the light: I could see what I was after on the desk quite clearly in the light from the hall.

As I bent over for it, I felt a tingling on my neck, less than a breath but much more than the vague sense one sometimes has of being watched. I straightened quickly, in some alarm.

It was dark outside. Not a clear, starlit dark either, but a cloudy shadow. It was a drab night. Desultory sodium-light from the streetlamps before and below me, that was all. No moon.

But the red glass at the centre of my window was shining.

It sent icy scarlet light onto the desk below, and onto me. I swear that was the source of the raised hair on my neck.

I gaped up at it. My mouth must have been slack. All the impurities and the scratches on the inside of that central panel were etched and vivid. It seemed to have a hundred shapes, all of a sudden, to look momentarily like a huddled embryo and a red whirlpool and a bloodshot eye.

I must have been staring at it for no more than three or four seconds when it stopped. I did not see it happen. I was not conscious of any light going out, anywhere. Perhaps it was extinguished as I blinked. All I know is that one moment it shone, and then it did not. My retinas retained no afterimage.

Perhaps it was an isolated light from some aeroplane or somesuch, that happened to shine directly and strangely through my window. I am thinking much more clearly now than when I started to write, and that seems the only possibility. Looked at like that, I do not know why I bothered to record this.

Except that when the room was lit up with that light, something felt very strange in the air. Very wrong. It was only three seconds, but I swear it made me cold, deep down.

8 October (Night. Small hours)

There is something beyond the window.

I am afraid.

I am no longer bemused or concerned or intrigued but truly afraid.

I must write this quickly.

When I came home in the evening (having thought all day about what happened last night, even when I denied that that was what I was doing) I felt a peculiar disinclination to enter my study. When I finally conquered it, of course, there was nothing untoward in there.

I looked nonchalantly enough up at the window and saw the sky through it, just as I should. Pitted and cracked by the old glass, but there was nothing out of place.

I dismissed my nerves and pottered around for a few hours, but I never relaxed. I think I was mulling over the odd light of the previous evening. I was waiting for something. That was not quite clear to me at first, but as the evening grew older and the sunlight was smothered, I found myself looking up more and more through the sitting room windows. I was thinking of what to do.

Eventually, when the day was quite gone, I decided to go into the study again. Just to read, of course. That's what I told myself, in my head, loudly. In case, I suppose, anything was listening.

I settled down in the armchair and leafed through Charlie's tedious book, that I am labouring to finish.

I glanced up at the window, now and then, and it behaved as glass should. I had turned off the main light, was reading by a little lamp to reduce the reflections. Beyond the window I could make out the occasional intermittent lights of some aeroplane passing from the left-hand windowpane through that central, much older one, and out again. They ballooned briefly as they slid behind old bubbles in the glass.

I read and watched for at least an hour, and then I must have fallen asleep.

I woke suddenly, very cold. I could only just make out my watch— it was a little after two in the morning.

I was huddled like some pathetic child in the armchair, in darkness. The bulb of the lamp must have blown, I remember thinking. I stood shakily and heard the book fall from my lap. I looked around, confused and shivering.

I think the white noise of rain was what woke me. It was coming down hard. I saw the dull shine of the streetlights glint and move slightly through the slick of water on the windowpanes.

I fumbled, trying to gather myself, and saw the room by red moonlight passing through that central pane. As I turned, I saw the moon briefly.

I stopped suddenly. My throat caught. I looked back at the window.

The old pane was dry.

Dirty rain was pounding against its neighbours, but not a drop spattered against it.

The moon was shining full in my face through the glass, distorted by its impurities. I was quite still.

After a moment I walked closer to the old window. All around me was the low, mindless sound of rain. I stopped just in front of the desk and looked up at that moon. As far as I could see through the buckled glass, it was in a clear, dark sky. I could see stars around it.

The sky visible through the rain in the other windows was a mass of cloud.

I moved my head slowly to one side, watching the moon. It moved slowly out of the old starburst window and past the dividing frame. It did not appear in the right-hand pane. When I moved my head quickly back, it returned, to vanish again on the opposite side.

The new panes and the old looked out over different skies.

I pulled the desk quickly out of my path and stood directly in front of the intricate frame. I put my hands to it, trembling, and brought my face up to it, and looked out.

I stared through the glass and the moonlight, and then with a flash of fear that made me sick I saw the top of a wall. Through the greenish glass below the red centrepiece, in the light of some ghost moon, I saw old bricks and crumbling mortar only a few feet before me, topped with broken glass.

Beyond that wall there was a low, angled roof sloping away into the darkness. I looked right, pressing my face against glass which was colder than the other panes. The wall stretched off as far as I could make out.

I fumbled behind me for the desk chair, pulled it over, and stood on it carefully without taking my eyes from the view. I looked down through the old window, tracing the black bricks below me. And there, perhaps six feet below the glass, was the ground.

I rocked with disorientation. Sure enough, to either side of me, the windowpanes still looked out over the London night, over the stretch of scrub and the dark slates fifty feet below.

But the patterned glass in the centre overlooked an alley, only a little way from the pavement. Scraps of rubbish skittered soundless across the cement.

With my ear pressed against the old glass, the silence that seeped through was greater than the pathetic puttering of the rain. My heart was beating so hard it shook me. I took in the dim sight in front of me with a numb foreboding that grew worse every second.

It became terror when I turned my head slowly, and saw that I was watched.

. . .

I saw them for less than half a second, the clutch of dark figures that stood motionless in the entrance to the alley. But in that moment I knew that their glowering unlit eyes were all on me.

I cried out and stumbled, tottering and falling.

I landed heavily and fell, then writhed until I could stand, and then I ran for the door, moaning, and I slapped the light switch and turned and the moon had gone.

The old window admitted the same view as all the others. Like its fellows, it was wet with rain.

It is nearly morning, now, and I do not know what to do.

I thought at first of telling somebody: Charlie, or Sam, or someone. But then I hear the same story told to me by a seventy-one-year-old, and I know what I would think: Alzheimer's, old-timers'. Or madness. Or blindness. Or a simple lie.

At best I would think I was being told a story in that irritatingly fey metaphorical register that some people adopt in their dotage (in which "I think often of my long-dead husband" becomes "I have lovely chats with your father").

I could only tell someone if they would come, and see it. And it might not happen again, or not while they were there, and then I would be left with their pity. I will not have that.

10 October

They are children.

They are taunting me.

That other city came back last night. I have avoided the study for two days, and I do not know what happened beyond that window. Let it come and go, I thought. Like tides changing outside a seaside house. No need for me to care.

. . .

I woke in the night, at some unspecified dark hour. I lay for a long time in bed, trying to work out what had disturbed me.

Eventually I heard it. A faint hiss. A whispering.

A voice was coming through the wall. From the study.

I lay there numb and cold with my eyes open. It came irregularly, furtive and insistent.

I sat up and pulled the top cover around me like a cloak. Mute and fearful I shuffled from my room and stood outside the study door. The sound was louder here, sliding insidiously through the wood.

I knew that I would not sleep again. I set my jaw, reached out, and opened the door.

The room was bathed again in that ghastly moonlight. It made my books and shelves look ancient and insubstantial. Everything was motionless, basking with the stillness of a dead thing. The moonlight extended from the old pane in a canal of dusty luminescence.

Through the rest of the window I saw scudding clouds, but it was a clear night in that other city. And as I stood there on the threshold of that freezing room, I heard that voice again.

OI MISTER.

It was a child's voice.

It was whispered, but it filled the room with ease. It resonated in weird dimensions.

I heard a thin tittering and a shushing noise.

There was cold outside me and inside me.

OI MISTER.

I heard it again. I inched forward into that terrible dark room. The desk was where I had left it. There was nothing between me and the coldly shining window.

There was another sound: a sharp tapping on the glass. I heard it again, and this time I saw a handful of little dark shapes appear from nowhere in the bottom of the old pane and rattle against it.

Someone, I realised, was throwing stones.

I crossed the floor in slow, tiny steps and picked up the chair, which lay where it had fallen. I mounted it and looked down as steeply as I could.

There was a quick, furtive motion in the shadows of the alley. Fear chilled me and blurred my eyes. I could see almost nothing in that great trench of darkness, but I made out the shapes of figures pushing themselves quickly flat against the wall directly below me, so that I could not see them.

And one of them spoke again.

OI MISTER YOU OLD CUNT. And there was a chorus of malignant giggles.

Another stone was thrown, much harder this time. I felt it through the glass, and stumbled back. I kept my footing. I screamed at them in my fear.

"What d'you want? Leave me alone!" I shouted, and was greeted with raucous and stifled laughter.

One by one little shapes pulled themselves from the wall and emerged into my line of sight. They were little more than shadows in that profound darkness. But I could see that they were children.

Unbelieving, I pulled myself down for a moment to stare through one of my other windows, but nothing had changed. I was fifty feet up, and the only wakeful thing this side of the horizon. I was staring out over little urban hillocks and clots of grass moving fitfully in the wind, and the endless maze of hunched houses all unlit and silent.

But up there in the other nightland that uncanny gang was hurling stones at my window, and hissing vicious abuse in spectral voices, and calling me old man, old man.

Quite suddenly I truly realised what was happening. For the first time that night I was fully aware that I was being taunted by *phantoms,* by *delinquent ghosts.* I seemed to wake, to feel the chill air and hear the rat-tat-tat of stones and the cruel words from a pack of children who *could not be there.* And I stepped off the chair as horror clotted in my gorge and I felt my legs nearly fold, and I walked as steady as I could to the light and turned it on, and when that did nothing to stem the flow of vitriol from the ghost city I slammed the door three times.

And when I turned back, thank God, thank God, it had all gone.

I do not know if the children fled in fear or if they are still there, waiting wherever the city has gone.

11 October

I went back to the shop from where the window came.

As I foresaw, the woman knew nothing, remembered nothing, could tell me nothing. She had had the window for months, part of a lot from somewhere she did not recall.

She looked at me, concerned by my manner. She asked if there was something wrong. I could not stop a fleeting, hysterical laugh at that, an incredulous grin. It must have been the most horrible rictus.

I was possessed by some unclear, nebulous emotions that I cannot define. A sense of urgency and isolation. A deep feeling that the past was done, that it was the present that should concern me.

What is the nature of that place?

I think of it in so many ways.

The window remembers what it used to see. That is clear. I do not know where I look out or when, but it must be the older view from that cracked pane (more cracked now, I realise, after last night's little broadside).

So am I living in a window's memory? Is this nothing but a repeat of the pointless brutality directed at some old man like me, who first lived behind that sunburst window? Perhaps this window looks out onto some imbecilic, repetitive Hades like a stuck record.

Or perhaps this time it is different. Perhaps those little roughnecks want to finish something off.

13 October

The little tykes. Ragamuffins. I imagine fat boys smoking and thin-faced girls. Dead eyes. Little ruffians.

The little terrors.

The *terrors.*

They will not leave me. They croon at me and mock my shuffling old-man walk. They scribble obscenities on the wall opposite, and on the bricks of my house, my other house that I cannot see. They piss and hurl stones.

I do not leave the study now. I am learning what I need to know for my defence. I wait for the ghost city to wax back to me, and when it comes I investigate it to the limits of my vision.

There is a drainpipe by my window, on my other wall, my ghost wall.

I have heard them scrabbling a short way up it, scraping the rust and mortar. I have listened to them whispering, daring each other to climb it. Calling me names, gearing each other up with hatred and poison to break my window and *scare me to death.*

I do not know what I have done or what he did—the man who lived in that other house. Perhaps he was just old and funny and stupid and lived where no one could hear him scream and beg.

I will not call them evil. They are not evil. But I am afraid that they are capable of it.

14 October

I sat in the study and waited all day and they came at last at night, and I cried for them to stop and stood on the chair with my pyjamas flapping idiotic around my ankles. I watched as one pulled chalk from its trousers and began to scrawl on the wall opposite my window.

It was too dark to see. But when they had made me cry they fled, and the ghost city stayed beyond my window until just before dawn, long enough for me to read what had been written for me.

YOUR DEAD OLD MAN.

15 October

I have gone out and looked around, and everywhere, in all the parts of the city, wherever I have been, youth seems to fill London.

I have heard animated swearing from girls and boys on bicycles and buses. I have seen signs that read "Only two children at a time" on the doors of small groceries. As if that were a defence. I have wandered the streets in a strange state staring around me at the little monsters that surround us.

For the first time in my life I see people look at me and glance away embarrassed. Perhaps I have not showered recently enough— I have been preoccupied. Perhaps it is just my broken walk. They could not know that I am newly like this. I was not this derelict thing until a week ago when the children came.

I am afraid of all these unchecked unbridled younglings. *None of them are human.* They are all like the ones who come to torment me at night.

I cannot look at them, at any of them, without this horrible fear, but also with a jealousy. A longing. I thought at first that this was new, that it had come through the window with that alien moonlight. But when I look at other adults looking at children, I know that I am not alone. This is an old feeling.

I have prepared myself.

I returned to the hardware shop, where the man who fixed my window in place did not remember or perhaps recognise me. I bought what I will need for tonight.

I have spent this day, this perhaps last day, walking slowly around with my hands behind my back (they sought out that old-man grip to go with my old-man limp). And when I saw that it would soon be time, that the afternoon was nearing its end, I shambled home again.

I am ready. I am writing this as the light wanes. So far the old pane, the haunted pane, shows the same sky as its siblings.

I am sitting just below the window with my walking stick by my feet and my new hammer across my lap.

Why me? I have pondered. I was not especially cruel I do not think, in any measured or repulsive way. I have had little to do with children.

During the night visitations, I have seen glimpses of flapping, ridiculous shorts half a century out of date, and discerned the old-fashioned, clipped voices of my merciless besiegers (the tone is not disguised even when sneering in wide-eyed sadism). And yes of course I have thought of the years when I was like them.

Perhaps it is as simple as that, that I look out at my own times running in those hordes. Is this to be that sort of banal morality tale? Am I my own abuser?

I do not remember. I can see myself running through rubble with others, and sifting for prizes and smoking vile things and torturing stray animals and all the rest, but I do not remember singling out some old man to be his personal harpy. Perhaps I deceive myself. Perhaps that is me, out there.

But I cannot believe that Hell is so trite.

I believe that I am just an old man, and that they have a game they have waited sixty years to finish. A game that makes them drunk with contravention. With wickedness.

I am watching and waiting. And when the sun has gone and the light behind that intricate pane flickers and changes, when I look down to see those spirits scamper to their stations with all that monstrous baleful energy, then we shall have a race.

. . .

Why not just break it now and have done? Shatter the damn thing.

I have thought of it a thousand times since this began. I have imagined hurling my shoes or books or self at that old glass and sending it into the sky in hundreds of pieces. Pattering down onto the grass so far below.

Or I could simply have it taken out again. I could replace it with a pane like all the others. I could return that glass trap to the bemused shopkeeper. I could leave it carefully in a skip for some other unsuspecting soul. I could sink it in the canal, a piece of disintegrating debris among so many, emitting its ghost light to the fishes.

But the children would still be waiting.

They are not *in* the window but beyond it. And they have not yet had blood. They have picked me. I do not know why, perhaps there is no reason, but they have picked me. They have me in their sights. I am to be the victim. They have been poised on the brink of this all my life.

Wherever I hide the window, they will be waiting. And if I break the glass into my own world, then nothing will have changed for them in theirs. They will stand in stasis in that hidden city and wait, and wait, and I am afraid of when and how they might find me.

They are just out to see how far they can go.

But if I watch, and strike at the right moment, if I am fast enough, I will take the fight to them.

I will strike a blow for old men.

If I can shatter the glass when their alley waits beyond, if I can smash it into *their* city, then things might be a little different. It might be a way in.

I want to emerge from the ruins of that window and drop (a short drop if you hang from the rim) into the alley (into the ghostland, immersed in the dead city, but I will not think on that) and I will wave my stick and run for them.

Bloody little *hooligans.*

If please God I catch one I shall lay it over my knee and by God I shall give it a hiding, a bloody good hiding, I shall teach it a bloody lesson, I will, I will thrash it, and that will, it will put an end to *all this nonsense.* I can't run away. I have to put a stop to this. They need to be taught a lesson.

(Oh but even as I write that, I feel so stupid. It is an idiot's plan. Insane. I catch a glimpse of the rucked skin on my old hand and I know that I can no more climb from the window and drop to the ground in that other city than I can leap mountains. What can I do? What can I do?)

I will try. I will do my damnedest.

Because the alternative is untenable.

I know what they are gearing up to. I know their plan. When the window changes, I will look out once more over that dingy alley, and their message, their chalk threat, will still face me. And I *must* make it up and out and at them tonight because if I do not, if I hesitate or I am slow, if I fail, if they are faster, if *I* do not go *out* . . .

They will come in.

AN END TO HUNGER

AN END TO HUNGER

I met Aykan in a pub sometime late in 1997. I was with friends, and one of them was loudly talking about the internet, which we were all very excited about.

"Fucking internet's fucking dead, man. Yesterday's bullshit," I heard from two tables away. Aykan was staring at me, gazing at me curiously, like he wasn't sure I'd let him crash this party.

He was Turkish (I asked because of his name). His English was flawless. He had none of the throaty accent I half expected, though each of his words did sound finished in a slightly unnatural way.

He smoked high tar incessantly. ("Fucking national sport: they wouldn't let me in fucking 'Stanbul without sufficient shit in my lungs.") He liked me because I wasn't intimidated by him. I let him call me names and didn't get my back up when he was rude. Which he was, often.

My friends hated him, and after he'd left I nodded and murmured agreement with them about what a weirdo, about how rude and where he got off, but the fact was I couldn't get worked up about Aykan. He told us off for getting moist about email and the web. He told us wired connection was dead. I asked him what

he was into instead and he took a long drag on his stinking cigarette and shook his head, dismissively exhaling.

"Nanotech," he said. "Little shit."

He didn't explain that. I left him my phone number, but I never
expected to hear from him. Ten months later he called me. It was
only luck that I still lived at that address, and I told him that.

"People don't fucking move, man," he said, incomprehensibly.

I arranged to meet him after work. He sounded a bit distracted, a bit miserable even.

"Do you play games, man?" he said. "N64?"

"I've got a Playstation," I told him.

"Playstation licks shit, man," he told me. "Bullshit digital con-
trols. I'll give you the ads, though. Playstation ads sing sweet
hymns, but you want a fucking analog control stick, or you're
playing once removed. You know anyone with N64?"

As soon as we met he handed me a little grey plastic square. It
was a game pack for a Nintendo 64 system, but it was rough-cast
and imperfectly finished, its seam bizarrely ragged. It had no label,
only a sticker scrawled with illegible handwriting.

"What's this?" I asked.

"Find someone with N64," he said. "Project of mine."

We talked for a couple of hours. I asked Aykan what he did for
a living. He did that dismissive smoking thing again. He muttered
about computer consultancy and web design. I thought the internet was dead, I said. He agreed fervently.

I asked him what nanotech stuff he was doing, and he became
ragged with enthusiasm. He caught me with crazy looks and
grinned at odd intervals, so I couldn't tell if he was bullshitting me.

"Don't talk to me about little miniature fucking arterial cleaning robots, don't fucking talk to me about medical reconstruction,
or microwhateverthefucks to clean up oil slicks, OK? That's bullshit to get people on board. What's going to be big in nanotech?

Eh? Like any other fucking thing . . ." He banged the table and slopped beer. "The money's in *games*."

Aykan had extraordinary schemes. He told me about his prototype. It was crude, he said, but it was a start. "It's old school meets new school," he kept saying. "Kids with fucking conkers, in the playground." The game was called Blood Battle, or Bloody Hell, or Bloodwar. He hadn't decided.

"You buy a little home injection kit, like you're diabetic. And you build up your own serum from the pack provided. Like when you play a wargame you choose how many fuckers on horseback and how many artillery, right? Well, you have different vials full of microbots that interact with your blood, each type with different defences and attacks, and there are miniature repair robots like medics, all of these fuckers microsize. And you make yourself a blood army, with electrical frontline, chemical attack forces, good defences, whatever you've decided.

"Then you go to the playground and you meet your little friend who's also bought Bloodwar, and you *prick your fingers*, right, like you're going to be blood brothers, and you each squeeze out a drop into a special dish, and you fucking *mix 'em up*." I stared at him incredulously while he grinned and smoked. "And then you sit back and watch the blood shimmer and bubble and move about. Because there's a war on." He grinned for a long time.

"How do you know who's won?" I asked eventually.

"The dish," he said. "Comes with a little display and speakers in the base. Picks up signals from the 'bots and amplifies them. You hear battle sounds and your troops reporting casualties, and at the end you get a score and you see who's won."

He sat back a minute and smoked some more, watching me. I tried to think of something sardonic to say, but was defeated. He leaned in suddenly and pulled out a little Swiss army knife.

"I'll show you," he said intensely. "You up for it? I can show you now. I'm primed. We know you'll lose because you've got no troops, but you'll see how it works." The knife waited above his thumb, and he gazed at me for the go-ahead. I hesitated and shook my head. I couldn't tell if he was serious or not, if he'd actually injected himself with these lunatic game-pieces, but he was weirding me out.

He had other ideas. There were spin-offs for Bloodwar, and there were other more complicated games, involving outside equipment like airport metal detectors that you walked through, that set off particular reactions from your tiny little internal robots. But Bloodwar was his favourite.

I gave him my email address and thanked him for the N64 pack. He wouldn't tell me where he lived, but he gave me his mobile number. I called it at seven the next morning.

"Jesus fucking Christ, Aykan," I said. "This game, thing, whatever . . . it's total genius."

I had been curious enough to rent a console from Blockbuster on my way home, to play the thing he'd given me.

It was utterly extraordinary. It was not a game. It was a totally immersing piece of art, a multilayered environment that passed through anarchic and biting political commentary, bleak dreamscapes, erotic staging posts. There was no "gameplay," only exploration, of the environment, of the conspiracies being unmasked. The viewpoint shifted and changed vertiginously. There were moments of shocking power.

I was stunned. I had pulled an all-nighter, and called him as early as I thought I could get away with.

"What is this shit?" I asked. "When's it coming out? I'll buy a fucking console just for this."

"It's not coming out, man," Aykan said. He sounded quite awake. "It's just some shit I did. Nintendo are bastards, man," he said. "They'd never licence it. No fucker'd produce it anyway. It's just for my friends. The hardest thing, let me tell you, the hardest thing isn't the programming, it's making the housing. If they read off CDs or whatever, no fucking problem. But putting the software into that poxy stupid little plastic square, and making it so it'll fit in the casing with all the right connectors. That's the hard bit. That's why I'm not doing that shit anymore. Boring."

I still own it, Aykan's guerrilla software, his illicit work of art. I still play it. Two years on I'm still discovering new levels, new layers. Later, before he disappeared, Aykan translated the scrawled title for me: *We Deserve Better Than This.*

Aykan's occasional emails to me often included web addresses for me to look up. I say Aykan's emails, although no name ever appeared in the "Sender" column, and they were never signed. Whenever I tried to reply to them, they would register as coming from a nonsense address, and the messages would bounce back to me. But Aykan never denied the emails were his, and sometimes even asked me if I'd received certain of them. He irritably dismissed questions about how or why he sent them anonymously. If I wanted to contact him, I had to do it by phone.

This was a time when mass-circulation emails were getting out of hand. Every day I'd get one or two urls to look up. Sometimes they were pornographic, with a message like "Did you know that was possible???!!!" from some sad lad or other I vaguely knew. More often they were links to some weird news story or other. Usually they looked too dull to chase up.

Aykan's, though, I always checked. They were pretty extraordinary. Essays, art pieces, things like that.

Sometimes he provided a password to get into hidden pages online, and when I visited them they were incomprehensible internal reports that looked very much like governments talking to governments, or rebel groups talking to rebels. I couldn't tell if they were hoaxes, but if not, I was rather alarmed.

"What's all this shit you keep sending me?" I demanded.

"Interesting, huh?" He sniggered, and put the phone down.

. . .

Sometimes he directed me to one or another of his online projects. That was how I realised that Aykan was a virtuoso of programming. Once, on one of our infrequent rendezvous, I called him a hacker. He burst out laughing, then got very angry with me.

"Fucking hacker?" He laughed again. "Fucking *hacker?* Listen bro, you're not talking to some sebum-faced little sixteen-year-old geekboy with wank-stained pants who calls himself Dev-L." He swore furiously. "I'm not a fucking hacker, man, I'm a fucking artist, I'm a hardworking wage-slave, I'm a *concerned motherfucking citizen,* whatever you want, but I'm not a fucking hacker."

I didn't care what he wanted to call himself. Whatever he thought he was, he left me awestruck—disbelieving, really, utterly bewildered—with what he could do.

"What search engine do you use?" he wrote to me once. "How often does your name come up? Try it now and then again tomorrow morning."

According to searchsites.com I appeared on seven websites, all of them work-related rubbish. When I typed in my name again the next day, I was nowhere. I looked up my company's website and there I was, halfway down the page. But when I ran my name through searchsites or runbot or megawhere, I had no luck. I had become invisible.

"What did you do, you fuck?" I yelled down the phone. I was excited, though, feigning anger badly.

"How's that, huh? I ran you through my hide engine." I could hear him smoking. "Don't worry, man," he said. "I'll take you out of it. But it's good, huh? Tomorrow I think I'm gonna run Jack fucking Straw through it, or maybe every fucking sex-related word I can think of." He put the phone down.

If he did run those words through his engine, it had stopped working. I checked the next day. But maybe he just hadn't bothered.

. . .

I spoke to Aykan several times, but a couple of months went by without me seeing him.

One morning I found another of his unmarked emails in my inbox. "HAVE YOU SEEN THIS FUCKPIG SCUMSUCKING PIECE OF SHIT?"

I had. It was the homepage of an organisation called An End To Hunger. I had been sent it at least twice already, as a recipient on mass emailings.

The site contained low-key, muted, and simple graphics, with a selection of harrowing statistics about world hunger. There were links to the UN Food Programme, Oxfam, and so on. But what made it such a popular site was its push-button charity donation.

Once per day, anyone visiting the site could click a little toggle, and in the words of the website, "feed the hungry." Alongside the button was a list of sponsors—all very dignified, no logos or bells or whistles, just the name of the company and a link to its homepage. Each sponsor would donate half a cent per click, which was roughly equivalent to half a cup of rice, or maize or whatever.

It all made me feel a bit uneasy, like corporate charity usually did. When I first saw the site I'd pressed the button. It had seemed churlish not to. But I hadn't visited it since, and I was getting irritated with people recommending it to me.

I called Aykan. He was incandescent.

"I've seen the site," I told him. "Bit gruesome, isn't it?"

"Gruesome?" he shouted. "It's fucking *sick* is what it is. It's fucking *beyond beyond*, man. I mean, forget 'politics lite,' this shit couldn't be parodied."

"I keep getting emails recommending it," I told him.

"Any motherfucker emails you that reply them right back and tell them to shove it up their arses till it hits the roof of their mouth, yeah? I mean by shit almighty . . . have you read the FAQ?

Listen to this. This is fucking *verbatim*, OK? 'Can I click the "Give Food" button more than once, and keep making donations?' 'We're sorry!' " Aykan's voice spewed bile. " 'We're real sorry! It's a shame, but you can't do that. Our sponsors have agreed for us to count one donation per person per day, and any more would be breaking our agreement.' " He made a noise like angry retching.

"Fuck 'em, bro," he said. "They tell us we can't be *naughty* and do it too *often?*" I didn't tell him I had donated that first time. He was making me ashamed.

I murmured something to him, some agreement, some dismissal and condemnation. It wasn't enough.

"This is fucking war, man," he said. "This one I can't let go."

"Run them through your hide engine," I suggested vaguely.

"What?" he said. "What the fuck you talking about? Don't talk horsefuck, man. I want them down and dead. Time for the big fucking guns, *hombre,*" he said, and put the phone down. I tried to call him back but he didn't pick up.

Two days later I got another email.

"Try visiting you shitting know where," it said. I did, and An End To Hunger would not come up. The browser couldn't find it. I tried again at the end of the day and it was back, with a small, pious note about how sad they were to be targeted by hackers.

Aykan wouldn't answer his phone. A week and a half later he called me.

"Man!" he shouted at me. "Go back to the bastards," he said. "I was . . . you know, I jumped the gun last time. Wasn't particularly clever, right? But it was like a fucking, what do you call it, I was doing a *reconnoitre.* But go back now, click the bastard button all you can."

"What did you do, Aykan?" I said. I was at work, and kept my voice neutral.

"I don't know how long it'll last," he said, "so get *all* your fucking friends to go visiting. For a *short time only* the shit-licking sponsors are going to be making a reasonable fucking payout. Ten bucks a fucking click, my friend, none of this half a cent bull. So go give generously."

It's impossible to say how much of an impact it had. Certainly for the next day or so I proselytised zealously. An End To Hunger kept it very quiet, when they found out. I like to think that it took the businesses in question the best part of a day to realise that their pledged donations had gone up by around 200,000 percent.

I wondered when Aykan would get bored of these games.

We spoke for a long time on the phone, one evening a fortnight or so later. He sounded exhausted.

"What you up to?" I asked him.

"Waging war, man."

I suggested that he was wearing himself out, that he should apply himself to other things. He got angry and depressed all at once.

"It really got to me, this one," he said. "It really *got to me.* I dunno why, but I can't . . . This one matters. But . . . I keep hitting the wrong enemy. 'Corporate sponsors don't actually care!' 'Big business is hypocritical!' That's not news to *anyfuckingbody.* Who doesn't know? Who gives a fuck about *that?*

"Do you ever stop to think about them, man?" he said. "Them in the AETH office. What must that do to your head? Like some kind of ghouls, man. What's that got to do to you?"

I changed the subject several times, but it kept coming back. "I dunno, man . . ." he kept saying. "I dunno what to do . . ."

It may have been the next day that he decided, but it was a good three weeks before he could make it work.

"Go and visit A* E** T* H*****," the email said. "Click and send the poor starving masses a present. See what happens."

I went to the site. Apart from a few minor updates, nothing seemed to have changed. I looked for some clue as to what Aykan had done. Eventually I clicked the "Give Food" button and waited.

Nothing happened.

The usual little message, thanking me on behalf of hungry people, appeared. I waited a couple more minutes, then left. Whatever Aykan had planned, I thought, it hadn't come off.

A couple of hours later I checked my email.

"How the fuck . . ." I said, and paused, shaking my head. "How the fuck, you insane genius bastard, did you do that?"

"You like that?" The connection was terrible, but I could hear that Aykan sounded triumphant. "You fucking like it?"

"I . . . I don't know. I'm very impressed, whatever."

I was staring at the message in my inbox. The sender was listed as "Very Hungry Foreign People."

> "Dear Kind Generous Person," it read. "Thank you so much for your Generous gift of half a cup of wet rice. Our Children will treasure every grain. And do please thank your Kind Organisers at An End To Hunger for organising their rich friends to throw rice at us—that is the advantage of employing Sweatshop labour and trade union busting. That way they can afford rice for us poor people. Whatever you do, do keep sitting back and not asking any questions of them, keep them happy, don't agitate for any corporate taxes or grassroots control or anything like that which would threaten the large profits that allow them to buy us Cups of Rice. With humble love and thanks, The Hungry."

"Every motherfucker who clicks the button's going to get that," Aykan said.

"How did you do it?"

"It's a fucking program. I stuck it on the website. It scans your fucking hard disk for what looks like your email address, and sends off the message when you draw attention to yourself by clicking. Try pressing 'Reply.' "

I did. The return address listed was my own.

"It's very impressive, Aykan," I said, nodding slowly, wishing someone else had written the letter, made it a bit subtler, maybe edited it a bit. "You've done a real number on them."

"Well it ain't over yet, bro," he said. "Watch this space, you know? Watch this fucking space."

My phone went at five the next morning. I padded nude and confused into the sitting room.

"Man." It was Aykan, tense and excited.

"What the fuck time is it?" I said, or something like that.

"They're onto me, man," he hissed.

"What?" I huddled vaguely on the sofa, rubbed my eyes. Outside, the sky was two-tone. Birds were chirruping imbecilically. "What are you on about?"

"*Our fucking philanthropic friends, man,*" he whispered tersely. "The *concerned folk* over at Feed The World central, you know? They've rumbled me. They've *found* me."

"How do you know?" I said. "Have they contacted you?"

"No no," he said. "They wouldn't do that—that would be admitting what the fuck was up. No, I was watching them online, and I can see them tracking me. They can already tell what country I'm in."

"What do you mean?" I said. I was fully awake now. "Are you intercepting their email? Are you crazy?"

"Oh man, there's a hundred fucking million things you can do, read their messages, watch who they're watching, bounce off internal memos, keep tabs on their automatic defences . . . Trust me on this: *they're looking for me.*" There was a silence. "They may even have found me."

"So . . ." I shook my head. "So leave it alone. Let it be, get off their back before you piss them off any more and they go to the police."

"Fucking *pofuckinglice* . . ." Aykan's voice swam in scorn. "They won't give it to the police, the police couldn't find their own thumbs if they were plugging up their arses. No, man. It's not the police I'm worried about, it's these Hunger motherfuckers. Haven't you clocked what kind of people these are? These are *bad* people, man. Major bad ju-ju. And anyway, *man,* what the fuck you mean *leave it alone?* Don't be such a shit-eating coward. I told you, didn't I? I told you this was a fucking *war,* didn't I?" He was shouting by now. I tried to get him to shut up. "I'm not looking for *advice.* I just wanted to let you know what was going on."

He broke the connection. I did not phone him back. I was tired and pissed off. *Paranoid prick,* I thought, and went back to bed.

Aykan kept sending his obscure emails, advising me of some new change to An End To Hunger.

The letter to donors did not last long, but Aykan was relentless. He directed me to their sponsors page, and I discovered that he had rerouted every link to a different revolutionary left organisation. He created a small pop-up screen that appeared when the "Donate" button was clicked, that compared the nutritional value of rice with what was rotting in European food mountains. He kept hinting at some final salvo, some ultimate attack.

"I keep watching them, man," he told me in one of his irregular phone calls. "I swear they are so on my tail. I'm going to have to be really fucking careful. This could get very fucking nasty."

"Stop talking rubbish," I said. "You think you're in some cheap thriller? You're risking jail for hacking—and don't shout at me, because that's what they'll call it—but that's all."

"Fuck you, bro!" he said. "Don't be so naive! You think this is a game? I told you . . . these fuckers aren't going to the police. Don't you fucking *see,* man? I've done the *worst thing you can do* . . . I've *impugned their philanthropy!* I've fucking sneered at them while they do the Mother Theresa thing, and that they can't fucking stand!"

I was worried about him. He was totally infuriating, no longer even coming close to conversing, just taking some phrase of mine or other as a jumping-off point to discuss some insane conspiracy.

. . .

He sent me bizarre, partial emails that made almost no sense at all. Some were just a sentence: "They'll love this" or "I'll show them what it really means."

Some were longer, like cuts from the middle of works in progress, half-finished memos and snatches of programming. Some were garbled articles from various encyclopaedias, about international politics, about online democracy, about computerised supermarket stock-taking, about kwashiorkor and other kinds of malnutrition.

Slowly, with a stealthy amazement and fear, I started to tie these threads together. I realised that what looked like a patchwork of mad threats and ludicrous hyperbole was something more, something united by an extraordinary logic. Through these partial snippets, these hints and jokes and threats, I began to get a sense of what Aykan planned.

I denied it.

I tried not to believe it; it was just too big. My horror was coloured with awe that he could even dream up such a plan, let alone believe he had the skills to make it work.

It was utterly unbelievable. It was horrific.

I knew he could do it.

I bombarded him with phone calls, which he never picked up. He had no voicemail, and I was left swearing and stalking from room to room, totally unable to reach him.

An End To Hunger had been ominously quiet for some time now. It had operated without interruption for at least three weeks. I was going crazy. There was a mad intensity to everything, every time I thought of Aykan and his plans. I was scared.

Finally, at ten minutes to eleven on a Sunday evening, he called.

"Man," he said.

"Aykan," I said, and sighed once, then stammered to get my words out. "Aykan, you can't *do this*," I said. "I don't care how fucking much you hate them, man, they're just a bunch of idiot liberals and you cannot do that to them, it's just not *worth it*, don't be *crazy*—"

"Shut up, man!" he shouted. "Listen to me!" He was whispering again.

He was, I suddenly realised, afraid.

"I don't have any fucking time, bro," he said urgently. "You've got to get over here; you've got to help me."

"What's going on, man?" I said.

"*They're coming*," he whispered, and something in his voice made me cold.

"The fuckers tricked me," he went on. "They kept it looking like they were searching, but they were better than I thought—they clocked me ages ago, they were just biding time, and then . . . and then . . . They're *on their way!*"

"Aykan," I said slowly. "You've got to stop this crazy shit," I said. "Are the police coming?"

He almost screamed with anger.

"*Godfuckingdammit don't you listen to me?* Any fucker can handle the police, but it's this *charity* wants my fucking head!"

He had invited me to his house, I realised. For the first time in years, he was ready to tell me where he lived. I tried to cut into his diatribe. "I know shit about these bastards you wouldn't *believe*, man," he was moaning. "Like some fucking *parasite* . . . You got no curiosity what kind of fucker lives like that?"

"What can I do, man?" I said. "You want me to come over?"

"Yeah, man, *please*, help me get my shit the fuck away," he said.

He named an address about twenty minutes' walk away. I swore at him.

"You been close all this time," I said.

"Please just hurry," he whispered, and broke the connection.

Aykan's house was one in a street of nondescript redbricks, and I was staring at it for several seconds before I saw that anything was wrong. The front window was broken, and fringes of curtain were waving like seaweed through the hole.

I sprinted the last few feet, shouting. No one answered the bell. I pounded the wood, and lights went on opposite and above me, but no one came to his door.

I peered in through the hole. I grabbed careful hold of the ragged glass frame and climbed into Aykan's house.

I stood, my breath shallow, whispering his name again and again. The sound of my own voice was very thin. It frightened me, such a little sound in that silence.

It was a tiny flat, a weird mixture of mess and anal fastidiousness. The bed-sitting room was crowded with Ikea-type shelves wedged tight with carefully ordered magazines and software, all exactly lined up. In the corner was a collection of extraordinarily powerful hardware, a tight little network, with printer and scanners and modems and monitors wedged into unlikely angles. The coffee table was revolting with ashtrays and unwashed cups.

I was alone.

I wandered quickly through all the rooms, again and again, back and forth, as if I might have missed him, standing in a corner. As if he might be waiting for me to find him. Apart from the shattered window, there was no sign of trouble. I waited and moped, but no one came.

After a few minutes I saw a green light winking languorously at me, and realised that his main computer was on sleep mode. I pressed Enter. The monitor lit up, and I saw that Aykan's email program was running.

His inbox was empty, except for one message, which had arrived earlier that evening.

It was listed as from AETH. I felt a slow surge of adrenaline. Slowly I reached out and clicked on the message.

We're so very disappointed that you don't consider our mission to improve the lot of the world's hungry to be a worthy one. We are motivated to try to help the poorest people on Earth, at a cost of nothing to our users. We consider this to be a winning situation for all sides. Without us, after all, the poor and the hungry have no voice.

It is a matter of great sadness to us that you do not share our vision, and that you have found it necessary to undermine our work. As you see, we have been able to trace you, through the sabotage to our website. We do not believe that this situation would be satisfactorily resolved through your country's courts.

We think it only reasonable to inform you that we take your conduct very seriously. We have our mission to consider, and we can no longer allow you to endanger those lives for which we work so hard.

We intend to discuss this matter with you. In person.

Now.

And that was all.

I waited in the cold, reading and rereading that message, looking around me in that quiet flat. Eventually I left. I debated taking the computer away, but it was too heavy, and anyway, it was really beyond me. I was never more than a day-to-day user. The kind of stuff Aykan had on there I'd never make head or tail of.

I called his mobile hundreds of times, but got only a dead signal.

I have no idea where he went, or what happened.

He could have broken that window himself. He could have written that email himself. He could have lost it completely and run off screaming into the night, with no one at all on his tail. I keep waiting, and hoping that maybe I'll hear from him.

He could be hunted, even now. Maybe he stays out of sight, keeps offline, uses pseudonyms, a thief in the night, letting dust blow over his online tracks.

Or maybe he was caught. Maybe he was taken away, to discuss the politics of charity.

Every week, some email or other recommends I visit An End To Hunger. The site is running well. Its problems seem to be over.

'TIS
THE
SEASON

C all me childish, but I love all the nonsense—the snow, the trees, the tinsel, the turkey. I love presents. I love carols and cheesy songs. I just love Christmas™.

That's why I was so excited. And not just for me, but for Annie. Aylsa, her mum, said she didn't see the big deal and why was I a sentimentalist, but I knew Annie couldn't wait. She might have been fourteen, but when it came to this I was sure she was still a little girl, dreaming of stockings by the chimney. Whenever it's my turn to take Annie—me and Aylsa have alternated since the divorce—I do my best on the 25th.

I admit Aylsa made me feel bad. I was dreading Annie's disappointment. So I can hardly tell you how delighted I was when I found out that for the first time ever I was going to be able to make a proper celebration of it.

Don't get me wrong. I haven't got shares in YuleCo, and I can't afford a one-day end-user licence, so I couldn't have a legal party. I'd briefly considered buying from one of the budget competitors like XmasTym, or a spinoff from a nonspecialist like Coca-Crissmas, but the idea of doing it on the cheap was just depressing. I wouldn't have been able to use much of the traditional stuff, and if you can't have all of it, why have any? (XmasTym had the rights to Egg Nog. But Egg Nog's disgusting.) Those other firms keep trying to create their own alternatives to proprietary classics like reindeer and snowmen, but they never take off. I'll never forget Annie's underwhelmed response to the JingleMas Holiday Gecko.

No, like most people, I was going to have a little MidWinter Event, just Annie and me. So long as I was careful to steer clear of licenced products we'd be fine.

Ivy decorations you can still get away with; Holly™ is a no-no, but I'd hoarded a load of cherry tomatoes, which I was planning to perch on cactuses. I wouldn't risk tinsel but had a couple of brightly-coloured belts I was going to drape over my aspidistra. You know the sort of thing. The inspectors aren't too bad: they'll sometimes turn a blind eye to a bauble or two (which is just as well, because the fines for unlicenced Christmas™ celebrations are astronomical).

So I'd been getting all that ready, but then the most extraordinary thing happened. I won the lottery!

I mean, I didn't *win* the lottery. But I was one of a bunch of runners-up, and it was a peach of a prize. An invitation to a special, licenced Christmas™ party in the centre of London, run by YuleCo itself.

When I read the letter I was shaking. This was YuleCo, so it would be the real deal. There'd be Santa™, and Rudolph™, and Mistletoe™, and Mince Pies™, and a Christmas Tree™, *with presents underneath it.*

That last was what I couldn't get over. It felt so forlorn, putting my newspaper-wrapped presents next to the aspidistra, but ever since YuleCo bought the rights to coloured paper and under-tree storage, the inspectors had clamped down on Aggravated Subarborial Giftery. I kept thinking about Annie being able to reach down and fish out her present from under needle-dropping branches.

. . .

Maybe I shouldn't have told Annie, just surprised her on the day itself, but I was too excited. And if I'm honest, partly I told her because I wanted to make Aylsa jealous. She'd always made such an issue of how she didn't miss Christmas™.

"Just think," I said, "we'll be able to sing carols legally—oh, sorry, you hate carols, don't you . . ." I was awful.

Annie was almost sick with excitement. She changed her online nick to tistheseason, and as far as I could work out she spent all her time boasting to her poor jealous friends. I'd peek at the screen when I brought her tea: the chat boxes were full of names like tinkerbell12 and handfulofflowers, and all I could see were exclamations like "noooo!?!?!? crissmass?!?! soooo kewl!!!!!" before she blocked the screen demanding privacy.

"Have a heart," I told her. "Don't rub your friends' noses in it," but she just laughed and told me they were arranging to meet on the day anyway, and that I didn't know what I was on about.

When she woke up on the 25th, there was a stocking™ waiting for Annie at the end of her bed, for the first time ever, and she came in to breakfast carrying it and beaming. I took enormous pleasure in waving my YuleCo pass and saying, perfectly legally, "Happy Christmas™, darling." I was glad that the ™ was silent.

I'd sent her present to YuleCo, as instructed. It would be waiting under the tree. It was the latest console. More than I could afford, but I knew she'd love it. She's great at video games.

We set out early. There were a reasonable number of people on the streets, all of them doing that thing we all do on the 25th, where you don't say anything illegal, but you raise your eyebrows and smile a holiday greeting.

Technically it was a regular weekday bus schedule, but of course half the drivers were off "sick."

"Let's not wait," Annie said. "We've got loads of time. Why don't we walk?"

"What have you got me?" I kept asking her. "What's my present?" I made as if to peer into her bag, but she wagged her finger.

"You'll see. I'm very pleased with your present, Dad. I think it's something that'll mean a lot to you."

It shouldn't have taken us too long, but somehow we were slow, and we dawdled, and chatted, and I realised quite suddenly that we were going to be late. That was a shock. I started to hurry, but Annie got sulky and complained. I refrained from pointing out whose idea walking had been in the first place. We were running quite a while behind time as we got to central London.

"Come *on*," Annie kept saying. "Are we nearly *there* . . . ?"

There were a surprising number of people on Oxford Street. Quite a crowd, all wearing that happy secret expression. I couldn't help smiling too. Suddenly Annie was running on ahead, then coming back to haul me along. *Now* she wanted to speed up. I kept having to apologise as I bumped into people.

It was mostly kids in their twenties, in couples and little groups. They parted indulgently as Annie dragged me, ran on ahead, dragged me.

There really were an astonishing number of people.

I could hear music up ahead, and a couple of shouts. I tensed, but they didn't sound angry. "Annie!" I called, nonetheless. "Come here, love!" I saw her skipping through the crowd.

And it was really a *crowd*. Was that a whistle? Where'd everyone come from? I was jostled, tugged along as if all these people were a tide. I caught a glimpse of one young bloke and with a start of alarm I saw he was wearing a big jumper with a red-nosed deer on it. I just knew to look at him he didn't have a licence. "Annie, come *here*," I was calling, but I got drowned out. A young woman next to me was raising her voice and singing a note, very loud.

"*Weeeeee* . . ."

The lad she was with joined in, and then his friend, and then a bunch of people beside them, and in a few seconds everyone was doing it, a mixture of good voices and terrible ones, combining into this godawful loud squeal.

"*Weeeeee*..." And then, with impeccable timing, all the hundreds of people sort of caught each other's eyes, and their song continued.

"... wish *you a merry Christmas we* wish *you a merry Christmas*..."

"Are you *mad?*" I screamed, but no one could hear me over that bloody illegal rumpty-tum. Oh my God. I knew what was happening.

We were surrounded by radical Christmasarians.

I was spinning around, shouting for Annie, running after her, looking out for police. There was no way the streetcams wouldn't spot this. They'd send in the Yule Squad.

I saw Annie through the crowd—goddammit, more people kept coming—and ran for her. She was beckoning to me, looking around anxiously, and I was batting people out of the way, but as I approached I saw her look up at someone beside her.

"Dad," she shouted. I saw her eyes widen in recognition, and then—did I see a *hand* grab her and snatch her away?

"Annie!" I was screaming as I reached where she'd been. But she was gone.

I was panicking: she's an intelligent girl and it was broad daylight, but whose was that bloody hand? I called her phone.

"Dad," she answered. The reception was appalling in this crowd. I was bellowing at her, asking where she was. She sounded tense, but not frightened. "... ok ... I'll be ... see ... a friend ... at the party."

"What?" I was yelling. "What?"

"At the *party*," she said, and I lost the signal.

Right. The party. That's where she'd make her way. I controlled myself. I shoved through the crowd.

It was getting more bolshy. It was turning into a tinsel riot.

Oxford Street was jammed; I was in the middle of what was suddenly thousands of protestors. It took me anxious ages to make headway through the demonstration. What had seemed an anonymous mob suddenly sprang into variety and colour. Everyone was marching. I was passing different contingents.

Where the hell had all these banners come from? Slogans bobbed overhead like flotsam. For Peace, Socialism and Christmas; Hands off our Holiday Season!; Privatise This. One placard was everywhere. It was very simple and sparse: the letters TM in a red circle, with a line through them.

She'll be ok, I thought urgently. *She said as much.* I was looking around as I made my way toward the party, only a few streets away now. I was taking in the demo.

These people were crazy! It wasn't that I didn't think their hearts were in the right places, but this was no way to achieve things. All they were going to do was bring down trouble on everyone. The cops would get here any moment.

Still, I had to admire their creativity. With all the costumes and colours, it looked amazing. I have no idea how they'd smuggled this stuff through the streets, how they'd organised this. It must have been online, which means some pretty sophisticated encryption to fool the copware. Each different section of the march seemed to be chanting something different, or singing songs I hadn't heard for years. I was walking through a winter wonderland.

I went by a contingent of Christians all carrying crosses, singing carols. Right in front of them was a group of badly dressed people selling copies of a left-wing newspaper and carrying placards with a photograph of Marx. They'd superimposed a Santa hat on him. "I'm dreaming of a red Christmas," they sang, not very well.

We were beside Selfridges now, and a knot of people had stopped by the windows full of the usual mix of perfume and shoes. The demonstrators were looking at each other, and back at the glass. Over on a side street, a few passersby were staring at the extraordinary spectacle. It brought me up short to see "regular" shoppers—it felt as if there was no one but the marchers on the streets.

I knew what the Selfridges-watchers were thinking: they were remembering (or remembering being told—some of them looked too young to recall life before the Christmas™ Act) an old tradition.

"If they won't give us our Christmas windows," one woman roared, "we'll have to provide them ourselves." And with that, they pulled out hammers. *Oh God.* They took out the glass.

"No!" I heard a man in a smart wool coat shouting at them. A contingent of the demo was looking horrified, laying down its banners, which read LABOUR FRIENDS OF CHRISTMAS. "We all want the same thing here," the man shouted, "but we can't support violence!"

But no one was paying him any attention. I waited for people to steal the goods, but they just shoved them out of the way along with the broken glass. They were putting things *into* the windows. From bags and pockets they were taking little crèches, papier-maché Santas™, gaudily wrapped presents, Holly™, and Mistletoe™ and they were scattering them, making crude displays.

I moved on. A man stepped into my path. He was part of a group of sharp-dressed types at the edges of the crowd. He sneered and gave me a leaflet.

INSTITUTE OF LIVING MARXIST IDEAS.
Why We Are Not Marching.

We view with disdain the pathetic attempts of the old Left to revive this Christian ceremony. The notion that the government has "stolen" "our" Christmas is just part of the prevailing Fear Culture that we reject. It is time for a reevaluation beyond left and right, and for dynamic forces to

reinvigorate society. Only last month, we at the ILMI organised a confer-
ence at the ICA on why strikes are boring and hunting is the new black . . .

I really couldn't make head or tail of it. I threw it away.

There was the thudding of a chopper. *Oh shit,* I thought. *They're here.*

"*Attention,*" came the amplified voice from the sky. "*You are in breach of section 4 of the Christmas™ Code. Disperse immediately or you will be arrested.*"

To my astonishment this was met with a raucous jeer. A chant started. At first I couldn't make out the words, but soon there was no mistaking them.

"*Whose Christmas? Our Christmas! Whose Christmas? Our Christmas!*"

It didn't scan very well.

I passed a group I recognised from the news, radical feminist Christmasarians dressed in white, wearing carrots on their noses: the sNOwMEN. A little guy ran past me, glancing around, muttering, "Too tall, too tall." He started to shout: "Anyone 5 foot 2 or under come smash some shit up with the Santa's Little Helpers!" Another shorter man started furiously remonstrating with him. I heard the words "joke" and "patronising."

People were eating Christmas™ pudding, slices of turkey. They were even forcing down brussels sprouts, just on principle. Someone gave me a mince pie. "Blessed be," yelled a radical pagan in my ear, and gave me a leaflet demanding that once we had won back the season, we rename it Solsticemas. He was buffeted away by a group of muscular ballet dancers dressed as sugar-plum fairies and nutcrackers.

I was getting close to the venue where the party was supposed to be, but if anything there were even more people on the streets now. The place was going to be surrounded. How would we get in?

Figures were moving in on the crowd. *Oh shit,* I thought, *the police.* But it wasn't. It was an angry-looking, aggressive bunch, smashing car windscreens as they came. They were dressed as Santa Claus™.

"Fuck," muttered someone. "It's the Red-and-White Bloc."

It was obvious that the R&Ws were out for trouble. Everyone else in the crowd tried to draw away from them. "Piss off!" I heard someone shouting, but they paid no attention.

Now I *could* see cops, massing in the side streets. The Red-and-White Bloc were drawing them out, chucking bottles, screaming, "Come on then!" like pissed-up Football™ fans.

I was backing away. I turned, and there it was: the site for the party. Hamleys, the toy store. The armed guards who normally protected it must have run ages ago, faced with this chaos. I looked up and saw horrified faces at the windows.

I should be up there, I thought. *With you.* They were the party-goers. Kids and their parents, besieged by the demonstration, watching the police approach.

And oh, there was Annie, shouting to me, standing under Hamleys' eaves. I wailed with relief and ran to her.

"What's going on?" she shouted. She looked terrified. The Yule Squads were approaching the provocateurs of the Red-and-White Bloc, banging their truncheons in time on tinsel-garlanded shields.

"Bloody hell," I whispered. I put my arms protectively around her. "There's going to be trouble," I said. "Get ready to run."

But as we stood there, tensing, something astonishing happened. I blinked, and out of nowhere had come a young man in a long white robe. Before anyone could stop him he was between the ranks of the Red-and-White Bloc and the police.

"He's mad!" someone shouted, but all the hundreds and hundreds of people were beginning to hush.

The man was singing.

The police bore down on him, the R&Ws made as if to shove him away, but his voice soared, and both sides hesitated. I had never seen anything so beautiful.

He sang a single note, of unearthly purity. He made it last, for long seconds, and then continued.

"Oh little town of Bethlehem, how still we see thee lie."

He paused, until we were straining.

"Above thy deep and dreamless sleep, the silent stars go by."

The R&W Bloc were still. Everyone was still.

"Yet in thy dark streets shineth, the everlasting light . . ."

And now the *police* were stopping. They were putting their truncheons down. One by one they set aside their shields.

"The hopes and fears of all the years are met in thee tonight."

More white-clad figures were appearing. They walked calmly to join their friend. With a start, I realised I was shielding my eyes. There was an implacable authority to these astonishing figures who had come from nowhere, these tall, stunning, uncanny young men. The white of their robes seemed impossibly bright. I could not breathe.

Now all of them were singing. *"How silently, how silently, the wondrous gift is giv'n. So God imparts to human hearts the blessings of His Heav'n."*

One by one, the police removed their helmets and listened. I could hear the frantic squawking of their superiors from the earpieces they removed.

"No ear may hear His coming, but in this world of sin . . ." The singers paused, until I ached to have the melody conclude. *"Where meek souls will receive Him still, the dear Christ enters in."*

The police were smiling and tearful amid a litter of body armour and nightsticks. The first singer raised his hand. He looked down at all the discarded weaponry. He declaimed to the Red-and-White Bloc.

"You should not have tried to fight," he said, and they looked ashamed. He waited.

"You would have been trounced. Whereas *now*," he continued, "these idiots have disarmed. *Now's* the time to fight." And he swivelled, and en masse, he and his fellow singers launched themselves at the police, their robes flapping.

The helpless cops gaped, turned, ran, and the crowd roared, and began to follow them.

"We are the Gay Men's Radical Singing Caucus!" the lead singer yelled in his exquisite tenor. "Proud to be fighting for a People's Christmas!"

He and his comrades began to chant: "*We're here! We're Choir! Get used to it!*"

"It's a Christmas miracle!" said Annie. I just hugged her until she muttered, "Alright Dad, easy."

Behind me the crowd were shouting, taking over the streets.

"That's the trouble with the Red-and-White Bloc," muttered Annie. "Bloody 'strategy of tension' my arse. Bunch of anarchist adventurists."

"Yeah," said a boy next to her. "Anyway, half of them are police agents. It's the first principle, isn't it? Whoever's arguing fiercest for violence is the cop."

I was gaping, my head swinging between the two of them as if I were a moron watching tennis.

"*What . . . ?*" I said finally.

"Come on, Dad," said Annie. She kissed me on the cheek. "You'd never have let me go otherwise. I had to get you to walk here or we'd have been too early. Trapped like them." She pointed at the still-staring prizewinners in Hamleys' top floors. "And then I had to run off or you'd never have let me join in. Come on." She took my hand. "Now that we've bust through the police lines, we can reroute the march past Downing Street."

"Well then it's the perfect opportunity to get *out* of here . . ."

"Dad," she said. She looked at me sternly. "I couldn't believe it when you won that prize. I never thought I'd have a chance to be down this way today."

"Someone grabbed you," I said.

"That was Marwan." She indicated the young man who had spoken. "Dad, this is Marwan. Marwan, this is my dad."

Marwan smiled and shook my hand politely, shifting his placard. MUSLIMS FOR CHRISTMAS, it said. He saw me reading it.

"It's not that much of a big deal for me," he said, "but we all remember how this lot came out for us when Umma Plc tried to privatise Eid. That meant a lot, you know. Anyway . . ." He looked away shyly. "I know it's important to Annie." She gazed at him. *Ah*, I thought.

"Marwan's handfulofflowers, Dad," she was saying to me. "Off the internet."

"Look, I have to tell you I'm pretty annoyed about all this," I said. We were getting close to Downing Street now. Marwan had said good-bye at Trafalgar Square, so it was just the two of us again, along with ten thousand others. "I bought you, I, I've lost a lot of, there's a big present in that party . . ."

"To be honest with you, Dad, I don't really need a new console."

"How did you know . . . ?" I said, but she was continuing.

"The one I've got is fine: I mostly use it for strategy games anyway, and they're not so power-hungry. Besides, I've got all the pinkopatches in my machine. It would be a pain in the arse to transfer them, and downloading them again is too risky."

"What patches?"

"Stuff like Red3.6. It converts a bunch of games. Turns SimuCityState into RedOctober. Stuff like that. I'm already up to level 4. The end-of-level baddy's a Czar. As soon as I can work out how to get past him I'll have got to Dual Power."

I gave up even trying to follow.

At the entrance to the Prime Minister's residence was a huge Christmas Tree™, in white and silver. Everyone began to jeer as we approached. The army were guarding it, so people made sure the booing was good-humoured. Someone threw Christmas Pudding™, but everyone sorted him out sharpish.

"*That's not what Christmas looks like,*" we all shouted as we went past. "*This is what Christmas looks like.*"

As the skies darkened, the crowd were beginning to thin a bit, before the police could regroup. We went through a contingent all in red bandanas, and joined in with their singing. "*Deck the halls with boughs of holly, tra la la la laaa, la la la la. 'Tis the Season for the Internationale, tra la la la laaaa . . .*"

"Still," I said. "I'm a bit sorry you didn't get to see the party."

"Dad," said Annie, and shook me. "This was the *best Christmas ever*. Ever. OK? And it was so lovely to have it with you."

She looked at me sideways.

"Have you guessed yet?" she said. "What your present is?"

She was staring at me, very seriously, very intensely. It made me quite emotional.

I thought of everything that had happened that day, and of my reactions. Everything I'd been through and seen—been a *part* of. I realised how different I felt now than I had that morning. It was an astonishing revelation.

"Yes . . ." I said, hesitantly. "Yes, I think I have. Thank you, my love."

"What?" she said. "You've guessed? Shit."

She was holding out a little wrapped package. It was a tie.

JACK

Now that things have gone the way they have, everyone's got a story. Everyone'll tell you how they or their friend, which you can see in the way they say it they want you to think means them, knew Jack. Maybe even how they helped him, how they were part of his schemes. Mostly though of course they know that's too much and it'll just be how they or their friend was there one time and saw him running over the roofs, money flying from his swag-bags, militia trying and failing to track him down below. That sort of thing. *My mate saw Jack Half-a-Prayer once,* they'll say, *just for a moment.* As if they're being modest.

It's supposed to be respect. They reckon they're showing their respect, with everything that's happened. They ain't, of course. They're like dogs on his corpse and they disgust me.

I tell you that so you know where I'm coming from. Because I know how what I'm about to say might sound. I want you to know where I'm coming from when I tell you that I *did* know Jack. I did.

I worked with him.

I was lowly, don't get me wrong, but I was part of the whole thing. And please don't think I'm talking myself up, but I swear to you I ain't being arrogant. I'm nothing important, but the work I did, in a little way, was crucial to him. That's all I'm saying. So. So you can understand that I was pretty interested when I heard we'd got our hands on the man who sold Jack out. That would be one way of putting it. That would be mild. I made it my business to meet him, let's put it that way.

I remember the first time I heard what Jack was up to, after he escaped. He was daring enough that he got noticed. *Did you hear about that Remade done that robbery?* someone said to me in a pub. I was careful, couldn't show any reaction.

I'd felt something when I met Jack, you know? I respected him. He wasn't boastful, but he had a fire in him. Even so, I couldn't be sure he'd come to anything.

That first job, he got away with hundreds of nobles and gave it away on the streets. He scored himself the love of the Dog Fenn poor that way. That was what had people all excited, told them he was something else than your average gangster. He weren't the first to do that, but he was one of few.

What got me wasn't so much what he did with the money as where he stole it from. It was a government office. Where they store taxes.

Everyone knows what the security on those places is like. And I knew that there was no way he'd have done something like that without it being a *screw you*. He was making a point, and my good bloody gods but I admired that.

It was then, in that pub, when I realised what he'd done, how he must have made that night-raid work, how he must have climbed and crept and fought his way in, with his new body, how he must have been able to vanish, weighed down with specie, that I realised he was something. That was when I knew that Jack Half-a-Prayer was no ordinary Remade, and no ordinary renegade.

. . .

Not many people see the Remade like I do, or like Jack did.

You know it's true. To most of you they're to be ignored or used. If you really *notice* them you wish you hadn't. It wasn't like that for Jack, and not just because he *was* Remade. I bet—I know—that Jack used to notice them, see them clear, before anything was done to him. And that's the same for me.

People walk along and see nothing but trash, Remade trash with bodies all wrong, shat out by the punishment factories. Well, I don't want to be too sentimental about it but I've no doubts at all that Jack'd have seen this *woman*—whose hands yes were gone and been replaced with little birds' wings—and he'd have seen an *old man,* not the sexless thing he'd been made into, and a young lad with eyes gone and in their place an array of dark glass and pipework and lights and the boy stumbling trying to see in ways he weren't born to but still a boy. Jack'd see people changed with engines in steam, and oily gears, and the parts of animals, and their innards or their skin altered with hexes, and all those things, but he'd have seen *them* under the punishment.

People get broken when they get Remade. I've seen it so many times. Suddenly, take a wrong turn by the law and it ain't just the physical punishment, it ain't just the new limbs or metal or the change in the body, it's that they wake up and they're *Remade,* the same as they spat on or ignored for years. They know they're nothing.

Jack, when it was done to him, never thought he was nothing. He'd never thought any of them were.

There was this one time. A foundry in Smog Bend, and there was a man there, some middling supervisor—this was years after Jack got free, and I only heard all this—who was causing trouble. Informing on guilders trying to recruit. There was gangs following organisers home, and scaring them so they'd not come back, or maybe retiring them permanently.

I'm not clear on the details. But the point is what Jack done.

One day the workers troop in and they take their places by the gears, but there's no klaxon. And they're waiting, but nothing happens. Now they're getting wary, they're getting very antsy. They know it's that overseer who's due in that day, so they're nervous, they ain't talking much, but they go looking. And there at the foot of the steps up to the office, there's an arrow put together out of tools. On the floor, pointing up.

So they creep up. And on the landing there's another. And there's a whole gang of men now, and they're following these arrows, soldered to the banisters, up on the walkway, trooping round the factory, until pretty much the whole workforce is up there, and they come to the end of the gangway, and there dangling is that supervisor.

He's unconscious. His mouth's all scabbed. It's sewn up, with wire.

People know right then and there what's happened, but when the man wakes up and gets unstitched he starts raving, describing the man who done this to him, and then it's certain.

That man was lucky he didn't get killed, is my thinking. There was no more trouble there for a while, I hear. That changed things. I think they called that one Jack's Whispering Stitch. It's things like that make you see why people respected Jack Half-a-Prayer. Loved him.

This is the greatest city in the world. You hear that all the time, because it's true. But it's sort of an untrue truth, for a lot of us.

I don't know where you live. If it's Dog Fenn, then knowing that Parliament's a building like nothing else, or that we've riches in the coffers that would make the rest of the world jealous, or that the scholars of New Crobuzon could outthink the bloody gods— knowing all of that doesn't do so much. You still live in Dog Fenn, or Badside, or what have you.

But when Jack ran, the city was the greatest for Badside too.

You could see it—I could see it—in the way people walked, after Jack'd done something. I don't know how it was uptown in The Crow—I expect the well-dressed there sneered, or made a show of not caring—but where the houses lean in to each other, where the bricks shed pointing, in the shadow of the glass cactus ghetto, people walked tall. Jack was everyone's: men and women, cactus-people, khepri and vod. The wyrmen made up songs about him. The same people that would spit in the face of a Remade beggar cheered this fReemade. In Salacus Fields they'd toast Jack by name.

I wouldn't do that, of course—not that I didn't want to, but you can imagine, in the business I'm in, I have to be careful. I'm involved, so of course I can't be seen to be. In my head, though, I'd raise a glass with them. *To Jack,* I'd think.

In the short time I worked with Jack I never used his given name, nor he mine. It's in the nature of the work, obviously, that you don't use real names. But then, what could be more his name than Jack? Remaking is the ruin of most, but it was the making of him.

It's hard to make sense of Remaking, of its logic. Sometimes the magisters pass down sentences that you can understand. One man kills another with a blade, take his killing arm and replace it, suture a motorknife in its place, tube him up with the boiler to run it. The lesson's obvious. Or those who are made heavy engines for industry, man-cranes and woman-cabs and boy-machines. It's easy to see why the city would want them.

But I can't explain to you the woman given a ruff of peacock feathers, or the young lad with iron spiderlimbs out his back, or those with too many eyes or engines that make them burn from the inside out, or legs made wooden toys or replaced with the arms of apes so they walk with mad monkey grace. The Remakings that make them stronger, or weaker, or more or less vulnerable, Remakings almost unnoticed, and those that make them impossible to understand.

Sometimes you'll see a xenian Remade, but it's rare. It's hard to work with cactacae vegetable flesh, or the physiognomy of vodyanoi, I'm told, and there are other reasons for the other races, so for the most part magisters'll sentence them to other things. For the most part, it's humans who are Remade, for cruelty or expediency, or opaque logics.

There ain't no one the city hates so much as the renegades, the fReemade. Turning your Remaking on the Remakers, that ain't how it's supposed to be.

Sometimes, you know, I'll admit it's frustrating, to have to keep all my thoughts to myself. Especially during the day, while I'm in at work. Don't get me wrong, I like my colleagues, some of them, they're good lads, and for all I know some would even agree with the way I look at things, but you just can't risk it. You have to know when to keep secrets.

So I stay well out of it. I don't talk politics, I just do what I'm told, stay well out of any discussions.

When you see, when you see how people looked up after Jack had struck, though, my gods. How could anyone not be for that? People needed him, they needed that, that release. That hope.

I couldn't believe it when I heard my crew'd got hold of the man who got Jack caught. I had to keep myself under control at work, not let anyone see I was excited. I was waiting to get my hands on the rat.

For a lot of people, the most exciting, the best thing he ever done was an escape. Not his first escape—that I can't help thinking would have been some tawdry affair. Impressive for all that but a desperate bloody crawl, his new Remaking still atwitch, all grimy, all stained by the grease of his shackles, and stonedust, lying in some haul of rubbish where the dogs couldn't smell him, till he was strong enough to run. That, I think, would have been as messy as any other birth. No, the escape I'm talking about was the one they call Jack's Steeplechase.

Even now people can't decide whether it was deliberate or not, whether he let it out to the militia that he'd be there, that he'd be stealing weapons from one of their caches, in the city centre, in Perdido Street Station, just so they'd come for him and he could show he could get away from them. Me I don't think he'd be so cocky. I think he just got caught, but being who he was, being what he was, he made the best of it.

He ran for a more than an hour. You can go a long way in that time, over the roofs of New Crobuzon. Within fifteen minutes news had spread and I don't know how, I don't know how it is that the news of him running moved faster than he did himself, but that's the way of these things. Soon enough, as Jack Half-a-Prayer tore into view over some street, he'd find people waiting, and as far as they dared, cheering.

No I never saw it but you hear about it, all the time. People could see him on the roofs, waving his Remaking so people would know it was him. Behind him squads of militia. Falling, chasing, falling, more emerging from attics, from stairways, from all over, wearing their masks, pointing weapons, and firing them, and Jack leaping over chimneypots and launching himself from dormers, leaving them behind. Some people said he was laughing.

Bright daylight—militia visible in uniform. That's a thing in itself. He went by the Ribs, they say, even scrambled up the bones, though of course I don't believe that. But wherever he went, I see him sure-footed on the slates, a famous outlaw man by then, and behind him a wake of clodhopping militia, and streaks in the sky as they fire. Bullets, chakris from rivebows, spasms of black energy, ripples from the thaumaturges. Jack avoided them all. When he shot back, with the weapons he'd just taken, experimental things, he took men down.

Airships came for him, and informer wyrmen: the skies were all fussy with them. But after an hour of that chase, Jack Half-a-Prayer was gone. Bloody magnificent.

. . .

The man who sold out Half-a-Prayer was nothing. You wonder, don't you, who could bring down the greatest bandit New Crobuzon's ever seen. A nonentity. A no one.

It was just luck, that was all. That was what took Jack Half-a-Prayer. He weren't outsmarted, he didn't get sloppy, he didn't try to go too far, nothing like that. He got unlucky. Some pissant little punk who knows someone who knows someone who knows one of Jack's informers, some young turd doing a job, whispered messages in pubs, passing on a package, I don't sodding know, some nothing at all, who puts it together, and not because he's smart but because he gets lucky, where Jack's hiding. I truly don't know. But I've seen him, and he's nothing.

I didn't know why he gave up Half-a-Prayer. I wondered if he thought he'd be rewarded. Turned out he'd have said nothing if they hadn't hauled him in. He'd been caught for his own little crimes—his own paltry, petty, pathetic misdemeanours—and he thought if he delivered Jack, the government would look after him, forgive him and keep him safe. Idiot man.

He thought the government would keep him out of our hands.

Most of what Jack did weren't so obviously dramatic, of course. It was the smaller, savager stuff that had them out for him.

It ain't that they were happy about the big swaggering thievery, the showings-off. But that ain't what made Jack a thorn they had to pluck.

No one knows how he got the information he did, but Jack could smell militia like a hound. No matter how good their cover. Informers, colonel-informers, intriguists, provocateurs, insiders and officers—Jack could find them, no matter that their neighbours had always thought they were just retired clerks, or artists, or tramps, or perfume-sellers, or loners.

They'd be found like the victims of any other killings, their bodies dumped, under mounds of old things. But there would always be documents, somewhere close by or left for journalists or the community, that proved the victim was militia. Awful wounds on both sides of their necks, as if ragged, serrated scissors had half closed on them. Jack the Remade, using what the city gave him.

That wasn't alright. It wasn't alright for Jack to think he could touch the functionaries of the government. I know that's how they thought. That's when it became imperative that they bring him down. But with all their efforts, all the money they were ready to spend on bribes, all the thaumaturgy they dedicated—the channellers and scanners, the empathy-engines turned up full—in the end they got lucky, and picked up some blabbering terrified useless little turd.

I made sure it was me first went in to greet him, Jack's snitch, after we got hold of him. I made sure we had some time alone. It weren't pretty, but I stand by it.

It's been a long time since I been in this secret political life. And there are conventions that are important. One is, don't get personal. When I apply the pressures I need to, when I do what needs to be done, it's a job that needs doing, no matter how unpleasant. If you're fighting the *sickness of society,* and make no mistake that's what we do, then sometimes you have to use harsh methods, but you don't relish it, or it'll taint you. You do what has to be done.

Most of the time.

This was different.

This little fucker was mine.

It's a windowless room, of course. He was in a chair, locked in place. His arms, his legs. He was shaking so hard, I could hear the chair rattling, though it was bolted down. An iron band filled his mouth, so all he could do was whine.

I came in. I was carrying tools. I made sure he saw them: the pliers, the solder, the blades. I made him shake even more, without touching him. Tears came out of him so fast. I waited.

"Shhh," I said at last, through his noise. "Shhh. I have to tell you something."

I was shaking my head: *No, hush.* I felt cruelty in me. *Hush,* I said, *hush.* And when he quieted, I spoke again.

"I made sure I got to take care of you," I said. "In a minute my boss'll be coming in to help us, and he knows what we're going to do. But I wanted you to know that *I made sure* I got this job, because . . . well, I think you know a friend of mine."

When I said Jack's name the traitor started mewling and making all this noise again, he was so scared, so I had to wait another minute or two, before I whispered to him, "So *this* . . . is for *Jack.*"

The leader of my crew came in then, and another couple of lads, and we looked at each other, and we began. And it weren't pretty. And I ain't supposed to glory in that, but just this once, just this once. This was the fucker sold out Jack.

I knew it couldn't last, Jack's reign (because that's what it was). I couldn't not know it, and it made me sad. But you couldn't fight the inevitability.

When I heard they'd caught him, I had to fight, to work hard, not to let myself show sad. Like I said, I was only a small part of the operation—I'm not a big player, and that's more than fine by me, I don't want to run this dangerous business. I'd rather be told what to do. But I'd taken such pride in it, you know? Hearing of what he was doing, and always knowing that I was connected. There are always networks, behind every so-called loner, and being part of one . . . well, it meant something. I'll always carry that.

But I knew it would end, so I tried to steel myself. And I never went to see him, when they stretched him out in BilSantum Plaza, Remade again, his first Remaking gone, knowing he'd be dead before the wound healed. I wonder how many in that crowd were known to him. I heard that it went a bit wrong for the Mayor, that the crowds never jeered or threw muck at the stocks. People loved

Jack. Why would I want to see him like that? I know how I want to remember him.

So the snitch, the tattletale, was in my hands, and I made sure he felt it. There are techniques—you have to know ways to stop pain, and I know them, and I withheld them.

I left that fucker red and dripping. He'll never be the fucking same. *For Jack,* I thought. Try telling tales again. I did something to his tongue.

As I did it, as I dug my fingers in him, I kept thinking of when I met Half-a-Prayer.

People need something, you know, to escape. They do. They need something to make them feel free. It's good for us, it's necessary. The city needs it. But there comes a time when it has to end.

Jack was going too far. And there'll be others, I know that too.

I knew it was necessary. He really had gone too far. But I can't talk to my workmates about this, like I say, because I don't think they think this stuff through. They just always went on about what a bastard Half-a-Prayer was, and how he'd get his, and blah blah. I don't think they realise that the city needs people like him, that he's good for all of us.

People have their heroes, and gods know I don't grudge them that. It ain't a surprise. They—the people I mean—don't know how hard it is to keep a city, a state like New Crobuzon going, why some of the things that get done get done. It can be harsh. If Jack gives people a reason to keep going, they should have it. So long as it don't get out of hand, which, of course, it always does. That's why he had to be stopped. But there'll be another one, with more big shows, more grand gestures and thefts and the like. People need that.

I'm grateful to Jack and his kin. If they weren't there, and this is what I think my mates don't understand, if they weren't there, and all them angry people in Dog Fenn and Kelltree and Smog

Bend had no one to cheer on, gods know what they'd do. That would be much worse.

So here's a cheer for Jack Half-a-Prayer. As a spectator who enjoyed his shows, and a loyal and loving servant of this city, I toast him in his death as I did in his life. And I exacted a little revenge for him, even though I know it was past time for him to stop.

It was a basic Remaking. We took that little traitor's legs and put engines in their place, but I made sure to do a little extra. Reshaped a suckered filament from some fish-thing's carcasse, put it in place of his tongue. It'll fight him. Can't kill him, but his tongue'll hate him till the day he's gone. That was my present to Jack.

That's what I did at work today.

When I met Jack he wasn't Jack yet. My boss, he's the master craftsman. Bio-thaumaturge. It was him did the clayflesh, who went to work. It was him took off Jack's right hand.

But it was me held the claw. That great, outsized mantis limb, hinging chitin blades the length of my forearm. I held it on Jack's stump while my boss made the flesh and scute run together and alloy. It was him Remade Jack, but I was part of it, and that'll always make me proud.

I was thinking about names as I knocked off today, as I walked home through this city it's my honour to protect. I know there are plenty who don't understand what has to be done sometimes, and if the name of Jack Half-a-Prayer gives them pleasure, I don't grudge them that.

Jack, the man I made. It's his name, now, whatever he was called before.

Like I say, in the short time I knew him, before I made him and after, I never called Jack by his name nor he me. We couldn't, not in this line of work. Whenever I spoke to Jack, I called him "Prisoner," and answering, he called me "Sir."

ON THE
WAY TO
THE FRONT

THE
TAIN

The light was hard. It seemed to flatten the walls of London, to push down onto the pavement with real weight. It was oppressive: it scoured colours of depth.

On the concrete river-walls of the south bank, a man was lying with his right hand over his face, squinting up through his fingers at the bleached sky. Watching the business of clouds. He had been there for some time, unmoving, supine on the wall top. It had rained for hours, intermittently, throughout the night. The city was still wet. The man was lying in rainwater. It had soaked through his clothes.

He listened, but heard nothing of interest.

Over time he turned his head, still shielding his eyes, until he was looking down at the walkway to his right, at the puddles. He watched them carefully, a little warily, as if they were animals.

Finally, he sat up and swung his legs down over the edge of the wall. The river was at his back now. He leaned forward until his head hung over the path and the dirty water that blotted it. He stared into the minute ripples.

The puddle was directly below his face, and it was blank, as he had known it would be.

He looked closer, until he could see faint patterns. A veil, the ghosts of colours and shapes moved across the thin skin of water: incomprehensible but not random, according to strange vagaries.

The man stood and walked away. Behind him the sunlight hit the Thames. It did not scatter: it did not refract on the moving river into little stabs of light. It did other things.

He walked in the centre of the paths and pavements, in clear view. His pace was quick but not panicked. A shotgun bounced on his shoulder. He swung it round and carried it to his chest, holding it as if it offered more comfort than defence.

The man crossed the river. He stopped below the arc of Grosvenor Bridge, and clambered up its girdered underside. Where it should have been a curve of shadows, the bridge was punctured, broken by thick rays of light. The man wrestled through the holes in its structure that recent events had left.

He emerged in a crater of railway lines. An explosion had spread broken bricks and sleepers in concentric circles, and the metal rails had burst and buckled into a frozen splash. The man was surrounded by them. He trudged past the bomb's punctuation, to where they became train lines again.

Months ago, perhaps in the moment of that interruption, a train had stalled on the bridge. It remained. It looked quite unbroken: even its windows were whole. The driver's door hung open.

The man gripped it but did not look inside, did not run his hand over the instruments. He hauled himself, with the door as a ladder, to the train's flat roof. And then he stood up, gripping his gun, and looked.

His name was Sholl. He had been awake for three hours already that day, and still he had seen no one. From the roof of the train, the city seemed empty.

To his south was the rubble that had been Battersea Power Station. Without it, the skyline was remarkable: a perpetual surprise. Sholl could see over the industrial park behind it—the buildings there much less damaged—to a tract of housing that looked almost as it had before the war. On the north shore, the Lister Hospital looked untouched, and the roofs of Pimlico were still sedate— but fires were burning, and trees of poisonous smoke grew over north London.

The river was clogged with wrecks. Besides the mouldering barges that had always been there jutted the bows of police boats, and the decks and barrels of sunken gunships. Inverted tugs like rusting islands. The Thames flowed slowly around these impediments.

Light's refusal to shimmer on its surface made the river matte as dried ink, overlaid on a cutout of London. Where the bridge's supports met the water, they disappeared into light and darkness.

Once, in a city seemingly deserted, Sholl would have explored, in fear and loneliness. But he had grown disgusted with those feelings, and with the prurience that quickly mediated them. He walked north, along the top of the train. He would follow the tracks down past the walls of London, into Victoria Station.

From some miles off, from the direction of South Kensington, came a high mewing sound. Sholl gripped the shotgun. A multitude lifted from the distant streets, many thousands of indistinct bodies. They were not birds. The flock did not move in avian curves, but spastically, changing speed and direction more suddenly than birds could ever manage. The things trilled and chattered, moving erratically south.

Sholl eyed them. They were animals, scavengers. Doves, they had been named, with heavy-handed irony. They could hurt a person badly, or kill, but as Sholl had expected, they ignored him. The flock passed over his head in unnerving motion. They were unclear.

Each dove was a pair of crossed human hands, linked by

thumbs. Cupped palms and fingers fluttering in preposterous motion. Sholl did not watch them. He was leaning out and staring into the Thames water below him, below the doves, the water in which nothing was reflected.

Of course the city was not empty, and at noon sounds of life and sporadic combat began.

Sholl was standing in the remains of Victoria Street, beside the immobilised bus in which he lived. It was a newer two-decker, its windows all grilled and caged, irregular bars welded across them. It had been inexpertly clad in plates of iron armour. Its number, 98, was still visible. Shreds of advertisement remained on its sides. Inside was food and fuel that he had stockpiled, his books, and the tat of survivalism.

There was small-arms fire coming from Brompton. He had heard that a small group of paratroopers had regrouped somewhere to the west of Sloane Square, and the noise seemed to verify that. He had no idea what they were fighting, nor how long they would last.

It had been some weeks since he had heard large artillery in the city. The resistance was breaking down. Now he could be almost certain that any gunfire he heard came from his own side. In the first few weeks of the war, the enemy had used weapons that were the same, functionally identical to those of the defending armies. It would have been—definitionally, Sholl thought sourly—a well-matched war, precisely matched, except for two things.

The imagos arrived from nowhere, in the heart of the city. Like Trojans, Londoners had woken with invaders among them. Troops had gone onto the streets. Gunships had shelled the city from the inside, levelling Westminster and much of the riverside.

The second factor in the imagos' favour was that they could break their habits. They started with the absolutely familiar weaponry, but soon discovered, or remembered, that they were not restricted to it, that there were other methods of warfare available to them. Their general had taught them how.

Standing in the broken streets north of Victoria, amid architecture brittled by war, tremulous and near collapse, Sholl began to see people. He glimpsed them at the windows of deserted shops: he saw them at the far ends of alleys.

The last Londoners. Millions were now gone. Dead, disappeared and fled. Of those who were left, some had become dangerous, like all terrified animals. Several times Sholl had almost been the victim of assaults, and as days passed there were more bands roaming and looting from the dying city. They would attack what fellow humans they met with a miserable kind of violence. But these fleeting figures were not those. Sholl shouted in greeting to a man he saw foraging for canned food in the glass and rubble ruins of a Europa food store. The man batted the air in Sholl's direction, demanding silence, an exaggerated motion of fear. His face was invisible. Sholl shook his head.

Sholl stood in the centre of the street, where he should not have felt safe. It was not bravado but a judgment. The enemy would continue their campaign against the backstreets where the last fighters held out, but had little interest in harassing London's fearful ratlike survivors. For which he might pass. Besides which, though Sholl did not yet fully trust it, he had another reason to think himself safe from the imagos.

Watching the cringing man running like a starveling from rubbish to rubbish, trying to get out of the light, Sholl made a decision.

He walked. His pack was heavy with books, tins and equipment he had taken from his bus, and he shucked it up in irritation, trying to make it comfortable. East along Victoria Street, past those houses still standing, charred cars and the spillage of war, past the uncertain monuments that the victorious invaders kept raising and forgetting. Up Buckingham Gate, bearing as directly north as Sholl could go.

．．．

There must have been thousands left in London, but fear had made most of them prey-creatures, who came out at night and moved in furtive bursts. Sholl thought very little of them or about them. There were a few others, more like him. He would see them very occasionally: men and women becalmed in the war's aftermath, standing without fear on roofs or wandering as if beyond caring by the edges of parks or rivers or darkened shops. He had seen enough of them die to know that not everyone with a similar insouciance to his own was safe from the enemy's attack.

And there were soldiers. Command had broken down almost instantly with the onset of fighting, but a few units survived, and persisted. In these late days they could be almost as dangerous as the invaders. In some places they had combined forces: in others they fought amongst themselves. They exchanged fire over control of some half-looted Sainsbury's, or an Esso petrol station. They might burst into view suddenly in a dust-bleached jeep pinned with guns, bursting out of the shell of a car park in their battered khakis, performing sweeps of an area they were trying to "secure."

They would level their guns at anyone human they saw, and shout at them to get down. Their intentions remained decent, Sholl suspected, or at least not malign: they were still trying with an imbecilic tenacity to defend London. He had even seen them in small triumphs. They rattled bullets into flocks of ravenous doves, spattering the pavement with the little hand-creatures and sometimes even saving the doves' intended prey. Even more powerful enemies fell to the soldiers, sometimes. They had brought down some of the flyers in the first weeks of fighting, had several times seemed to kill (it could be difficult to tell) what must have been imago commanders. But the logic of defeat—and they were defeated—had fragmented them.

The soldiers made themselves live in a future where they had won. They experienced each second as a memory, preemptively. The rat-people, in contrast, the Londoners become vermin, lived only in a present that terrified them. Sholl did not know where in history he lived, he and the few others like him. He felt uncoupled from time.

In some parts of London, the soldiers seemed to feel the pressure pulling them toward warlordism, and they fought it with inappropriate bonhomie. They would lean out of their fortified warehouses or basements, and yell cheerfully at any of the terrified and starving citizens they saw, inviting them in. In earlier but still recent days, Sholl had spent time with a unit camped out in Russell Square, in what had once been a dormitory for overseas students. The soldiers had made it into barracks, pasting their schedules and rotas on its noticeboards, on top of handbills for skiing trips and Italian lessons. They leaned out from upper floors and shouted at the few terrified locals, wolf-whistling the women.

They had tried repeatedly to contact some central command, some bunker or committee, but their superiors were gone or silent. Including Sholl, there had been four civilians with them, whom the troops had mocked with good humour, and tried to train. The commanding officer was a young Liverpudlian who had spent most of the day grinning at his troops, but whom Sholl, walking at night, had heard in the small hours trying to raise Liverpool on his radio, weeping into the static. "Fucked if I know, mate," he had said on the day Sholl left, as if Sholl had asked him a question.

There were squads camped out in grand houses in Kensington. They seemed cowed by their surroundings. They could not relate to the cool private gardens or the streets' tall white facades. Even where the war touched the architecture, where it was scorched or bullet-pocked, or where the attacks of the enemy had changed its material into something new, the areas seemed sedate, and the soldiers uncertain rather than pugnacious.

In Bermondsey the remnants of some regiment were bivouacked in Southwark Park. Sholl had been impressed with that. The invaders, as well as the doves and other scavengers that had spilt out into London with them, concentrated their attacks on streets and backstreets. For the most part, Sholl had observed, they avoided parkland. But despite this, and the seemingly obvious advantage that might have offered them, most of London's soldiers ignored the green spaces. Sholl wondered if the training in "urban warfare" had trapped them, if they could not relate to their task if they did not have side streets and deserted buildings in which to retreat.

He had approached the Bermondsey encampment, therefore, hoping to find something other than these neurotic everyday routines. He did, but it was no more useful to him. Machine guns had shredded the bushes beside him as he approached. He had lain where he had thrown himself, half-hidden by a tree that he knew would provide no defence from another such onslaught. "*Fuck off,*" had come an amplified voice. Some figure in camouflage, just visible beyond the bombed land that surrounded the camp, standing on a crippled tank with a megaphone to his lips. "*Fuck off out of our park you fucker.*"

Sholl had retreated. The mud craters that surrounded the soldiers, he had realised, were not evidence of some hard-won battle against the enemy: they were as far as terrified Londoners had reached, trying to join the panicked, paranoid troops, and where they had been destroyed.

It had taken him a month to find the right people. He had travelled by day in his bus, when it had still moved, and then on foot, ignoring the dangers. Sometimes he heard fighting, between Londoners and the enemy, or human bands, and sometimes it was close, but usually a street or two away, around a corner, out of sight.

Sholl kept an *A–Z* map of London on him always, and amended it as he learnt about the city's changing shape. He blocked out those areas he would not go: the imago strongholds; where the gangs were; the savage new communities where even human intruders were accused of being vampires, and burned or beheaded. In the rest of the city, Sholl made notes. Itemising what he found, he tried to track down, to anticipate, where certain other things might be. He was not searching randomly: he had a plan.

Where a building was gone or ruined, he crosshatched it out in black. Where it was made into something new, or where a new thing had appeared, he stuck numbered red crosses: he added a legend in tiny script on the inside front cover, naming what he saw.

#7, he had written, for the structure that now dwarfed the Brixton Prison. *Jebb Ave. filled with something like cuckoo-spit. Funnel-tower still rising—threads snagging chimneys. Something inside moving.*

In white dabs of Liquid Paper, Sholl marked and numbered the camps of London's soldiers.

He watched them from the top deck of his bus, or from surrounding buildings, through binoculars. He made notes about them, too.

#4: ≈ *30 men, one tank, one big gun. Morale v. bad.*

On four occasions, from as far away as possible, Sholl had watched the soldiers fighting. Once their enemy had been another human unit, and the exchange of fire had ended with a handful of dead on each side and desultory shouted curses. Watching these desperate men and women wrestling with their shaking weapons and churning each other into meat-froth had broken Sholl's reserve and shocked him, and made him tremble.

The other three times, the battles had been the result of some bizarre incursion of the enemy. Once, the humans had managed to retreat. Twice, they had been wiped out. And those times, though the carnage was no less bloody or loud than when humans killed humans, Sholl had watched it with detachment. Even when the invaders had spun away through space just past him, so that he felt them, ignoring him, shimmering and cleaning themselves of blood.

It had taken Sholl a month. Days watching the soldiers doing their recces through the brick ruins of London, even here and there rescuing people—men and women half-eaten by doves, distractedly maimed by invaders. In the evenings Sholl would lock the doors of his bus and by torch read the books he had looted.

(His library was mixed. He was surprised to discover a renewed appetite for fiction. Mostly, though, he read and obsessively reread books on physics, which he worked through trying to understand what had happened to light, and puerile military guides called *SAS Survival* and *Extreme Combat.* He had a collection of *Soldier of Fortune* magazines, which he still regarded with contempt, even as he read them. The science he found terribly hard, but he had worked through doggedly, and had been surprised to find himself understanding. He took in the science and the survivalism stolidly, as medicine.)

It had taken Sholl a month, picking his way through the dwindling safe routes of the city, avoiding imagos and the gangs, watching soldiers, to find a group with the shades of self-consciousness, of purpose but uncertainty, that he was looking for. A group close enough to the enemy.

Like the Bermondsey soldiers, the troop that Sholl approached were quartered in parkland. They were much more secure, though, in the thickets in the south of Hampstead Heath. Sholl came up the trails of Parliament Hill, with London behind him. It was not very far before three sentries rose from scrubby bushes and halted him.

The frightened young men roughed him a little and rummaged in his rucksack, and when they had decided (according to what science Sholl had no idea) that he was not vampire, one of them ran and returned with their commanding officer. Sholl had watched the troop several times, from the rooftops of Gospel Oak, and he recognised the man by his grey hair and his bearing.

They met in a copse a little way from the path, not hidden but out of immediate sight. Sholl was held by two young soldiers, who gripped his arms without much purpose. Their officer faced him, and over the man's left shoulder Sholl could see down and across London, all the way to what had been the Post Office Tower, then Telecom Tower, and was now something else altogether: a distorted beacon in the killing fields of central London. This late in the afternoon, there were regular sounds of fighting, gunshots and small explosions. Lights glimmered in the city. Flocks of doves spasmed over the bombed-out and imago-corroded roofs.

The officer nodded sharply at Sholl. "Come to join us?" he said.

"I came to ask," said Sholl, "whether you'd join me."

It was a humiliation and a punishment.

Let me start again.

It was a humiliation and a punishment.

(I am out of practice in my own voice. It is the classic danger for the operative under cover, for the spy, to lose track of where you end and the role begins. I would like to use our original voice, but for ease and speed I will stick to what I have used for so long.)

(Although in fact, of course, that voice that my people use, that I now find so hard—this voice—is no more ours than this. It is nothing but evidence of our bars. It was our *prison argot,* it was our slang, and while we used it—forced as we were—we forgot our own mountain language.)

It was a humiliation and a punishment. I would not want to minimise that. We have told stories and stories about our imprisonment, for centuries. But for a long time, it's true, our chains were loose.

We were trapped, and what we had wanted, what we had fought for, was lost to us, but for thousands of years we had the run of our prison—mostly. We were banished: but there are worse things. We could shape things, we could make our place ours, and become what we wanted.

Except beside the lakes, where we could always see siblings trapped in communion with you. And where, sometimes, we were called. Water was our worst degradation and punishment.

If you drank from your crude bowls it was not so bad. One little part of us would momentarily be crushed into the banal shape of your mouth, but we were free beyond those few inches and could gesticulate hatred at you. But when you leaned over the lakes, and entered them, we were pinioned to you, trapped into our mimicry, gazing dumb up at you. We knew when you were approaching the water, were forced to you, nodding from our world through the water into yours, silent and powerless, visual echoes.

Even then, we could strain against it.

As the water moved our forms were freed a little, and could warp with hatred. *Enter the water,* we would think fiercely, our new faces mumming your stupid thirst, *get into the water,* and when you did and shattered its surface, we became halfway free. Still sutured to you by threads we could not break, but as the lake's surface burst into drops, so did we. We could strain against your shapes.

For a long time after we lost our war, water was our only torment.

Then you learnt to polish obsidian, and trapped us in its black sheen. Its hardness made us cold, and fixed us without even small ripples of freedom into your likeness. But still you could only show tiny parts of us at a time, and you could ossify only our faces. And then, though our borders were fixed, the dark stone gave us a more subtle freedom, one that could unsettle you. Though it fixed us in unfreedom like amber, when you looked in the obsidian you saw, not yourselves, but us, watching, with our loathing. Obsidian revealed us as shadows.

Carbuncle, you used, and phengite, and emeralds and lead, and copper, tin, and bronze, and silver, and gold, and glass.

For thousands of years you trapped us imperfectly, and each of your jails gave us our little freedoms. We glowered from the dusk of black stone. When we were cast in bronze, we made ourselves relish the burnish that you gave our skins, knowing it disguised us. We rejoiced in rust, and as our bodies passed behind its imperfection we warped luxuriantly. Verdigris and discolourations, and scratches and pockmarks gave us licence, and though we were constrained, we could also play.

Silver was the worst. Jewellery we could bear. The little multiples of us you made in the facets of your gems, the strange elongated bodies we became in your rings were fleeting, and so strange to you, and so unnoticed that we had the space to play. But in the silver and specula you caught us.

A few of us who suffered the ignominy of whole walls of silver, in the high homes. The *specula totis paria corporibus:* mirrors equal to the whole of the body. We were racked on the preening of the Roman rich.

What you cannot know is how it *hurt.*

For we who are not, or were not, our bodies: we, for whom flesh is, or was, only one possible clothing. We might fly or invert ourselves through the spines of grass, we might push ourselves into other ways of being, we might be to water as water is to air, we might do anything, until you looked at yourselves. It is a pain you cannot imagine—very literally, in the most precise way, you cannot know how it is to feel yourself shoved with a mighty and brutal cosmic hand into bloody muscle. The agony of our constrained thoughts, shoehorned into those skulls you carry, stringy tendons tethering our limbs. The excruciation. Shackled in your meat vulgarity.

We cursed the slaves that lifted your mirrors, in those early days, cursed them and envied them their freedom. Our hate smouldered. We watched you as you watched yourselves. We held your eyes with ours, those eyes you forced us to wear. Until there were more and more of the larger mirrors, and you introduced us to a new shame, as the polished silver became so very slowly more common, until not every glance into it was an occasion, and you might enter your room (snarling us with shocking violence to you) and glance at us and then *turn away.* And we would be made to turn, and look away from you, at nothing, so that we could not even hate you to your face.

Sometimes you slept near your mirrors, and held us in place, in pain, with even these insufficient eyes closed, tied to your stupor for hours.

. . .

We did not fear glass. Why should we fear that dirty, algae-coloured stuff, that made only the tiniest imprisonments? Punctuated by bubbles and stains, blown in curves and dusted with lead and tin, a finger-length in diameter, glass did not frighten us.

Through our meaningless, occasional imitations, we saw what you did. Cleaning the glass with potash and burnt ferns, limestone and manganese. We did not pay much attention. It only made your mangling of us in little concave chambers more precise. We did not pay much attention.

We looked back later and realised how remiss we had been. We should not have been surprised at the source of our trouble.

Venice was our nightmare. Where there was no reflection we could make our world as we wanted it, but where mirrors or metal or water saw your buildings, we had no choice but to throw up our own analogues—sometimes instantly, with all the agony and effort that took. In most places your eyesores came and went momentarily, as you moved your specula, your points of reflection, and glimpsed some wall or tower. But Venice, city of canals, forced us to live in your architecture. Even in the forgiving prison of water, which let our bricks and mortar lap and ebb against your designs, we were uniquely constrained. Venice hurt us.

It was under the protection of Venice, more than half a millennium ago, that the epoch of our humiliation became that of our despair.

In the fires of Murano (observed from the analogue you made us keep of it, in puddles and in the local commodities themselves), washed by estuary salt and silicates in new concentrations, industrious men made crystal glass. And while those accidental alchemists stared in piggish awe at the white, white-hot stuff they had made, their paymasters in the city of canals mixed tin and quicksilver, and made the tain.

Once, we were exiled to a landscape that was ours. It was only broken in places by rippling pools of distortion where there was water, where we might be called to perform our mute play of you. And then there were tiny moving snares, the first mirrors, but when we could evade them, where we were not cursed and tied to someone of substance, still they could not harness us. The rest of our retreat, our prison, was ours, to decorate and shape and inhabit as we wanted, only glimpsed occasionally by you through your little holes, the spaces that sucked us into your shapes. The rest of our world was ours, and you would not have recognised it.

And then the tain.

Glass democratised. Though we fought it, though we sought to keep it arcane. Glass became mass, in scant centuries, and the tain, that dusting of metal that stained its underside, with it. You put out lights at night and trapped us even then in your outlines. Your world was a world of silvered glass. It became mirrored. Every street had a thousand windows to trap us, whole buildings were sheathed in tained glass. We were crushed into your forms. There was no minute, and not a scrap of space where we could be other than you were. No escape or respite, and you not noticing, not knowing as you pinioned us. You made a reflecting world.

You drove us mad.

Once there was a room of mirrors in Isfahan, hundreds of years ago. Lahore's palace was ringed by Murano glass and Venetian tain. *What misery is this?* we thought when those places were built. We would stare at each other, each of us trapped in that place, our bodies fractured, staring at each other, scores of us taking the same form, scores snared when one person entered those rooms. *What have they done?* And then there was Versailles. Our bleakest place. The worst place in our world. A dreadful jail. *It can be no worse than this,* we thought then, stupidly. *We are in hell.*

Do you see? Can you understand why we fought?

Every house became Versailles. Every house a hall of mirrors.

So far from the dangerous heart of town, the soldiers of the Heath were able to relax discipline a little. In the little false forests of the park, those not on guard duty played cards and smoked, read, listened to cassettes.

Between the little tents was a variety of equipment and furniture, in disrepair and in good condition. Stacking plastic chairs and wooden desks that looked pilfered from schools, ranged randomly: trunks and boxes, all map-stained by weather.

The unit was swollen with incomers, with Londoners who had joined up to fight. The full-timers spoke with accents from around the country, used the jargon unthinkingly and tersely, moved their equipment without effort. The others, men and women whose uniforms were imperfectly pieced together and amended, who walked and swung their weapons with self-conscious care, were recent volunteers.

Sholl saw a girl in her midteens, wearing a Robbie Williams T-shirt above her camouflage trousers, uncertainly hefting her rifle, while a burly Mancunian private showed her, gently, how to take aim. There was a group of young men listening to hip-hop on a cheap machine that stripped it of bass, looking at maps, bickering in the slang of south London estates.

The CO gave Sholl lager, and good food, and let him sleep. Sholl was surprised at his own exhaustion. Before the officer left him, they talked, in the most general terms, about the war. Sholl was careful not to discuss his plans, not to preempt himself. But along with what he said was communicated something calm, a sense of something preparatory. He did not discuss his plans, but with his unexplained invitation—*whether you'd join me*—with his measure, he set himself apart.

When he woke, Sholl emerged from the tent into the damp

clearing, and quietly toured the camp. The men and women of the unit were in their groups, as before, quietly working or playing, but he saw them watching him. Sholl knew instantly that they suspected him, though they could not have said of what. His conversation with the CO, his invitation, had been reported.

He exchanged a few greetings. Steam rose from cooking and laundry, and smoke from small fires. Sholl watched it, so that he did not yet have to meet the soldiers' eyes. They wanted something from him, and knew that it would be forthcoming. He had not come to them like the other frightened Londoners; he had not arrived as a refugee to be made safe. He had brought them something.

The change in the camp was not overt, but it was clear. The soldiers were expectant. The soldiers watched Sholl as if he were a Jesus, with nervous, hopeful interest, and scepticism and excitement. Sholl's mouth was dry. He was not sure what to do. The officer approached him.

"Mr. Sholl," he said. "Would you like to talk to us? Would you like to tell us why you're here?"

Sholl had thought it would take a little time to come to this. He had wanted a day to feel for the mood of the camp, before he spoke. He had expected to be interrogated by the commander alone, or perhaps with a few lieutenants. He had prepared himself to persuade that audience. He had not thought that with the breakdown of structures, primitive democracy would assert itself.

The CO knew he was in charge by nothing but the approval of his troops. He was not a stupid man; he understood that "need to know" had become a dangerous condescension. There was no one to court-martial the insubordinate, and there never would be any more. He needed his women and men to agree with his orders.

He sat with them and leaned against a tree and smoked. They did not look at him. They were still turned to Sholl.

Sholl sat. The legs of the chair sank an inch into the wet earth. Sholl put his head in his hands and tried to make himself ready.

He tried to turn the confrontation into a discussion. He started by asking questions.

"We try to get messages to other units. We're still scanning for word from the government, or top brass or whateverthefuck." The commander's voice failed for a second. The idiocy of the state-ment was obvious. Everyone knew that there was no government, and no one in charge of the army's ragged remains. Sholl nodded as if the remark made sense, not needing to press the point.

His questions were answered. Messianism still clung to him—not sought, but useful—and the soldiers told him what he wanted to know guardedly, and waited, knowing that soon he would tell them why he was there.

"So you're trying to get your orders, I understand that," said Sholl. "But what do you do day to day?"

They patrolled the edges of the Heath. Unlike the maddened Bermondsey renegades (of whom they had heard, and at whom they were disgusted—"We should go fucking sort *them* out, never mind the fucking imagos," someone shouted) they welcomed what few civilians made it to join them. There were very few. There were no children. No one had seen any children for weeks.

They patrolled the Heath, and when they saw the enemy ha-rassing or murdering humans, they tried, where they could, to in-tervene. They made some minor incursions into the streets that were roamed by murderous imagos, trying to find survivors. "We know where there are some—in a school up by the hill, we think—but we can't get to them. There's a nest of vamps in the tube station." That, Sholl already knew.

The vampires and other imagos had not come up onto the grassland, and so the troops were still alive, but that was just contin-gent. They might come any time. The soldiers patrolled and waited and scanned the airwaves with their crappy radios, and waited.

"What *happened?*"

The question came at Sholl suddenly, breaking through his own queries about the soldiers' habits—how many, how often, where, why. The man who asked it had no reason to expect an answer from Sholl—a drab-faced newcomer sat among soldiers—but he asked it again, and others echoed him, and Sholl knew he had to answer.

"What happened? Where did they come from? What happened?"

Sholl shook his head.

"From the mirrors," he said, telling them what they already knew. "From the tain."

He used the language he had stolen from his physics books, a language of laws and propositions named after the living and dead who had formulated them, and made it seem as if he spoke it fluently. A cheap shot. He told them (regretting the jargon instantly) that *en one sine theta one still equals en two sine theta two.* Except in certain circumstances.

Except in the case where *en one equals minus en two.* Except for reflection.

There is something called the Phong Model, Sholl said. It's a graph. It's a model to show how light moves. The shinier the surface, the more precise and bright the reflected light, the narrower the range in which it can be seen. The model used to describe how light bounced off concrete and paper and metal and glass, its angle of specular reflection narrowing, approximating the angle of incidence, its bright spot brightening, as the surfaces became more mirrored.

But something happened, and now Phong describes a turning key.

It used to be a sliding scale. Asymptotic. An endless approximation to infinity or zero. It's become a threshold. As the reflected brightness grows more precise, as its angle of exit narrows to more closely mimic its entry, it's approaching an edge, it is becoming a change of state, he said. Until a critical moment is reached: until light meets the sheen of a gloss surface, and everything alters, and the light unlocks a door, and what was a mirror becomes a gate.

Mirrors became gates, and something came through.

"We know that," one of the men shouted. "We know that already. Tell us what happened. Tell us how it happened."

That, Sholl could not do. He could tell them nothing they had not heard from the vampires that taunted them sometimes: they were the most comprehensible of the imagos.

The soldiers stayed, though, still watching him. They wanted him to be special: they were anxious to forgive him. They asked him questions that allowed him to be circuitous, to seem vaguely wise. He had travelled through London's ruins, that they only looked out over. He could tell them much more about the city than they could learn from their cautious and pointless sorties.

"I want your help," Sholl told them suddenly. Many of them looked away from him. The officer held Sholl's eyes. "I've got a plan. I can *end* this. But I need you to help me."

Still the men and women waited. There was no revelation in this. Sholl could only stumble on. He started to tell them what it was he wanted to find, where he wanted to go, and with that, finally, he provoked a few gasps from them. Some of them expostulated. He told them what he wanted them to do, what he wanted them to achieve, and where they must go.

Even now that he had roused them, there was very little of the discussion Sholl had expected. The soldiers on the heath wanted to be convinced. But they were not suicidal. They needed more than his exhortation.

He spoke in elegant insinuations, avoiding details but giving them enough to entice them. He was afraid to proceed alone, and he whispered at them, secrets, things he had heard, things that only he could do. He waited for them to be intrigued, and to join him.

To his astonishment, and dismay, they did not.

You made us *hurt* each other, and ourselves. You made us blood each other, when you fought in front of your looking glasses. You ignored them, and us, but we could not resist. When you conducted your knifings, your shootings dead. When you slit your own throats and watched the blood leak out of you, and out of us. We *stabbed* each other, for your vainglorious whims, and accompanied you in suicide. And where your mortuaries were glazed, you trapped us there, and made us rot with you.

We fought you. There were ways.

Your world mirrored, and caught us in more webs of light. We had to make your houses, your clothes. Where you had animals we had to make them too, moulding the matter of our world into the cowed shapes of your dogs and cats, animating them, dandling them like marionettes as your pets snuffed mindlessly and licked the mirrors. Exhausting and humiliating. But vastly worse was when you looked at yourselves. Then, we could only make puppets of us. Your sentience demanded it, our presence, unknowingly.

The bonds and boundaries were not stable. In the beginning, when reflection was rare, each event was a trauma, and we had no strategies. Where there were two mirrors or more they pulled chains of us together and locked us all into identical mimicry, in recursive tunnels of only one of you. As the tain spread, we learnt to fold our space, so fewer of us were snared.

Where tiny parts of you were fleetingly reflected, the snippets of us that took your shapes were almost disengaged, almost independently born. There were never fast-fixed rules, hard lines: we learnt strategies. But some things were unchangeable. Where you were reflected, always, one of us at least was stitched to you.

Endlessly we were drab copies. The impurities and stains that had given us some relief were taken. As we tried to hide behind one, we were laid bare in another. Even where we stretched and warped we did it at your whim, forced into *your* pathetic parodies of your own outlines, in bent circus mirrors.

But some of us, some few, some ones and twos, found we could break free. By a caprice we never understood, as we were watched by you our unconscious tormentors, some of us found the strength to rebel.

It would start and finish in an instant. Our revolts. A rush of freedom, a sudden certainty that we could move, a look up and a luxuriant stretching out and murder, a coming through. You would not withstand us, little men and women staring up dumb as your own faces came for you, your own arms crooked and pushing through the mirror.

And when you were done and finished, we were in your world.

A parliament of spies. It was a troubling victory. We were fixed, fast-frozen in these idiot bodies.

The mirrors broke with our passage. We found others. Pressed ourselves against them, staring into the empty rooms beyond the glass, and whispered into them. Whispered until our siblings heard us, and in that way we would make murmured plans. We received orders and gave them, and squabbled over them. We were deep under cover, and our tribes cajoled and begged us, and made the case for their strategies.

Some of us killed ourselves. We could do that, in the bodies that encased us. We could die. It was a horrid revelation, but the temptation of that new experience was too great for some.

We went to war. A fifth column.

There were plans we could make. To keep the tain covered, to slow the encroaching empire of mirrored glass. It made for strange allegiances.

We joined the Venetian ranks. Hidden, we infiltrated the camp of our own dumb torturers, kept our hatred battened down. This was not the time for rage but for politics and strategy. Having watched over the means of our misery, having seen it devised, Venice wanted it for itself, and made it forbidden knowledge. They coddled the glass-men of Murano, hid them behind enticements and threats, hostaged their families and would not let them leave. And even while they continued to make the mirrors, we swallowed and helped the floating republic keep them. The monopoly thrived on scarcity, and if we could not have no mirrors, we would fight to keep them rare.

So when through perfidy the tain-makers escaped, we were there to help Venice, to guide the assassins, to be assassins ourselves. When the French could not mimic the expertise and instead stole the experts, made their own mirror factories, it was we who poisoned the glassblower, we who gave the metal-polisher fever until he died. We killed the escapees, desperate, fighting for Venetian merchants against the merchant-state of France, each little victory scored against history.

Mirrors could not be corralled. We fought and strove and fought and agonised and lost, at every step.

We walked among you. We learned tricks.

There have been escapees, infiltrators on your side of the partition for as long as we have been in prison. Some of us escaped from the water, the polished obsidian, the bronze and glass, and hid beside you. But never so many as broke your silvered glass.

We wore your faces, left-to-right. Mostly your friends, no matter how they loved you, could only stare at us a little, with a consternation of which they could make no sense. Staring at your reflection in flesh, knowing that something was altered but not able to see quite what it was, what of you was wrong.

And where there were marks or scars or tattoos, where our reflected nature was impossible to hide, we disappeared, and became new people. With our task.

Mirrors betray us. When we came through, we murdered those whose bodies had bound us, and there was no one among our tormented comrades left behind in our place, no one forced to mimic us from beyond the glass, as we had mimicked you. There was nothing in the tain made to take our shapes: we were invisible in the mirror, we had no reflections. When you saw that, you screamed, and called us things. We are the patchogues: that is our name. But you called us vampires.

Gongsun defeated us. Your champion. Gongsun, Gongsun Xu-anyuan, Ji Xuanyuan, Huangdi. They are all his names. The man who defeated Chiyou with his south-seeker, who wrote a book of sex, created writing, made tripods that stood to mimic infinity. He who made twelve great mirrors, to follow the moon into the sky and capture the world. To capture us. The Yellow Emperor.

It was our fault. It hurts to say it. We thought we could win. The first attack was ours.

And when all was done and your champion, your Yellow Emperor, had led you to victory—at bloody cost, at least—he set free his mirrors. Snared us. Until then the worlds had bled, had oozed into each other. We had walked without pause from our plane to yours, through the doors of light, through the glimmerings of water and the flat gateways of stone and polished metal. Until your champion, with arcane sciences that I cannot begin, I cannot begin to understand, until he separated us and locked us apart. A world to play in, but punished with the enforced mumming of your vanity.

He changed history. He made it so that it had always been so. And you forgot us, and cast us as images, and ignored us, and stared at yourselves.

I have seen my people debased. Entities more powerful than your moon made to smear scarlet wax and fat on peeling lips, lick it off lumpy teeth, made to preen with you. Bulked into spasming fibrous meat and mutely raising and lowering iron bars, without complaint, unable to complain, as you stared at yourselves, at them, made to wear your sweat-wet clothes and jostle mindlessly from machine to machine as you worked to change your shapes. You have put mirrors by your beds, or over them, and trapped my people in your clammy fuck-embraces. You made us fuck each other, stare at the eyes of our siblings with shared hatred and apology as the bodies you made us wear did the corporeal things you did.

For six thousand years, and forever, you have held us down. Each of us alive and watching, and waiting, and waiting, undying all that time. You didn't know, but not knowing is no excuse. And you have taken our freedom away in slow increments, until in a sudden flurry of three centuries you sped it all up, and took away our last escapes, and made our world yours.

One day, we whispered. We had whispered it forever.

When it came, the time was not one day but many, stretched out over months, a luxuriant, languorous release, in pieces, in parts and parcels, and the more infuriating but ultimately the more wonderful, liberatory, for that.

The streets were wet again. It was like a warning. London was never so alien as after the rain, its tarmac and slate turned into what would once have been mirrors.

Sholl walked through the remains of Hampstead, past empty outlines of shops spilling glass and the last remains of their produce. By a bookshop, he trod through a slush of decaying paper pulp.

There was water still in the air, a mist that coalesced and ran down Sholl's face. The pavements tilted away from the Heath, and he could feel himself descending.

He kept swallowing, and changing his grip on his gun. He was surprised at the extent of his fear. He had not thought he would be alone. Even so, he did not consider changing his plan. It was irreversible.

Sholl listened hard as he walked, but he could hear only soft noise of the air. He felt closed in, hearing his own actions very close as if they reverberated back from walls, as if he were walking a corridor, a rut, channelled inexorably. He listened to his walking, his feet falling and rising. A gentle slap and plash before him, and behind him a faint wet parting. He breathed in deep, and held it for a long time, past several feet of brick and broken window, and exhaled, a tremor still audible.

Something moved away from him, up the wall, in a lizard motion not quite like anything Sholl had ever seen. He was approaching the junction by the underground station. This close to Hampstead's heart, the fauna of mirrors were playing.

The street curled leftward, bringing the crossroads into view. For a last few seconds Sholl would not look at it. He focused instead on the water around him, on the puddles and slick asphalt. The light was hard, even through the clouds, but of course no light rebounded, there were no specular highlights. The rainwater washed the city free of dust and went into its cracks, and stained it camouflage, darkening it. Sholl tramped through the wet that did not reflect him. On water-blackened streets, with the outlines of everything still rain-sharpened, as if London were an etching, though the matte wet colours ate the light.

Sholl had to look ahead in the end.

The tiles of Hampstead Underground had once glinted. Now their dark green changed as water drooled from it. It was hidden with a smearing of grey urban ivy. The station's metal mesh gates were bent wide open, snapped, splaying from the dark entrance like roots from a cave. In the unlit interior Sholl could just see the ticket booth, the stainless steel doors to the lifts stalled open, pitch within.

Before the station, the crossroads was full of moving things. Through the shadows Sholl saw that the station itself thronged with them, and they spilt into the open air, foraging in the ruins.

The mindless animals of the war, the residue of the fighting. Like rats in trenches, they were overrunning. For centuries they had been spawned in thousands, little resonances of reflection, shed by passion in makeup compacts, dresser mirror triptychs, glazed gym walls. Imago spoor, they had lived fleetingly and been destroyed within moments, an endless pell-mell life cycle. But when reflection became a door they were set free; they could live. They could breed. They were the detritus of reflection. Vanity's castoffs, the snippets of human forms thrown up and ignored in the echoes between mirrors.

Human hands clutched and unclutched along the gutter. They picked their way through the mud, leaving tracks of fingerprints. Up the hill, Sholl saw a mouldering human corpse. Several of the hands picked their way across it with fingertip grace, and settled on its flesh, lowering themselves and gnawing at it with their nails. They were grazing.

There were little clouds of colour-smeared lips like plump butterflies, that ebbed through the air, each motion with the exaggerated kiss-pout of someone applying lipstick. Eyes, human eyes, spasmed into existence and out again, moving through folded space, winking stupidly as they went.

There were teeth in big horse-grins, that Sholl half saw. With a peristaltic wave a biceps clenched and unclenched through the centre of the junction. Like aggregates of spiderwebs, the imagos of hair drooled from windowsills, billowing, against the wind. There were doves overhead, flapping their fingers energetically.

These were mindless scavengers, that had come in the aftermath of the fighting, and their numbers had increased. They spilt out of the mirrors and did not die. Ignored images and afterimages, gone feral.

Men and women walked among them, unperturbed by the stranger presences. Their clothes seemed extraordinary—suits, jeans and shirts, drab everyday wear, exactly as it would have been before the war. They were vampires, imagos in human form. They did not speak to one another. Sholl pressed himself against the wall beside him, watched from behind the brick.

Each vampire concentrated, moving in its own shuffling path, tracing repeating patterns with autistic precision, ignoring its siblings completely. The vampires muttered to themselves.

The men and women moved in gradually changing patterns, like clockwork winding down, and the vermin, the refracted glimmerings of people, fluttered and crept by them. Sholl watched. Way overhead, just below cloud, a sudden point of focus came into clarity and was gone. An imago, a full imago, in its own barely perceivable form. Miles to the south, Sholl heard a huge ripping sound.

Sholl was very afraid. He had never yet deliberately faced the imagos. And though the vampires were the most comprehensible, and the weakest of them, they were still stronger and more savage than any human. And they hunted. When vampires moved into an area, the surviving humans moved out or died.

He sighed, his breath quivering. He felt in his pockets for his torch and ammunition, his cuffs; then he hefted his shotgun and stepped into view.

There was a tiny increase in the sound of the vampires. They did not stop their motion, but simultaneously, they looked sidelong at Sholl, watching him with what looked like unease.

He levelled his gun at one of them, a vampire in a clean baker's smock. It winced, and tried to shrink away, but continued in its monotonous circuit. Sholl pulled the trigger.

The gun seemed to sound for a long time. The baker-thing was lifted, was hurled high in an arc of blood. It squealed very high like a pig. All the vampires made the same noise.

When the baker landed, it drummed its feet and hands on the pavement like a child having a tantrum, spattering blood around it. There was a cave in its chest from the shot. Its shoes scrabbled on concrete. It shook its head hyperactively, keening through gritted teeth.

Sholl reloaded, watching the vampires. They were grimacing, emitting a grating sound. They moved back and forward on their heels, staring at him. Their faces were screwed up with concentration. Sholl stepped forward.

His heart was striking hard. He felt very cold. His fear was so strong it was as if he could not breathe.

As he approached the closest of the vampires, he forced himself not to slow. It backed away. It was a woman in a frumpy, blousy dress. It dropped to all fours and moved from him with animal motion.

Sholl leaped forward and made a grab for the woman's arm. It screeched and jumped, floral fabric billowing. It landed on a windowsill, six or seven feet up, and crouched, hissing.

Quick with adrenaline, Sholl spun. Every second, every split second, he expected a vampire blow to take him down. He twisted, to see what was behind him, and behind him, and behind him, holding his breath with fear. But the vampires were paralysed, were staring at him with an unreadable expression.

Shaking, Sholl went forward again, for the next nearest vampire, reaching out to grasp it. The wildlife, the shards of human forms, scattered, fleeing the crossroads too fast to see. And the vampires, now, bolted. Loping four-limbed at a sped-up pace, scrambling up strange angles of wall, snapping back into the darkness of Hampstead Underground Station, howling and growling, so that in a fraction of a second, only Sholl and the wounded baker-vampire were in the road.

The baker snapped its limbs and was suddenly reeling on its feet. Sholl came for it and it wailed in what sounded like terror and ran, backward, much faster than any man could move, facing Sholl all the time. Matter jostled loose in gouts from its terrible wound, and it left blood and shredded viscera on the road.

Sholl watched it disappear. He was elated. He turned, pirouetting alone in the middle of the road. Sounds of triumph and survival came out of him, delighted sounds he could not control. They had not touched him.

He fired his gun into the air and whooped. London swallowed the noise, denied him an echo.

Sholl still had to do what he had come here to do. He had to get what he needed. He stared into the entrance to the station, into the eyes of the vampires still watching him, just visible as shadows. Sholl's fear came back to him. He swallowed. *What does it matter?* he thought. *If the very worst happens, what does it truly matter?*

He stepped forward, toward the tiled steps, toward the darkness, where many of the vampires and the fauna of mirrors had fled.

As he entered the station there was a collective whine from the things within. The hands scuffed through the dust and hid in the darkness of holes and corners, the eyes and lips winked and kissed out of sight.

The vampires howled and swung, simian, into the lift-shafts and away to the caverns in the station's end, toward the stairs. The chamber was ghosted with echoes. The cables still holding the ruined lifts sounded like huge instruments as the vampires grabbed them and clambered out of reach and sight.

Sholl walked into the stillness. He stepped over the skeleton of a London Underground employee, still coated in the rags of its blue uniform. Sholl stood by the electronic gates, and listened.

He needed to move fast. He could still feel his own fear. It was undiminished, as if his sudden bravado did not replace it but overlaid it.

Like a fare evader, Sholl vaulted the gates and stepped to the back of the dark station. It was very cool. He stood in front of the jimmied lift doors, listening to drips, strange sounds of steel. There was rubbish on the floor, a scattering of discarded tickets. Sholl headed toward the back of the station, toward the staircase.

The spot from his torch foraged like an animal, like a guide dog picking out a path for him between the broken metal and obscure imago detritus—unidentifiable rotting things, organic constructs spun out of nothing. The station floor was sticky. Sholl made the only sound, walking into the darkest part of the corridor, descending a little preliminary flight of ten steps, in absolute blackness now, approaching the shaft and the black iron of the spiral stairs, the scuffed paint of its handrail curling close to the cylindrical wall, clockwise down and out of sight.

A pillar of pipe- and rust-scarred metal threaded through the centre of the coiling stairway. Sholl stood on the top step, and angled his torch down through the thin gap between the right-hand rail and the pillar. The light met more stairs, and he moved it till it pushed past the handrail directly below him, and then again, and then it died, three coils of the stairs down, long before it touched the bottom. Nothing moved in the beam. Nothing sounded.

I saw them come this way, thought Sholl.

He set his foot on the second step down. It made a little noise. He waited, and then continued.

Sholl descended slowly. He brought both feet together on each step, and paused before moving on. He listened to his breath come fast. He was suspended. The steps rose rapidly behind him into darkness. He shone his torch back the way he had come, fearful that he was being followed. He became uneasy about the dark pillar beside him. He imagined that something was hiding behind it, a few steps below him, moving at his pace, keeping just out of his sight. Sholl moved left, until he was touching the shaft's curving wall, straining himself to see as far down ahead as possible.

He went like that, skirting the wall, lower and lower toward the cold train tunnels, quite cosseted by darkness. His pace lulled him, the slow spiralling descent became hypnotic. There were tiny sounds at the edges of things, as the feral imagos, the little ripped images of hands and eyes and genitals, crawled away from him. Perhaps they were other things, too: the last of the rats or mice, hiding from the predatory reflections.

The light that bobbed from step to step suddenly touched something that moved. The shock of it made Sholl cry out, and flail with the torch as if it were a sword, until its light picked out a face, a line of faces, a mass of them, lips thinned and resolute, eyes distended, and fixed on him.

Soundlessly, the vampires clogged the stairs. He could not count them—twenty at least, in their incongruous clothes, standing still, waiting for him. They watched him as he moved the torch from one face to the other. The constriction of each pair of pupils, in turn, was their only motion.

Sholl breathed fast with his heartbeat. He waited for the vampires to attack him, but they did not come closer. Nothing moved in the shaft for a long time. Finally, Sholl descended one step. The vampires responded in perfect time, like a macabre dance troupe, shifting backward together, staying out of his reach. He came forward again, and they moved back in time with him, and they began to make a sound, a faint humming, an anxious and unpleasant noise.

Anger rose in Sholl. He pointed his gun into the mass, but he did not shoot. He approached them more quickly, and they increased their own pace, their soundtrack becoming louder.

With a sudden lurch, Sholl almost threw himself down the stairs at the human figures, letting his shotgun swing back on its sling. He snatched out so quickly that his hand closed around the lapel of the nearest vampire. The creature screeched and moved away, yanking free of Sholl's grasp and scuttling past him up the stairs. Sholl's momentum took him on, and he had to fight to keep his feet, hurtling down, the torchlight swinging from wall to wall, showing the coldly set features of the vampires. Sholl snatched as he ran, and felt cloth and even flesh and bone in his grasp, but again and again it was pulled free.

He swung his shotgun. It clattered against the wall.

Sholl shouted wordlessly, and grabbed desperately for the figures that were scattering, spreading out. They evaded him. He stumbled down the stairs, grabbing for the handrail. He reached the bottom unexpectedly: the floor changed, disrupting his rhythm, and he fell onto the concrete plateau. His torch skidded away from him, its beam random.

From the floor, Sholl craned his neck. Darkness loomed over him, moving forward and backward as the torch rolled. Ranged around Sholl were scores of figures, the vampires, hollowed out by shadows. He bellowed and rose, hurling himself at them, deeper into the tunnels, following a sign that said THIS WAY TO TRAINS.

The vampires surrounded him out of his reach, retreating with him, into the darkness, never touching him, staying beyond his fingertips when he lurched.

Sholl swung his shotgun like a club. He wanted to fire into them, to rain them in bloody bone over each other, but he was afraid that they would scatter, and he needed to reach one, to take one. He screamed in fearful rage, and in frustration.

The torch was a long way behind him now. It was a little point of glimmering at the end of the passage. He walked in pitch and the vampires were as indistinct as ghosts. Sholl ran at them, and they were gone from his hands, glowering from the darkness.

Get out of here, he felt them think. *Get out of our house. Leave us alone.*

Sholl stamped like a child and screamed again. They would not get close enough to touch. They just stood at the very edges of light and waited for him to go. He raged at them, becoming exhausted, stumbling farther and farther into their dark. He leaned against the walls and felt despair.

Something came out of the silent crowd around him. He heard it approaching, pushing through the immobile vampires. It made a low sound as it came, and Sholl looked up, into the darkness, not with the terror that made sense but with some kind of hope. He stared into nothing as running footsteps echoed toward him.

Like something rising out of murky water, a face became momentarily visible, inches from him. Dirty white in the darkness, crossed with scars. Sholl did not have time to register its expression before he was hit hard, and he flew backward.

He lay dazed in the cold dirt. He knew he needed to get up. The thought was looping in his head that one of them had *touched* him. It had hurt him yes but it had *touched* him; it was not staying out of reach. It was what he wanted, and needed. He was excited but afraid again, knowing that he could be killed.

His attacker was circling him. Sholl could hear it. He made a sound like mewing and rolled, trying to stand. He was hit again, the momentum pushing him to the tunnel's wall.

Adrenaline came through the new pain, and he was standing, arms out to fight. There were noises in the tunnel, of consternation, of whispered bickering. Sholl could hear tugging. Bodies buffeted against one another. Something was passing through the vampires, a concern. At the back of the tunnel, in the purest black, a voice was raised (the reflection of a larynx forced, unhappily, to make human sounds).

With a little harsh bark—not at Sholl but at its companions—the attacker broke free of its crowd. Sholl could see an insinuation of it, a shadow in the darkness. He raised his arms to meet it, and when the cold face emerged up close to him he discovered that he was ready. He swung the shotgun, stock out like a mace. He smacked the face aside.

Sholl was elated. To have *touched*, to have *connected*. He swung his gun again, toward the ground where his attacker must have fallen. He wielded the barrel with force that surprised him. He was not conscious of anger, but of focusing on a task.

The vampire that had touched him cried out when Sholl's makeshift club slammed into its leg. The percussion on the bone was loud. The wounded thing grabbed Sholl's shin and hauled him, but Sholl was ready again, and he brought himself down on the prone figure.

They tumbled into each other. They rolled in the dust and muck. Sholl grabbed for the imago's head, careful not to slip his thumbs into the thing's mouth, but to grip the skull and bring it down, twice, on the concrete. His opponent was punching Sholl in the face, but it did not have the worst of imago strength, or that strength had left it, because the blows connected and they only hurt.

Then Sholl was choking, the vampire pinioned beneath him but reaching up, gripping Sholl's throat. Sholl heard his own breathing stop. He was hitting his attacker, but not hard enough, and he knew that he was in danger. He heard a faint twittering, like birds, and he was sure it was in his own head.

Terrified of dying, he felt for his shotgun. By the time he had it in his fingers, he was weak. He brought it down on the vampire's head, and the grip on his throat loosened. The gun bounced from the skull to the floor, and fired down the tunnels.

In the frozen moment of light Sholl saw the faces of the crowd. They loomed over him and his dazed attacker. So far as he could read emotion in those faces, faces that wore human features without facility or empathy, they looked stricken. Discomposed and desperate. Their mouths were open. He realised that the sound like birds was not his imaginings, that they were making it. Trilling and staring down. One or two of them were reaching for him in his fight, but with hovering, tentative and crooked-fingered hands, so that he knew they would not bring themselves to touch him, they could not. And then the light was gone, and he was left only the afterimage.

Sholl was strengthened by their anxiety. He dazed the imago beneath him with another brutal blow and stood, rescuing his shotgun, refilling it. Sholl dragged the half-conscious vampire back the way he had come, toward the little light. It began to wake, and he hauled it high enough that it could crawl, and took it around corners until he saw the bottom of the spiral stairs, with the torch at their foot.

The vampires came with him. They followed Sholl and his captive, keeping a few feet away but becoming visible as they turned in to the fringes of torchlight. They kept reaching out with that unconvincing motion, not committing but terrified of this capture that they witnessed, distressed by what they were watching. They moaned.

Sholl locked the vampire's arms to the banisters before it came to. He used two pairs of cuffs. That would not hold any imago at full strength, Sholl knew, but not all the invaders were so uncannily powerful, and he hoped that this one's injuries would keep it weak. He beat it twice in the face with his shotgun, watching the blood come up under the skin, and out, with satisfaction.

He shone his torch into the bleary face. The stitchwork of scars marred features that would—with normal feeling animating them—be pleasant enough, Sholl suspected. Beyond the illumination, the other vampires watched anxiously, but they would not come closer.

When the vampire had strengthened a little, its head rolling less, moving with more certainty, Sholl clicked his fingers until he caught its eye, and as it began to snarl and strain against the chains, he put his shotgun to its neck, and pushed hard enough to bruise.

"I don't know," he said, "how bad it'll be for you if I fire." In the tunnel so far underground, his voice was stark. "I don't know what'll happen to you, or how long it'll take for you to fix."

He looked carefully at the worm-white face. It moved constantly below the skin, as muscles worked. The vampire strained but the doubled handcuffs held. The other vampires waited.

Nervously, Sholl let his captive try and fail to break free.

"Why did you touch me? Why won't *they* touch me?"

He did not like to speak it, as if doing so would break whatever power he had, but in any case the vampire did not reply. Sholl prodded its neck again. He knew he did not have long, and he thought quickly for other tactics. He could not bully this thing into speaking, but perhaps he could make it think that there was no point to its silence.

Even with an enemy so opaque, so alien as the imagos, even with the fog of war, it had been possible to learn a great deal about their campaign. In the early days of the conflict, the vampires had seemed much more like humans. They had lived among humans for years, sometimes centuries, and they had picked up habits. In the first weeks of the war they had often—standing at the head of the incoming force, on some terrible machine, taking stock of the aftermath of a massacre—taunted the defeated armies, had raged about their own oppression, and crowed that it was coming to an end.

As they had passed time back among their own kind, that

mimicked behaviour had died, replaced with increasingly incomprehensible actions, without analogue or meaning in human terms. (The vampires had become pathetic. Trapped in the bodies they had loathed for centuries, the imago spies, who had perhaps been key to freeing their kind, could not become themselves. They were stuck, pretend humans and now pretend imagos.) But Sholl had listened very carefully in those early days, and had talked to others who had heard things, sometimes demanding information of them as they died. To his captive audience, now, Sholl showed off what he had learnt.

He told the tethered vampire when and how the imagos had been enslaved, at the hands of a myth, an ancient human thinker-king. He told it how it and its comrades—the vampires who called themselves patchogues, the spies, those-who-cross-over—had been the advance guard. How the unfettered imagos that had at last broken out had become their generals, all answering to one, their forms melting away gradually from anything recognisable to human eyes, as they regained their own dimensions, leaving the patchogues behind.

At the head of them all was their over-power. The military genius who had won the campaign: a champion. The imago they called Lupe, the Fish, or the Tiger. Waiting here, in London, at the heart of the campaign, as its troops finished off the last resistance. Sholl told his captive that too.

The vampire's face did not change, and neither did any of its fellows'. Sholl had reached the point of his interrogation.

"I have something," he said. "For the Fish of the Mirror. Where is it?"

Nothing spoke.

"Where is the Fish of the Mirror?"

Sholl punched the barrels of the shotgun hard into the chained patchogue's temple, making it rock and snarl. When Sholl spoke, though, it was as if he had been conducting a quiet discussion.

"What can I do? You're not scared of me. None of your siblings are scared of me. Lupe won't be afraid. What can *I* do to it? I can't hurt the Fish of the Mirror, can I? I want to give it a gift. Where is it?

"I want to *give it a gift.*" His captive stared at him. Sholl was beginning to rage. He hit the vampire in the face repeatedly as he spoke. Each time, its head snapped quickly back and it stared at him full on again, without fear, uncowed. "I want to give it a *gift.* I'll fucking give it something. Don't you want it to have something it can't fucking forget? A present. Where's the Fish of the Mirror? Where? I'll give it something. I have a fucking *gift* for it, something it can't refuse. Where is it? Where is the Fish of the Mirror? Where? Where is the Fish of the Mirror? *Where* is the Fish of the *Mirror?*"

And suddenly, in a voice that was shockingly human, the captive told him. It took full seconds for Sholl to realise what had happened. He began to smile. *Of course.*

He had won. The vampire did not believe he could hurt the Fish of the Mirror. What did it matter if he knew where it was? Perhaps it was the vampire's alien psychology, that made it give in to his taunts, or perhaps it wanted to see what he would do with the information—what betrayal he would attempt, and fail at. It would not believe he had no plan.

But Sholl saw that his captive seemed to have shocked its comrades. The other vampires were twitching nervously, and rolling their heads on their necks like sick dogs. Here and there Sholl heard them howl. He looked up, directly up, watching the black coil of the stairs disappear over his head, hearing the silence and the little drips and scratches of underground sound, and the mouth-noise of the vampires. He became terrified, very suddenly, and when he directed the torchlight into the faces of the things that surrounded him, picked them out one by one and saw them watch him unblinking, their mouths slack or grimacing, he was weak.

"Why don't they touch me?" he whispered. He hated his plain-
tive voice. "None of them. No imago in London. And why do you?"

He looked back down at the chained creature below him, and
let out a cry as he saw that one patchogue braver than the rest had
crept closer, close enough to touch, and that it was reaching out
now and grasping the handcuffs. Sholl stepped backward and levelled the shotgun, but he was too slow: the vampire had burst its
comrade's chains and it ululated briefly as it hauled the bloodied
captive onto its shoulders and rescued it, loping at ridiculous
speed into the dark corridors.

Sholl fired into the shadows, and in the brief hot light he saw
the pellets tear open several of the vampires, sending them
screaming into one another, but he knew that he had missed his
attacker and its rescuer. They had gone much quicker than he
could follow, becoming invisible in their siblings and the dark.

The smell of sulphur was rank on him. After their first screech,
even the wounded vampires were silent. The ranks closed, and all
that had changed was that now the faces closest to his, staring at
him, were splashed with their neighbours' blood.

In the darkness under the earth, Sholl stared at them, and
waited for them to come at him, but still they did not.

It took Sholl less time to come up than it had to descend. Then he
had walked in terror of where he was going—now he wanted pas-
sionately to get out.

He took the stairs at a slow jog, stopping every few score feet
and taking his breath. Every time, he would turn and look behind
him, and even after what he had just seen and done, the ranks of
silent faces following him still made his stomach pitch, the blood-
messed vampires in their everyday clothes like an honour guard.
They kept their distance precisely, wordlessly trailing him, making
sure he was going.

They came with him as far as the station's entrance, gathering
just inside the building. They stared at Sholl as he stumbled into

the early evening, spreading himself wide as if even that waning light energised him. Behind him the patchogues touched each other nervously now and then, in absentminded social behaviour unlike anything human.

Sholl stood exhausted in the junction beyond the Tube entrance. The imagos did not follow him, and the vermin of mirrors had not returned. The crossroads was empty.

Tottering, Sholl turned back toward the station. He rubbed his face as if just waking, and gazed at the wide-eyed vampires that waited for him finally to go, hating him from the shadows. Sholl was elated. He had gone *in* and he had come *out*. He had gone down and come back up, and he had brought with him what he wanted, the knowledge. He knew where he had to go.

He raised his arms like a scarecrow and staggered a few steps back the way he had come, back toward the vampires, running at them as if he were trying to mock-scare a child. They bolted away too fast to see. Sholl rushed them and laughed when they hid, waited a few seconds until one or two heads began to reemerge, then repeated his wild charge, disappearing them again.

After two of these ridiculous games he was distracted by tiredness, and he crossed the junction toward the ruins of an estate agent's office, sat heavily in its shadow. For some seconds Sholl could hear nothing except his own breath. He huddled and tried to regain his strength. He could not think about what he had yet to do.

The snare of rapid-fire weapons woke him out of sudden sleep with a sucking gasp. He rose and turned. A jeep had burst from a side street and pulled up in front of the Tube, the woman behind the wheel keeping the engine running. Two of the Heath soldiers were tearing across the road toward him. There were three others behind them, standing poised together a little way in front of their vehicle before Hampstead Station, pouring fire into its entrance. Bullets burst tiles and bricks and tore the edges of the metal gratings ragged.

From inside came howls as vampires were wounded or perhaps killed. They emerged in ones and twos, riddled with bulletholes and blood, moving in reptilian bursts, trying to close in on the men attacking them, held back only by the rate of fire. Their faces were immobile and their hands crooked into hard claws, even where they held in innards torn loose by the onslaught. They circled the soldiers with obvious murderous intent, despite their injuries, and the men backed slowly toward Sholl, making sure that they did not reload simultaneously, that there were no moments without gunfire pushing back the vampires. The soldiers were retreating in controlled panic. They could not hold off the vampires for long, and they knew what would happen when they failed.

Their two comrades ran low toward Sholl, keeping their profiles small, trained to avoid bullets that were not what would kill them here. They held out their arms and screamed at him to come. He fell into them, yelling wordlessly, buoyed by their presence, let them drag him, throw him across the back seat and leap in after him. The others came in then (everyone landing untidy across one another and fighting their way into seats), screaming *go go go*, and the jeep spasmed forward and roared.

Sholl was laughing. For many yards the vampires followed them, their passage audible as they chittered, and things broke in their wake. But the driver was a virtuoso, and slowly the vampires were left behind. Sholl supposed himself to be in some kind of shock, but his euphoria did not feel at all pathological to him. The soldiers had come for him. They had come back and waited.

He lay back and listened to them, as the jeep hurtled north, toward the safety of the open ground. *affirmative I fucking told you* and *did you see? did you?* and *couldn't go near, like they were scared*.

Sholl could see the edges of trees. Sholl could feel the texture change under the tires. They were on earth, on grass, by water, out in the cool air, and the soldiers had come for him.

They would not touch you. You came into our nest, and my siblings would not touch you. I do not understand.

When they pulled me away from you I was dazed, until in a dread in the sightless black where they brought me to safety, laid gently on the sleepers by the cold rails, I remembered what I had told you. I felt shame, I feel shame, but none of my people has yet told me I was wrong.

What can you do? What can you do, you insane man that came here, that came down here, in our deeps? You can't touch the Fish of the Mirror. How could you harm it? Did I do wrong?

Why would they not touch you?

There I was in darkness, at the bottom of the world, with the others, we patchogues in our nest, until we heard you. We *felt* you. Descending. We felt you descending and we came to meet you, and I was eager to have you succumb to us. I will not tolerate your kind. I will not allow any of you to live, after what you did. And when you came—I was not surprised or impressed with what you must have thought your bravery, the dangerous ramblings of an animal with stunted instinct—I waited. But you were not touched.

You kept coming, and coming, into our unlit place. They would not touch you.

I was made to watch. I was not synchronised with this. I was like a toothless cog, turning in an engine but not *gripping,* not cohering. They would not touch you, and it affronted me. I asked and asked them why in little whispers, in our own language, in your language, and whichever sibling I asked responded with a faint wordless evasion.

They would not tell me why, because I should know why.

For a long time, I thought I could not touch you, as they could not. And then as you reached our basement and began to swing inelegantly at us (what did you want? what were you trying to find?) I felt an energy come through me, like nothing so much as the energy that came to me when I saw the mirror burst and the fear of the thing that mocked me, and I knew that it was not that we could not touch you, but that my siblings *would* not, and that I *would*.

They did not like it. They would not stop me but they did not like it, and they watched uneasily, but I was too angry not to, you coming here as if you were not about to die.

A slippery trick had you on me, blinding me and hurting this dreadful head that I hate, that traps me. I was not humiliated—I am not like you and your brief and contingent victory means nothing at all, less than nothing, means as little as air. I was not humiliated but I was afraid, and not of you (what would you do but just perhaps kill me, which would only be something new?) but of my siblings, and not of them but of their sudden new *fact*, the fact that they would not touch you.

They watched me touching you, one two, fingers closing on your throat, but they would not join me. They only waited, for you to go. It was an unpleasantness.

I could not parse the expression that you took when I told you what you wanted to know. I have remembered it many times. I have seen it, I have thought it through. I have reconstructed it, and made my siblings mimic it so that I can see it again. It is very unclear to me. I do not know what you are thinking. Your face, the expression you took seems to me to hold delight, but also—is that horror? Fear of course (there is always that whenever I see you feeling anything) but I am sure that is horror I see, too.

What will you do? I wonder what it is that you will do.

I still wish I knew why they would not touch you, and why I would.

We spent a very few minutes together, and I hated you for all of them, but I wish you were here again. I would try to find out why they will not touch you.

Sometimes I imagine trying to see what of you my siblings *would* touch.

If I opened you to them, would they touch you then? Is your skin the barrier? If I took that for them—because *I* will touch your skin—would they touch the red core of you? Would they touch your inner places, the fragile palpitating things that make you?

But you would not last that, and though I hate you, I truly want to know the limits. So I would keep you whole, and keep asking my question. One of my people will tell me, would tell me, some time. Why they will not touch.

They do not shrink from me. I have watched and listened for any sign, for any sign. When I could tell, when I *saw* how it was, how it was going, I watched for it, but they do not shrink from me.

Since you came here and I touched you and they would not, I have gone farther and farther away. I feel something closing. It is closing around me. I have been part of something, I thought, but one by one I feel the bridges that link me breaking. I have felt myself more and more, have been more and more in myself, of myself, stuck more than ever within my constraints of skin. My light was part of a constellation, I thought, and in slow turn I have seen the other stars go out until I am alone in my universe, and I am frightened.

They are still by me and with me, my siblings, my others, but a connection has gone, and I'm alone. I thought that it must be them. I watched to see them judge me and punish me for my ill-thought, arrogant declaration to you. They must have cut me out, I thought, but they did not. They do not shrink from me: they are as they ever were, and in body I'm part of this company. We do and speak to each other as we did.

It is not they who have closed but I. I've cut myself away. I'm alone, and lonely. What frightens me is that I've not become lonely now, but have looked inside and seen that I was, already. How long has that been going on?

Now then. Now then now then. What's all this, then? How long has this been going on?

Snips of your moron culture fill me. At inappropriate times. At all times, really. I resent my emotions—which are worthy of the word, which aren't the little bubbles of whim that you call feelings—I resent that my emotions remind me of the detritus from your entertainments or your mannered interactions.

I'm thinking that I have been alone. That I wasn't part of all this. They don't shrink from me but I don't think I can come back in. I still don't know how this happened. I can't think about it for very long. I am afraid of how alone I will be.

There is an escape. Down, to where the cold rails are. I walked in the same place as once did little grey mice so filthy they were like animate dust. They have been taken now by the fauna of mirrors. I am used to the darkness, it's like something physical. I smacked the walls and the rail with my stick, to make sure there was nothing—no stalled train, no bodies, no fallen bricks—in my way.

I walked north on the train lines. Very slowly, as if to leave the city.

I'll go for a time, I said, to see what it is in me that's closed the doors. When I decided, lying on the platform's edge, in the darkness under Hampstead, I wondered how to take my leave, and that brought with it, that query, a wave of horror at the fact that I did not know the answer. That such a question occurred.

What do I know? Where shall I go? Will I be alone? How long have I been so?

I'll go away, for a time. I think of you often. Your gun and light, your obvious fear as you stumbled into us. The questions you asked, that could do you no good, that I answered for you in arrogance. I hated you then and I hate you now, but I remember you. Why would they not touch you?

When he came back to the Heath, and rejoined the camp, the celebrations—the joy—caught Sholl up easily. He arrived, batted side to side by the jeep, to see all the soldiers lined up and waiting. As the vehicle jounced through trees, they cheered. Sholl saw their officer clench his fists with passion that was unfeigned and incredulous.

They partied that night, turning up the volume on their cheap stereos and churning the earth into mud with dancing, and Sholl partied with them, high on their enthusiasm. There was a paradox to his own pleasure, though, which he became aware of. He had been truly delighted that the soldiers had appeared, that they had been sent. He had thought he was alone, but they had followed him, out of sight, and watched him cross the junction, and enter the station to the vampires' lair. They had sent back word of what they had seen, and waited for all the hours it took for Sholl to reemerge, and then they had risked their lives to fetch him, because of what they saw him do.

The soldiers were proficient. He had not known he was being tracked, that he was in their sights all the time he walked. The CO was too intelligent, too cautious a man to throw himself in with strangers, no matter how they talked. But Sholl had communicated something, not the authority he had intended but something, that had given the officer pause enough to send soldiers after him, to learn. And when they saw what he could do— struggling through their awe—they came in to save him.

But they had not saved him, of course. He had not been in danger, unlike them. And what came to Sholl was that forcing him to go—as he had thought—alone, had proved to him that he could, which he had not been sure of, at all. He had not wanted to test it, but had been given no choice. And now that he knew he did not need the soldiers, they wanted him.

What—would he turn them away, now? Of course not.

Thinking about what had yet to be done (as he turned absent-mindedly on his toes, with a beer and sandwich in his hands, dancing with one of the women) Sholl considered that he did not know everything he would face. The piratical last Londoners themselves, let alone the imagos. And perhaps whatever it was that kept him safe would ebb. Perhaps there would be imagos he had never faced before, that would touch him.

There were other thoughts, too, other reasons that he felt he needed the company to be with him, but they were very faint and hard to read, and he did not consider them deeply. All around, he could hear conversations about himself.

"Motherfucker went for them and they ran!"

"He wasn't scared, they were scared!"

". . . wouldn't touch him . . .

". . . fucking straight past them . . .

"They wouldn't touch him."

Sholl knew what was happening to him, in the eyes of the soldiers; he could see the transformation. They tried not to stare. They looked at him obliquely, but he could see their expressions. They were jealous—some so much that it was all they could feel. But for most of them, their awe was more powerful.

He did not like it, and became all the more profane in his words and his louche dancing, but he knew that he could not erase the feeling in them, that it was too formless and wordless to be countered (they would deny anything put to them, that came close to stating it). And besides, he needed it. He had counted on it. But that did not make it good to bear.

Sholl could command the army unit now, and they would obey him. He knew he should not tell them too much, that unspoken and secret things were important to their construction of him, but his discomfort with their barely hidden reverence made him talkative.

He told the CO that they would go south, loud enough for the soldiers to hear. He used tones that could just have been suggestive, so that the officer himself could turn around and make the orders. Sholl pretended to think himself only an advisor. Everyone was complicit in this.

They never asked him how he knew where to go. He had gone into the underworld, and come out bloodied, with the knowledge. He grimaced at the theatrics of it.

Sholl never explicitly announced their goal, but by inexorable rumour, it was less than a day before all the soldiers had some half-understanding, some inchoate knowledge of where they were going and why. They knew that something waited for them, and that they were coming for it, as guerrillas. Sholl did not try to find out what they thought they would find. Their excitement was enough for him. He had them doing something, and they were giddy on it.

They knew that the journey they were about to make was deadly, and that some of them would likely die. They were heading toward London's terrible heartlands, into the streets. They would set off early, and if they made Camden Town, just over two miles south, by nightfall, Sholl would be satisfied. That would be halfway. Then the same the next day, and they would find their target, and enter by darkness. That was the plan.

Beyond a certain number they would be a liability, but the process of elimination was difficult. There were too many volunteers for the mission, and men and women designated to stay, to care for refugees and keep camp, were livid, and would not listen to mollifying nonsense about it being the most important job of all. But eventually—Sholl stayed away from the process—the unit was chosen. Three vehicles, each carrying six soldiers. Some tripod-mounted guns, a rocket launcher, a handful of grenades. Sholl, the commander, twelve men and four women. Most had been professional soldiers, and the others were young and tough. It was an elite unit. Strapped in what body armour and weapons they had. With a nameless emotion, Sholl decided he would not learn their names.

The jeeps set out at six in the morning, breaking out of the trees, with the whole camp lined up to wave them off. Sholl had watched carefully and unobtrusively, while he gathered the things he had brought: almost none of those who were coming made long good-byes. They patted friends and lovers brusquely, as if they were on another quick recce.

When it came to Sholl to take his leave, he turned and took in the mucky clearing, with its washing and cooking, its dingy tents, the refugees, the soldiers ersatz and trained. They were all watching him. He raised his hand very slowly, turning to take in every face he saw. *You will not see me again,* he thought. He could tell that they knew.

That first day, Sholl saw that his escort was perhaps indispensable after all. The route they had picked out was dangerous. The alternatives were worse: Primrose Hill was continually tunnelled through by some great maggoty imago; Kentish Town was a wasteland of heat and burnt-out houses that smouldered endlessly, in some arcane transmirror pyrosis. But Camden, where they had to go, was the running ground of apocalypse scum, the worst spivs from the dead market's stall-holders, the least politicised of its punks. They had fetishised their own brutalisation, exaggerating their piercings and their outlandish hair and giving themselves mock-tribal names out of *Mad Max 2.*

The tension was hard as Sholl's troop penetrated the city. The little convoy of jeeps made slow way, flanked by guards on foot, tersely yelling information to one another, watching the upper windows. It took them hours to pass through the tight streets. Each major junction was scouted, each possible lair investigated and secured.

Twice they saw imagos: once a thing that momentarily took a form reminiscent of a flock of birds; the other a glowering point of precision on the ground. The birds-thing watched them, unafraid but uninterested, from the end of a long crescent, before stalking away with childish, clumsy steps. The other circled them (they scouring the ground frantically to watch it, trying to track the spot where they could see too clearly), coming closer in a predatory motion. Sholl was steeling himself to walk into its path, banking on his power, but with flawless aim the officer blew up the point of road where the thing manifested, and mercifully it dissipated.

They came to Camden ready for human trouble. With depressing predictability (the soldiers had been miming readiness to one another for many yards) the Camden gang burst out at them from below the bridge over the canal. The soldiers met them with careful bursts of fire. Sholl was in the leading vehicle, and he saw all of the brief fight. The rabble of punks fired crossbows and shotguns, but they were murdered without effort.

When several of them had fallen, the rest gave up and ran, abseiling from the bridge into waiting barges, which moved away sedately enough for the leading soldiers to drop grenades into them almost at leisure. When two of the barges had been destroyed, the CO looked up anxiously at the sky, for doves or airborne imagos, and yelled sharply over the shrieks of dying raiders, telling his soldiers to stop and to move on. Sholl was sure he was motivated as much by pity as urgency.

The exchange of fire had been so one-sided that Sholl was surprised to discover himself adrenalised. The soldiers, too, breathed shakily: they had seen plenty of combat and misery over the last weeks, but not many firefights, and few against their own kind. It was late afternoon when they came to the end of Camden High Street and they stopped for the night. They camped in the concrete forecourt of a council estate on Crowndale Road.

Since the soldiers had taken Sholl from Hampstead Tube, and installed him, unspoken, at their head, there had been several nights. Celebrations and preparations, and now this, their last night together. Sholl knew it, and he wondered who else did.

They built a fire. Sholl pushed it with a stick, watched its sparks.

When the light fell and they finished eating, Sholl started them telling stories. Everyone alive had the kind of story he wanted: set just before the war broke out, as things began to turn, the shocks of knowledge. The moment the reflections went wrong.

"First time," said one man, interspersing his words with smoking, taking his time, "I knew first time. You think something like that, something so insane, you'll think you're mad, you'll think of excuses, but I knew first time that it was the world that was wrong, not me. I was all covered in shaving foam, and I look down to rinse it, and when I look up again my reflection was *waiting* for me. It hadn't looked down at all. It had pulled the razor sideways, was bleeding all across its foam, staring at me. I didn't even check for blood on my cheek. I knew it wasn't me anymore."

"I heard noises," said a woman. "It kept on mirroring me, but I could hear noises. Coming from in my makeup mirror. I can't believe it. I don't believe what I'm hearing. So all slowly, I put my ear up to it. For ages there's nothing, and then, totally far off, and echoing, like it's at the other end of a long corridor, I can hear the sound of a knife being sharpened."

A man had stood in front of the mirror in his morning nudity, and had seen aghast that where he was detumesced, his reflection was erect. Another's reflection had spit at him, the gob sliding down the wrong side of the glass. And it was not always their own reflections. One woman told in a voice still hollow at the memory how she had spent long disbelieving minutes at breakfast looking to the mirror beside her husband and back at him, watching his reflection meet her eye—not the eye of her reflection but her own eye—and mouth obscenities at her, calling her *cunt cunt cunt* while her husband read his newspaper, and now and then glanced up and smiled.

Eventually they asked Sholl what he had seen, how he had known. He shook his head.

"Nothing," he told them. "Nothing ever changed. It never disobeyed me. I just woke up one day, and it had gone."

Very soon after that, all the reflections had all gone. Some had come out in the shape of their last mimicking, some had taken hybrid forms, but they had all come out, and nothing was left visible behind the mirrors.

The second day was easier than the first. They moved in little starts. They did not go direct: Sholl had heard rumours about what was in Euston Station. To avoid it, they continued down to where St. Pancras and King's Cross met in a wedge. There were a surprising number of people in that once-unsalubrious zone. It had become a little commune, perhaps fifty people living together in what had been the WHSmith in King's Cross Station. There were more, Sholl knew, camped out across the fanning train lines at the back of the station: a tent town had arisen among the brick piles and sheds, adrift in weeds in that open cut in the city.

The soldiers spoke briefly to the locals, bartered cans of soft drink and alcohol from them, examined the little hand-signed notes they used as currency. The people here were nervous, but not terrified. There was something in the angles between Pancras Road and York Way that the imagos did not like, that kept that zone relatively clean. Sholl breathed it in deep, and wished he could stay.

There were nomads from Clerkenwell in the area, the locals said. Men and women were eager to follow mystics, and one such group was nearby, and the soldiers had better be careful. They cut down south, moving cautiously, determined not to be lulled, until they reached the stepped concrete of the Brunswick Centre. They waited there for two hours, in the courtyard at its heart, but the cult they had been warned of did not appear.

The soldiers prepared themselves. This close to their target, they lost their heart, they became afraid to go on, to bring the mission to an end. Though he did not want to, Sholl kept considering the patchogue that had told him where to go. He wondered why it alone had touched him.

Sholl and his soldiers waited, for as long as they could, savouring the little journey they had shared: and when they could not put it off any more, they went on. Past the uprooted trees of Russell Square: down Bedford Place, become an avenue of statues, that the imagos had uprooted from around the city and placed there at regular intervals, their features and outlines changed—Nelson, torn from his column, laughing hysterically, "Bomber" Harris urinating—and then right, toward their target.

I didn't think I would be gone so long, or so far. Or is that true? Did I?

I thought—I think I thought—that I'd travel far enough to get away from those of my siblings that know me and knew me, and find others, and see things in this reconfigured city, at its outskirts, and make sense. Of everything. And be in it again, open my doors. And I have seen my people at every place, in all their forms, the patchogues—the patchogues like me—all trapped in their prison uniforms, the other imagos in whatever they wish. It isn't quite fair, is it, that we who came through, with that strength, who were the first agents in the war, benefit less than those weaker.

Like the Fish of the Mirror. It's general now, but it was weaker, I suppose, than we who came through.

Everywhere I go, I'm with my people. I see *you*, too. At the corners of things, scurrying where we've not yet met you and destroyed you. I feel the hatred I always do. But I am not sure now where it stops, where I am, where that hatred is and where I begin.

I discover that I do not want the society of kin. I want to be alone. ǝuoʅɐ ǝq oʇ ʇuɐʍ I, I want to be alone.

The rails have taken me out of the underworld, into the opened-up flat city of the big sky, the ring of London where buildings sprawl low and uneasy and it is not like a city but like a found landscape, not like a suburb but like an accident, like spillage on the hills. I've kept walking. I have continued to walk.

There's smoke in the sky behind me from the heart of the town. Here the backs of houses that abut my railway line, the synagogues and warehouses, cemeteries and other things look only momentarily emptied—everyone here, all of you, have just stepped out for one second (there are cold lights burning in many houses, I do not know how). Where I see you now you do not belong, *you are as much intruder as me.* You're creeping. These are no longer your houses, and you don't know how to be in them. You would rather hide in a basement, in a cellar, in a broken cinema where the signs are shattered, because that way you know that you are *hiding.* From me.

Neither of us knows what to do with the city anymore.

I come to the end of the line, and it is dark, and London has lowered itself to the night. There are woods. There are woods here.

Still north, barefoot on the tar roads. Past open-doored cars sleeping like cats. The trees come up to shroud me. Over the biggest road (what am I looking for?) and on to green. Forests at the border. Deserted schools and playing fields, and through trees that tussle together not as if to block my path but as if it is a game.

The moon's up—I can hear my siblings in the south, playing. Like whales. I can hear them but I can't see them, and it is a relief.

There are paths in this greenery, I have been following them, and the trees pull apart to uncover a secret for me, and I see it and I know what it is I've been looking for.

We never knew—or I was not told—quite what happened, how we came free. I know some things. The Fish of the Mirror was the mastermind. It was its genius that broke us all out, rather than only a misfit few renegades who had to be spies, and are now reminders.

Light falls as light always fell. It scatters. It rebounds from what it touches. But as it touches off tighter, where its integrity is more sustained, and more sustained, the key turns, until where there is sheen, light transmutes, and makes a door.

Pushing through the mirror was something, was a pleasure you can't imagine. All the patchogues say so. A complete feeling. Something very whole. But it is not the mirror that reflected: it was the tain. That is where the imagos were. In the tain. Coming through the mirror was a one-way trip: we broke the glass as we passed. We showered those whose forms were our prisons with jagged splinters as we arrived, so that they were bleeding and crying out before we touched them.

When we looked up, all exhilarated from our liberation struggle, we turned and saw the door was closed, that only a fringe of glass and thin silver was left at the edges of what had been a mirror.

Now, all mirrors are open doors, always. The imagos, those who aren't trapped in your bodies, can pass through glass without harm to it or them: they can slip into the tain. But not us. If we push into the tain we will break it.

There are other doorways. Mirrors that are not blocked to us with a skin of glass: but they are hard to find. Sheets of chrome or aluminum so pressed, so polished that scuffs don't disfigure them, that they are portals, with the tain open to the air. I do not know where any are.

Coming over this little hill, though, I know why I've come here. I have come here, I've found this place so that I can go home.

The moon rises over the little pond before me, and the pond is absolutely, unnaturally still. I am almost afraid to breathe (but trapped in this body, I must). The trees that brought me here circle the water, showing it to me, and I know that in the days before the war I would have looked down and seen the twin of each of those trees. I look down now, imagining it, and I'm staring into water so still, lit by moonlight so absolutely pure, it's like a little god.

I want to go home. The bondage is broken: there's nothing tethering the other side anymore. It's undiscovered now, a continent absolutely strange. What forms it might take. After centuries of mocking-bird topography, the tain has been freed. It might be any shape now: the thought of that makes me hanker. It could be *anything*. I look hard, staring through the darkness of the doorway, through the water, and I swear I can see through, past the veil that obscures, through to the other side, and I *swear* that I can see trees.

If I'm gentle, if I'm quick, if no wind comes to disrupt this perfect tain, then I can go, I can go home. My passing will disrupt it but I'll be gone. I need time, or space, or something, to work out why I do not want to be with my imago kin any more. I'll go where it's untethered, where it can all be different.

In my bare feet I run down this little grass angle, down this scrubby incline, picking up my feet so as not to send dirt or boscage into the water, not to disrupt it, to disrupt it only with me, and I run and leap. I am poised. I am poised, and now I am descending, and as the water, as the tain comes up at me, I can see through it, I can see through it faintly, to what I swear is a rising crater of dirt and grass, to trees, to a moon and clouds, to everything that is here around me, everything but me. I am falling toward the tain, but no one is falling toward me.

The soldiers were to launch their attack in the small hours. They were still not sure of what it was Sholl wanted to do. They only knew that he had a plan, and that they had to get him inside. Sholl knew that he could not think about it too hard, about what the men and women were doing: the faith they had and what they were prepared to do, for him, without ever knowing his story.

He spent the hours before their assault talking quietly to the officer. Sholl told him that he did not have to come, or bring his troops. Sholl was ready to go, and the soldiers could wait for him. Sholl meant it: he would have been sincerely relieved had his companions stayed where they were, refused to come one step farther with him. But he was not surprised by the officer's refusal, and he greeted it with as much resignation as sadness.

The soldiers performed their routines, like tics—checking and rechecking, strapping ammunition, sighting along rifles—and Sholl stood in the darkness of the shop in which they waited and stared across at their target. He did not know the morals or rules of the new terrain: he suspected that they were unknowable. Still, he understood a kind of logic to the Fish of the Mirror's choice of lair, and the fact that he understood it did not convince Sholl that it was therefore wrong.

It could be a kind of neurotic, a kind of masochistic pleasure. To be surrounded by the evidence of your imprisoning: to roam corridors like time machines, in which the differing shapes and colours of your jailers from a thousand years ago stretched up to those of yesterday, and your pleasure derived from the fact that you passed them, and remembered them, but were free. Making a home in the shell of a jail. It was bitter, but it made a kind of sense.

The Fish of the Mirror lived in the British Museum. At its heart, the vampire had told Sholl. Surrounded by the detritus of men and women from the ancient Americas, from the East, from old Greece and Egypt. Material culture that the imagos had been forced to make, wherever it was reflected. The Fish of the Mirror lived in corridors made of time, of incarceration, and it moved through them, quite free.

He did not know what else was inside. Perhaps nothing. There was no movement on the white steps, on the lawn before the building. The gates were open.

"Let me go alone," whispered Sholl with sudden, absolute conviction.

When he said it loud enough to be heard they argued with him, at first respectfully but soon with great heat.

"You cannot go in there alone!" the commander yelled at him, and Sholl bellowed that he would go where he wanted, alone or not. The soldiers marshalled moral arguments against him—*it's not your fucking fight, we need this, you don't get to order us*—and all he could do was play the messianic role they had given him. He spoke obliquely and hinted at things he could not tell them. He spoke with righteous anger. He felt contempt for himself, for this act, but he felt pride under that, because he was trying to save them. When he finally bellowed at them that he would *go alone*, he used all the authority they had ceded to him, and they were shocked and silent.

Sholl walked away from them, stepped out of the broken window of the shop and stood alone in the street, in full view, without weapons. He showed the soldiers what only he could do.

It was deep night: the moon silvered him. Sholl turned back to his companions in the darkness of the shop and muttered something to them: it was meant to be conciliatory and warm, but he saw only betrayal on their faces. *You don't understand*, he thought, and raised his hands in an attitude of the most vague, the most uncertain benediction, then turned and walked away quickly, crossing Russell Street, passing through the threshold of the museum's gates and onto its drive, past the lawn where the ruins of public sculptures were bruised with verdigris. He was in the grounds, he was in, and he walked faster toward the steps and the doors that were open and very dark. He had never been so afraid or excited.

As he began to ascend the stairs, Sholl heard quick steps on the gravel behind him. He spun, horrified, crying out *go away* before he had even seen who was following him. It was the commander, and most of the soldiers. *You don't go in alone* the officer was screaming, his weapon held so that he could have been threatening Sholl, or protecting him.

Sholl began to run back toward him. He was not surprised by the soldiers' decision, and he felt shame. They were still approaching him when he saw their faces change. Their expressions were blasted suddenly wide, staring at what was emerging from the museum. Sholl heard something bursting out behind him, but he did not turn back. His run faltered as forces overtook him. He came to a stop at the bottom of the stairs, and spread out his arms as if he would hold back a tide, but the imagos swept past him, in a frenzy like he had never seen, and descended on the soldiers.

The imagos were dressed in a flickering, a strobing sequence of forms, of people, of the people throughout history, staccato aggregates of their own oppression. They were a wind of flint-axe chippers, of pharaohs, of samurai, of American shamans and Phoenicians and Byzantines, helmets with placid faces and splinted armour, and tooth necklaces and shrouds and gold. They came down in a vengeful swarm, and the soldiers fired with tough and stupid bravery, ripping apart moments of flesh and blood that only folded in and refocused and became again. The bodies of the imagos were shredded endlessly as they came but these were not vampires—these were the unfettered fauna of mirrors, for which meat was an affectation.

No one could have expected this. It was like nothing imaginable. It would have been reasonable for the soldiers to pass the museum's threshold thinking they had at least a chance of retreat.

They screamed as the imagos reached them. *Stop!* screamed Sholl, but the imagos did not obey him. They would only not touch him. They ignored him and continued. *Stop! Stop!*

One by one the soldiers were taken. After five, six of them had died in blood, or been pushed into space that was folded away to nothing, or frozen and made gone, Sholl turned away. It was not callousness that made him walk stolidly back up the steps, with the massacre going on behind him. He could not turn round, he could not watch what he could not stop, for shame.

He had not been shocked to turn and see the soldiers there. Guilt blasted him. *Why did you let them come?* it spoke. *Company? Protection? Sacrifice?*

Sholl shook his head violently and tried very hard not to think of what was happening. He was trembling almost too much to stand. He pushed at the museum's half-open door, and the motion was timed precisely with a wet screech behind him, that sounded like the commander. Sholl hovered at the museum's threshold. *I didn't know. I told them not to come,* he said inside him. He had been right not to learn their names.

His face creased as he walked into the darkness, leaving the gunfire behind him, and the imagos playing.

It was not far, through the dark. In the echoes of his footsteps, and the faint sounds from the fight outside. He knew where the Fish of the Mirror must be.

He passed the south stairs to his left, crossing into the enormous pillared hall, where signs for toilets and cafés were still intact on the walls. Sholl discovered he was crying. It was just here, now, he was here, ready to face the power of the imago forces, the controller, the Fish of the Mirror. He drew breath, focused on his plan. The Reading Room was ahead, and after deep breaths, Sholl entered.

The Reading Room. The round chamber that had been at the heart of the British Library, and then remade into a pointless focus for the museum. Its dome was way overhead. Most of its shelves had long ago been stripped: they housed only ghost books. The massive room was lit by the moon through the skylight, but that was not how Sholl could see every edge of everything, every curlicue of detail in the chamber. It was all etched in shadow on shadow, and he could see it all, in the black sunlight that poured out of the presence hanging in the room's centre, like a darkling star, invisible but utterly compelling, evading deliberation, not quite seen, insinuating its own parameters, patrolling the moiling cylindrical space with feline, piscene ease. The Tiger. The Fish of the Mirror.

Its vast, unsympathetic attention turned slowly to Sholl. He felt himself becoming more precise as it considered him, more exact. He bristled from its thoughtful application.

He could not breathe.

Will you *touch me?* he thought.

Enough. It was like pushing through ice, but he made himself move. Step forward through his awe. This was what it came to. He had not come here, unarmed, to stare. He had a plan.

They must have known. Without any doubt, they must have known the truth. So was it a game? Did they not mind me?

For a long time after the jailing of the imagos, their world was nothing like yours. Except where there was water, things were shaped in very different ways, in other dimensions. For a very long time. But the imperialism of the tain, earth's specularisation, meant less and less space for the other world to be other. Places of imago aesthetics grew smaller and fewer. The mimicked land spread.

Ways were found to minimise the hurt. When one woman tilted one looking glass in Rome, must the whole imago universe pitch like an unstable ship? Where one man faces thirty windows, did thirty imagos have to be lashed powerless? Solutions were found. There are strategies, even in prison.

Let the mirrors, the tains themselves, let them move, pitch between the worlds. Let them bend space, so that one imago may seem fractured, but will always match one of you. From caprice to precision.

The prison's rule went from one of great freedom with occasional, arbitrary and greatly cruel punishment, to one of structure and limitations and no freedom at all. With the imperialism of mirrors, all this became necessary. I see this now. I've understood it. I didn't know, before. Faced with the mindless dynamism of the mirror, a new strategy was found, and it gave the imago world a certain shape.

When I came through, I burst through the tain, and hurled onto steep slopes. I rolled with momentum, afraid that gravity would take me back across, and leave me bobbing in the water back on the other side.

I stopped and breathed mirror air. I shook.

I made my way up a path, amazed by the feel of earth underneath me, by the colour of the night sky, by the trees. I walked very slowly. I was afraid of what I might find. I gripped the ground with my feet, I listened to the wind. I emerged from the woods and set out for the city, nobno⅃.

Right is left, here, and left right, so the signs say ʏᴙTᴎƎ Oᴎ and Ǝvɪ⅁ ʏᴀw, but the city is in every other way the same. There was no tiny part of the world that was safe from mirrors, so the imagos finally gave in, and made a reflection.

I held my breath for so long when I came here—when I came *back*, I want to say, though that would be wrong. It is as if London has been blotted, and I walk in the paper.

I wander through Islington—it gets tedious to always give it its mirror name—and along the railway lines toward Kensal Rise. The sun rises behind me, on the wrong side of the sky. I suppose I have come home.

This place is more like London than London now: there are no changes here, no imago exudations, no signs of the war. It is like London was. There are no fires. There is only the grey, silent city, abandoned, on the wrong side of the mirror. A vacant likeness. Very often, my feet make the only sound.

The imagos, all giddy with freedom, are gone, through the open doors, for revenge and emancipation's sake. The fauna of mirrors have gone. There are no birds here: there never were, only little shards of imago-matter made to copy them. No rats. No urban foxes, no insects. But strangely, the city is not quite empty.

I am not the first here. Others have made their way through. I have caught glimpses, at the edges of streets, or climbing in the reflected trees. Only a very few, here and there: men and women, gone feral in ragged wool and fur, running through the streets, but not as if they are streets. I do not know if they are rebel imagos, or escaped humans. Some vampires must hate being meatbound too much to live with their siblings, and any human would find this place a sanctuary now.

These are my fellow citizens. They are frightened—I am too, I think—but we are all safe here. There is nothing here that wants to kill us. I am not a danger any more. We can walk these empty, mirrored streets, retracing favourite routes in looking-glass script, as if unwinding our memories. We can get on with being alone.

The glass of the mirror ruptured, tearing apart my face, when the patchogue burst out of the tain, but I was very quick. I met it, my own snarling face. I wasn't subdued or driven out of my mind by it. *I had never trusted that image anyway.* That was why it found me where it did, in the toilet of a hospital, near my ward of melancholics and hysterics.

We rolled and choked each other in the debris of its passing. We struggled below the urinal, smashing open the doors of empty cubicles. Though we—they, I mean, the vampires—are strong and hard to kill, I managed it, with long edged bludgeons of mirrored glass. I stabbed and sawed, scoring my fingers, and felt my muscles tremble with the effort, but after long minutes I lay in blood more its than mine, and my doppelganger's head was taken off, and it was dead, and I was exhilarated and terrified. But without reflection.

Afterward, I tried to tell. But I came out all wet with blood and the patients, my old cohorts, screamed murder, and then they saw that I'd nothing in the tain, and they screamed that I'd become a monster. They called me vampire. My *friends.* They stared at me all bloody, at the emptiness in the glass, with terror so frantic I ran.

I've lived a long time. I don't know why. Maybe it's our imagos that kill us. Even trapped in mimicry, maybe their hatred reached past the glass and slowly throttled us, after our scores of years and ten. Only I killed mine, so I kept not dying. I've lived a long time, alone. For years, and years, not knowing what I was, more afraid of all of you than I'd ever been before, and resenting you more, a *tide* of it, bitter and growing, and alone.

This is my first time beyond the mirror, but I know all the imago histories by heart. I have had them told to me. Whispered through cold glass. All the stories of old Venice. I'd have loved to have been there. All the stories of the Yellow Emperor. I've mopped floors and disinfected stalls for years, in all manner of places, so I could work close to my siblings in the mirrors, and whisper to them when you weren't about, when the shop closed or the train arrived. It's perversely safe in those places. No one noticed me to notice I had no image.

There are strategies, to not being seen being unseen, to having no reflection. A way of moving, little dances of avoidance. They're hard to learn, and a master recognises another. When I saw her, the woman in the station, I made her my new sister instantly, as I watched her bobbing elegantly away from glazed walls and windows. I sat her down in the café and made her teach me what she was, what I would be. For a very long time she'd say nothing. When finally she realised that I wouldn't betray her, when she saw the tremor in me, the excitement, this making sense, this *community*, she told me enough—what I needed to know.

I went turncoat without regret. I was sick of you all. That night I uncovered the mirror in my lodgings, pressed up close to its empty face, and whispered into its glass, *what would you have me do?*

I've been a spy for a long time. Living days in your toilets, nights sleeping with my ear to the glass, hearing stories. They must—I don't believe that they could not—have known what I was, that I wasn't as other vampires. But they rewarded me when they came through, letting me live as one of their crippled scouts. I've seen them, the imagos, killing every human they see, and they have always left me. I lived among them. They *saved* me. From the man they wouldn't touch, whom I touched. Showed myself up. And now I have turned away, and run, and hidden from them.

After long years of feeling nothing, I find that I feel shame.

And I swear that I don't know for whom: I don't know which of my betrayals makes me ashamed. Am I a bad man, or a bad imago? Which is it that hurts me?

I find a comfort in this nearly empty city. Now that the illusion, the silly little game I played (myself as monster) is over, I find a comfort being simply alone.

There's nothing unique about me now. On the other side, no person has a reflection now. But if I went back to be as them, that would make me prey. I don't find myself frightened by that— more indifferent. I'm disposed to stay here, in this city where I can be alone.

I wonder who he was, that man my siblings, the imagos, wouldn't touch. I wonder why they wouldn't, and what he'll do.

I like it in this nearly empty London. The air's cool. There is food—tins and bottles in all the deserted stores, their wares printed in mirror-writing.

I've taken to climbing towers, and looking out—when light's waxing and waning—looking out over the inverted horizon, tracking the river, that curves the wrong way, and the skyscrapers, on the wrong side of the city. It's calming. The city all unlit and coursed through with wind, like a natural formation. Glass bows fractionally, in window frames, in the bluster. From up high, I sometimes see the other citizens, the escapees from all the chaos on the other side. I recognise some of them: we pass each other once or twice a day, at opposite ends of the street, and I know they recognise me.

We don't smile, our eyes don't meet, but we know each other. We are quite safe here: we don't fear each other.

Sometimes I stare into puddles (I'm careful not to tread on them), try to see through the obscurity. I wonder what is happening in London Prime.

One of the refugees to my quiet city does the same. I've seen him, standing over the water, hands on hips, squatting and watching. A man bearded through lack of care, wrapped in what was once an expensive coat. I've watched him, and seen him see me, but we haven't yet spoken. We stand at opposite ends of the street, staring intermittently each into his own water, and it is as if we are in the same room, about to meet.

The sun is going down over my quiet London, over in the east.

This is a surrender, Sholl thought. *That's how this should be told.*

Refraction is the change in direction of a wave—like light—when it passes into a new substance. *There was nothing we could do,* thought Sholl. *We had nothing. We have to change direction.*

The Fish of the Mirror listened to him.

We surrender, Sholl told it again. That had always been his intention.

Is that it? Is that *the plan?*

Sholl did not know whose voice it was he gave the words to. The question was stark.

What would you have me do? he thought.

He did not tell himself that he had not lied to the soldiers, that he had promised them nothing about his plan: he had told them nothing, but he knew that he had lied.

The Fish of the Mirror turned and came closer, expanding, unlight passing through it. It listened without comment. It granted him audience, and heard his petition.

I won't let us be destroyed, he thought. *We can do this. They* listen *to me.* He did not know if that was true. He knew only that they would not kill him, and that therefore he could make his offer, and his request.

No one else could get close enough, for long enough, to try. This was the only chance they had. No one else could possibly have even been heard.

He did not debase himself, did not plead, nor bluster. There was no trick. He came, the self-appointed general of London, spokesperson for humanity, recognising the fact that his side had lost the war, and asking for peace, as a conquered people.

You don't need to kill us any more, he thought. *You win.*

It was the sobbing of the Liverpudlian officer into his radio that had put the idea in Sholl's head. He had stood in the corridor beyond the radio room after midnight, stricken, listening to the man cry and scan the static for a sound. The relentless white noise wore down on Sholl.

What if everyone was waiting, he thought, to make contact, to hear their commands, and there was no way for word to come through? Perhaps the government still sat, in exile, in a bunker underground, making decisions completely without meaning, or perhaps they were all dead. It made no difference. They couldn't speak to their troops. There was no one to make decisions. Soldiers are paid to fight, and so the dispersed troops tried to, in bandit raids, being slaughtered when the imagos bothered. But fighting was not all that soldiers did: sometimes they surrendered.

Their job, now, Sholl became certain, was to surrender. What if the imagos were not carrying out a meaningless slaughter, but were fighting the war because no one had declared it over? Just like the soldiers. Waiting. For a decision that no one could take, and an order that could not be given.

What if there was no one left to give the order to stop? Would the war continue until stilled by entropy, or until the last human was dead?

Until that descent into Hampstead Tube, Sholl had not known for certain that the imagos would not touch him, but for weeks it had been clear to him that he had lived much longer than he should. He had made less and less effort to hide, and the fauna of mirrors, imagos and scavengers, always avoided him, shied away from him, without respect or fear, but as if noting something.

What is this? Sholl had thought. Aghast, he had decided that he was chosen for something. For this. He granted himself authority to speak for his people. To surrender. Judas-messiah.

He made no demands, but he offered terms that seemed reasonable: the terms of abject but dignified surrender. An end to hostilities. Tribute, in kind or obedience, in *prayer* if the Fish of the Mirror required. Whatever was necessary. And in return, humans could live.

Perhaps we'll be nomads, he thought. *Or farmers, or serfs, ploughing up London's ruins. A little colony of the imago empire. A backwater, eventually, with the freedom granted to those who are no trouble. We could make plans then—* but Sholl stopped himself. That was not why he was here. This was not strategy or double-bluff; it could not be. This was a surrender.

Am I Pétain? Collaborator? Will children use my name as a curse? But there will be *children.*

We'll live, we'll spread the word that we've lost, and we'll live, in ghettos if we have to, but we'll live. A new history. What will we be? But we will be.

Someone had to decide. It was this, or die, like we're dying.

He thought of the strange imago that had helped him, still not understanding its motives. He thought with shame again of the soldiers outside, who had come with him against his orders, as he had suspected they might, and been slaughtered by the Fish of the Mirror's imago guard. The guard that had let him pass, waiting for him to do whatever it was that they expected.

Perhaps I've got this all wrong. Perhaps this isn't why they leave me alone at all—what if the chosen one misunderstands what he's been chosen for?

It was too late for that now. His offer—his suit for peace, his *surrender*—had been made. Sholl bowed his head respectfully and stepped back. He tried to feel like a leader. The humans had nothing with which to bargain—no strength at all. The only thing that

Sholl could do was make his forces soldiers, defeated soldiers, rather than bandits or vermin. That was all he had. If the Fish of the Mirror chose, it could ignore Sholl, and hunt down the last Londoners, to the last child. All Sholl had was his surrender. An extraordinary, arrogant claim that it was his to surrender. In all his humility was this last puffed-up pretence. It was all he had. He begged. Searing, he begged mercy, general to general.

The Fish of the Mirror glowed. Sholl stepped back, his hands up and open. He waited for his conqueror to consider.

This is the story of a surrender.

. . . the world of mirrors and the world of men were not, as they are now, cut off from each other. They were, besides, quite different; neither beings nor colours nor shapes were the same. Both kingdoms, the specular and the human, lived in harmony; you could come and go through mirrors. One night the mirror people invaded the earth. Their power was great, but at the end of bloody warfare the magic arts of the Yellow Emperor prevailed. He repulsed the invaders, imprisoned them in their mirrors, and forced on them the task of repeating, as though in a kind of dream, all the actions of men. He stripped them of their power and of their forms and reduced them to mere slavish reflections. Nonetheless, a day will come when the magic spell will be shaken off.

The first to awaken will be the Fish ["a shifting and shining creature . . . glimpsed in the depths of mirrors"]. Deep in the mirror we will perceive a very faint line and the colour of this line will be like no other colour. Later on, other shapes will begin to stir. Little by little they will differ from us; little by little they will not imitate us. They will break through the barriers of glass or metal and this time will not be defeated. Side by side with these mirror creatures, the creatures of water will join the battle. . . . [I]n advance of the invasion we will hear from the depths of mirrors the clatter of weapons.

JORGE LUIS BORGES
"The Fauna of Mirrors"
from *The Book of Imaginary Beings*

The patient awoke about midnight and had just entered the dimly lit bathroom when he saw the reflection of his face in a mirror. The face appeared distorted and seemed to be changing rapidly, frightening the patient so much that he jumped through the bathroom window.

LUIS H. SCHWARZ, M.D.
and STANTON P. FJELD, PH.D.
"Illusions Induced by the Self-Reflected Image"

ACKNOWLEDGMENTS

My sincere thanks to Emma Bircham, Mic Cheetham, Simon Kavanagh, Peter Lavery, Claudia Lightfoot, Colleen Lindsay, Jemima Miéville, Jake Pilikian, Rebecca Saunders, Max Schaefer, Chris Schluep, Liam Sharp and Jesse Soodalter.

My deepest gratitude goes to all the editors who commissioned and/or published some of these stories: Benjamin Adams, Michael Chabon, Pete Crowther, Eli Horowitz, Ian Irvine, Maxim Jakubowski, Pete Morgan, Bradford Morrow, John Pelan, Mark Roberts, Nicholas Royle, Peter Straub, Jeff VanderMeer, and Tony White.

I would like to point out that the historical detail in the story "foundation" is accurate and a matter of record. The U.S. Army did bury Iraqi soldiers alive, using tanks mounted with plows. Among many other sources, see Patrick Sloyan's article "How the Mass Slaughter of a Group of Iraqis Went Unreported," *The Guardian*, 14 February 2003.

SOURCES

"Looking for Jake" in *Neonlit: The* Time Out *Book of New Writing*, Volume 1, ed. Nicholas Royle: Quartet, 1998.

"Foundation" in the *Independent on Sunday* "Talk of the Town" magazine, 27 April 2003, ed. Ian Irvine.

"The Ball Room" (which was co-written with Emma Bircham and Max Schaefer) is original to this collection.

"Reports of Certain Events in London" in *McSweeney's Enchanted Chamber of Astonishing Stories*, ed. Michael Chabon: Vintage, 2004.

"Familiar" in *Conjunctions*, 39 (*The New Wave Fabulists*), eds. Peter Straub and Bradford Morrow, 2002.

"Entry Taken from a Medical Encyclopaedia," under its original title "Buscard's Murrain," in *The Thackerey T. Lambshead Pocket Guide to Eccentric & Discredited Diseases*, ed. Jeff VanderMeer and Mark Roberts: Night Shade Books, 2003.

"Details" in *The Children of Cthulhu*, ed. John Pelan and Benjamin Adams: Del Rey Books, 2002.

"Different Skies" in *Britpulp!*, ed. Tony White: Sceptre, 1999.

"An End to Hunger" in *The New English Library Book of Internet Short Stories*, ed. Maxim Jakubowski: Hodder and Stoughton, 2000.

" 'Tis the Season" in *Socialist Review*, 291, December 2004, ed. Pete Morgan.

The Tain, PS Publishing, 2002.

"Go Between," "Jack" and "On the Way to the Front" (illustrated by Liam Sharp) are original to this collection.